BE I WHOLE

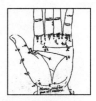

BE I WHOLE

G I T A   B R O W N

MACMURRAY & BECK
Aspen, Colorado

Song on page v written by Ferron. © 1980 Nemesis Publishing.
All rights reserved. Used by permission.

Copyright © 1995 by Gita Brown
Published by:
MacMurray & Beck, Inc.
400 W. Hopkins, Suite 5
Aspen, Colorado 81611-1609

Printed and bound in the United States of America

Library of Congress Cataloging-in-Publication Data
Brown, Gita, 1958–
  Be I whole / Gita Brown.
     p.   cm.
  ISBN 1-878448-66-8
  1. Family—United States—Fiction. 2. West Indian Americans—Fiction. 3. Creek Indians—Fiction. I. Title.
PS3552.R685515B4   1995
813'.54—dc20   95-18009
                                                        CIP

MacMurray & Beck Fiction; General Editor, Greg Michalson

Be I Whole designed by Susan Wasinger.
The text was set in Goudy by Pro Production.

There's god-like
And war-like
And strong-like
Only some show
And there are sad-like
And mad-like
Who have life we know

But by my life, be I spirit
And by my heart, be I woman
And by my eyes, be I open
And by my hands, be I whole

—FERRON

chapter one

With her knees upraised and her elbows propped there, she pulls the pipe from her lips.

"Listen to this that I'm going to tell you," she says.

Her slender chocolate-brown fingers cup the warm pipe bowl and a thick cloud of smoke covers her face. Her watery eyes appear fixed straight ahead.

"This is a tale of my mothers. They told it to me, I heard it, and I now tell you. The way my mothers told me and later died, I now tell you, so that you can hear it and tell it after me. It is a parable, not a tale. A parable. But we pretend and call it a tale."

The talebearer is offered tobacco but she shoos it away.

"I don't want tobacco for this," she says. "I give it as a gift."

So first, you see, there was Papa Job. Papa Job wasn't the kind of man who walked around with wet stains under his armpits. He was the kind of man who kept himself smelling of American soap. He wore brown pants that barely reached the ankles, the hems held up by safety pins and paperclips. The matching brown shirt he wore was always clean, though the collar nibbled away ragged at the edges.

Every night Papa Job oiled and stocking-capped his black head and combed his black eyebrows bushy and low over his eyes and then his thick mustache. The most beautiful region of his form was the palms of Papa Job's hands, which were the purest pink, imprinted with bold fatelines; the body skin on him, brown as shoe polish. It was Papa Job's ritual to eat and then to sit at the end of the bed in the dark with his ankles crossed and his long brown toes curling and twisting against each other. Cupping his hands over the harmonica, he played the low-est, blue-est melody God ever wrote on a two-dollar instrument. Outside the bedsheet that curtained the window was the land of immigrants and ghost slaves.

Everything was grey-colored in 1951. All the people wore grey and black colors: the ladies with curled bangs and ankle-length skirts and the men with bag-size pants. The cars with the fat round hoods was black metal. The trolley beating up and down the streets was grey steel. And the ghost people, the slave children, they were stepping over the train tracks to get to the beauty parlors and barber shops.

There are many black-and-white photographs in the basements of Detroit. The photographs will show you the color of things at that time and the ghost slaves that be during the 1950s.

Papa Job rented a small building that had once been a bar on the corner of Linwood and Davison. It was surrounded by dirt and enclosed by a fence. Barbed wire rolled over the top of that fence. His neighbors would pass the fence and run mock, "Where you think you are, West Indian? In a prison, man? In a prison? Say, black West Indian, where you think you from?"

The renovated bar squatted on the corner of street-lined rows of tenement buildings, bombed-out windows, gaping holes in a grey sky. A woman in widow's weeds would lean on folded arms from one of these windows, a grey curtain tied in a knot behind her. She would open her mouth and roll out a blues song.

> I tell you widow woman
> Is just as good as dead
> I tell you widow woman
> Is just as good as dead
> Nothing but some ghost man
> Laid up in her bed
>
> One night that whiskey bottle
> Took my man and gone
> One night that whiskey bottle
> Took my man and gone
> Left me with six chil'run
> Now living's just too long
>
> Some days you know I can't tell
> If it's colder inside or out
> Some days you know I can't tell
> If it's colder inside or out
> It ain't the holes up in these walls
> It's the lonely I'm talking about

The widow's voice floated down like the snowflakes on the thin cold glass of Job's fenced-in windows. His one-room house was once a corner-corner bar, now renovated. Sometimes the ghosts of drinking men would pass cool across his face as if asking him to join them in their drinking. But Papa Job wasn't a drinking man. He read by candlelight. He read any kind of book he found in trashcans and he read from a tattered Bible. But he didn't believe all what was written in that book. He studied the Bible more than he read it, to separate the true from the lie. That was his way. He hated any kind of lie.

We all have a history and so Papa had. When Papa Job was seven years old, his elder sister shined his face with Vaseline and waved good-bye to him. Standing in the snow on street corners, he polished shoes, sold newspapers, and smiled showing all his teeth.

At twenty-five he got half-sole shoes with cardboard inside, crunching ice and snow. He went to work at the Tuller Hotel in his knee-length black coat and black hat. At the hotel he put on a red bellboy's uniform. He carried people's luggage and yes sirred, yes ma'amed everybody from dawn until dusk. He saved up his money religiously. And he headed straight home to his renovated bar after work. When darkness rolled over, out of it creeped forth every wild thing of the earth: the aimless ghost slaves who wandered hungry, who mounted up and went down again, their courage melting away. When daylight arose, they withdrew themselves and lay down in their dens.

Papa Job's landlady was the only one to get inside Papa's tall steel fence. She was a full-busted black woman with a short ribbed neck. Tiny pieces of lint lived in the folds of her neck. She had shaved eyebrows that were penciled back in in black. This landlady was once the proprietor of the bar he now lived in. Every other week she would come to collect the rent, slipping and sliding on the ice and snow. She would lean against his door frame in her crushed velvet black coat and her black leather pumps that were too tight. A red mark ringed the back of her swollen feet. Even leaning, she towered over Papa Job's five-foot-six height. Papa smiled up at her with teeth white as milk and held the door open only a tiny bit. Her warm breath came to him smelling of hard liquor. She stood there a while and chatted a bit, "Cold weather we're having, eh?" Then she stuffed her bosom with his currency and wobbled off on pointy heels.

By January the snow was coming down heavy. Winter's tongue rifted and rustled white outside his window. Beneath the wood floor of his dwelling was a musty cellar where he saved and stored canned vegetables to keep from going hungry during the harder winter months.

This night Papa Job lifted the trapdoor and climbed backward, step by step, down the ladder to his cellar. The cellar was dark. The floor was cold concrete. Black water pipes like lamp posts stood here and there, holding up the beamed ceiling where black waterbugs lived. Papa Job's house slippers crunched down on bugs that had died and dried on the concrete. There were three tiny windows against the brick wall. The windows barely reached above ground. Papa Job went over to a dusty handmade wooden shelf. He kept many rows of canned goods on the shelves. The cans were rusting and covered with cobwebs from sitting for so long. As his eyes moved from one shelf to another, Papa noticed that one of his cans of yam was gone from there and he wondered who got so low as to take his yam like that. He looked up at the tiny-tiny windows above his head. None of the windows were open and none of the panes broken. Papa Job stood there thinking, turning that can of yam over and over again in his mind.

The next evening Papa Job's empty stomach bumped the ladder rungs as he descended again to his cellar. He stepped onto the cement floor and felt a waterbug squish beneath his slipper. He scraped his sole on the rung to remove it. Then he shuffled over to the shelf of cans. He was going for a can of beans but found only an empty ring in the fine dust. The can had been there last night. He saw it last night. Now he swore to catch the one who was thiefing his food and kill him.

The following evening he left off from his bellboy job early. When he got home, he took his machete, brought over from Nassau, a pawned .45, and a baseball bat. He lifted the trapdoor in the floor, descended the ladder, and hid in a spot where he could see from all sides. He waited and the cellar air chilled him. Then he heard the trapdoor squeak open, splintered shafts of light came down, he heard the rubbery squeak of boots on the ladder rungs. Now he was awake. He clutched his weapons. And in his heart he thought, "It's you or me, Anancy." Anancy was a little trickify man told about in stories on the Island. "Yah, Anancy, it's me or you."

The wintry air opened up for the person who booted past. Papa Job listened to the crunch of bugs. Another can slid off the shelf. His fists tightened on his three weapons. His feet sprang forward. Flurried motion. A cobweb waited, netting his face. He tripped over the bat. His weapons splattered across the floor. Papa Job shouted. She darted. A woman! Papa held onto the hem of her poncho and pulled himself to his feet.

He said, "What you be doing thiefing me property without me say-so?"

Her woman's voice came out as cool as the wintry air. "I didn't do it."

But he shouted, "You're a thief, man!"

"The devil placed that in your mind," she frowned. "Let me go. From now on I won't bother you. I'll go someplace else."

She tugged her poncho out of his hand and tottered a little backward.

She was a tiny woman, the color of blackberries, and high-cheekboned. Her long slender neck held her head like something breakable. She was chesty, with small hips. She had a way of standing akimbo, her belly extended, her palms on her backside, and her elbows jutting out behind her like wings, that reminded him of the Islands. She was young, maybe early twenties, carrying a shopping bag in the crook of each arm. She wore a black felt hat, a man's hat. Long thin braids were wet on her shoulders and speckled with beads of snow. She had thin brown lips, a long angled nose. Then Papa Job gave her eyes a look. Her pupils flashed gold with flecks of brown. His heart began to beat fast, bap bap bap. But his voice came out harsh when he spoke to her.

"Why should I let you go?"

And she answered, "Why would you want to keep me?"

And Papa Job said . . . Well, he couldn't find nothing to say.

She removed tobacco from a pouch at her waist and lit a black chipped long-stemmed pipe.

Papa Job's eyes flickered over her. "Hmm, it would be good to have this one for a wife," he thought.

Her eyes fastened on him. "How do you know I want to *be* your wife?" she asked. Then she took a long deep draw from her pipe.

Papa Job swallowed. "I wasn't thinking—I didn't say—" he stammered.

She eased her behind onto the bottom step of the ladder. "I am of the Ki," she went on, "and you—you are from the Island, but you are not of the Ki."

"So, she was of the Ki," Papa Job thought, "those people who sat under the beamed roof of the Eastern Market. They send the young ones like her out to thief for them." He remembered the Ki as a little boy, but at that time they were mostly called the black gypsies.

He remembered how he and his elder sister, Claomie, would filter in with people milling about in the hot of the Eastern Market. Tired people dragged tired children, shoving wire carts and laboring with big bags full of smaller brown bags.

Claomie, his sister, wore a burgundy scarf tied loose under the chin. She carried a brown leather bag over the crook of her arm. She had come to America by herself and found work and raised Papa Job like her own child.

"What we get at a market, Claomie?" Papa Job would ask, looking up at her.

And Claomie always replied the same thing. "For eighty cents me get me pinto beans to make soup, four scallions, a garlic, ripe banana. Fifty cents for gungo peas and a bag of dried pineapple to sweet your tooth, Papa."

Papa Job and Claomie would file slowly under the high-beamed roof and pass stands of produce. Papa would watch the farmers calling the customers, their stomachs contracting hard with each word.

"Come on now! Git your watamelons! Twofo dolla! Twofo dolla! Ya bust em, ya buy em!"

And the grapeseller's eyes darted back and forth, fixing upon everyone that passed. "Who want grapes he'ya! Grapes! A quarta a pound! Quarta a pound!" He caught Claomie's eye. He swung up a batch of grapes.

"Quarta a pound, lady!"

His hard belly pressed the edge of the table. His eyes urged her to touch and feel and buy, buy, buy. His thick fingers shook open a bag. Claomie leaned over to touch the grapes. The grapeseller snatched them up and thrust them into the bag.

"Yes, ma'am! Ya want these?"

But Claomie turned away from the table, leaving the unanswered question like a bad smell in the air.

Papa Job clutched the backdress of Claomie and his face bumped against the blue and yellow print. They stopped by more open crates and stands and Claomie's grocery bag got filled up with the items she wanted to buy. She continued going, continued going down the line, until she got to the far end of the beamed roof.

It be quieter down there.

At the far end, huddled on the ground in a tight cluster, were ancient black faces; women wearing gold earrings, holes punctured all the way up the earlobe; men wearing long braids down their backs, bartering off medicines sealed in canning jars, green roots as long as an alligator's tail, or bottled oils of myrrh, aloes, and cassia.

Papa Job stood at Claomie's side, fist full of Claomie's dress.

"Who they?" Papa Job asked.

"They Haitian, Papa. Black gypsies. I'm going to get me fatelines read by them. But don't call them gypsies, call them the Ki."

"You mean like as a don-key?"

"Yah, donkey."

Claomie sat down on the ground of mashed litter within the group of bartering Ki. She pulled her leather bag onto her lap and started rummaging through it to pay the Ki. She handed the man a pile of pennies.

Papa Job's fingers now scooped up the cold loose pennies in his pants pocket. He crouched down. He pulled the Ki woman's palm to him and pressed the pennies there. He saw her long dangling earrings, snakes coiled around a pole, and the head of the snakes brushed her shoulders. "I want my fatelines read," he told her. "I want to know who I will marry and when."

The woman shrugged. "How should I know how to read it?" She watched him through cool, heavy lids.

"Hmm. Well, I also heard the Ki sell juju," he said. "What would you give a man if he want a woman but she don't want him? What juju do you have for that?"

Her eyes turned crafty. "There is no juju for that," she said.

He stood up. He slid his hands in his pockets. "I don't believe you," he said. "You just don't want to be telling me about it."

She puffed from her pipe and watched him closely.

Papa Job grunted. "Keep the money."

She hesitated, unsure of him, then quickly counted the pennies in her palm, pulled up her grey woolen poncho, and shoved the money into her skirt pocket. He saw that she wore three layers of skirts all with different prints and her boots were laced all the way up to the knees. His palm slid down the back of his head.

"Are you happy?" he asked. "You couldn't be happy. You are a hungry woman."

"Happy?" she replied in a yawning, casual manner. "What is happy, hm?"

"Sa-tees-fied, mamba. Or are you unhappy?"

"Hmm. No, I am not unhappy. But give me a bite to eat and I will be sa-tees-fied."

She steadied her pipe between her teeth, lifted herself from the rung, and picked up her bags.

Papa Job followed her swaying backside up the ladder.

At the wooden table, Papa Job forced his eyes down on his bowl.

"Ahhhhhhhhhh, my God," he whispered, "the incense smell of this woman."

The woman gazed up at him coolly and with a small smile. "You say that?"

But what else was she to say to that? She pay him no mind. Together they ate beans and corn and drank black coffee while a red candle burned down, hardening many paths along a green bottle.

Papa's one-room walls could have been plastered together with wet earth. The walls were black or else thickly layered with soot. The room was shaped like a tunnel; on the left a long wooden bar once used for drinking, and behind the bar were many rows of shelves reaching the ceiling; along the middle wall was the front door of battered wood; and along the right wall was a closet with hinges but no door, inside the closet strung with three shirts and three pairs of pants was a rollaway bed raised on its grey metal stand. A bureau beside the closet shelved a pair of bongos, photographs taped to the mirror. A porcelain sink had been piped through a gash in the wall. And next to the sink was a little room that held only a toilet. Above the toilet a naked bulb hung down low from a gold chain.

Papa Job and the Ki woman sat at an eating table near the stove.

Papa swallowed the food in his mouth and looked up.

"Do I sew, hm?" she asked, finishing his thought again.

She leaned over to study the paper clips holding up his pants legs.

"Ah, me see it now," she said, straightening her back.

Papa Job frowned. "I don't ask you to do no sewing."

"Yah. You ask," she sighed. "I know your mind." She used her fingers to push the beans on a fork and dropped them red down her throat. "I don't do much sewing, man. I bleed too much. What else?"

Papa Job crossed his ankles, slid his interlaced fingers between the warmth of his two thighs, and held them there. He liked this black gypsy, he certainly did.

The woman still hadn't removed her black hat nor her grey poncho. He watched the candlelight flicker on her silver snake earrings.

"Which island are you from, eh?" Papa Job asked.

"Far far across the water," she replied. "Too-too far for a name."

"You are from Haiti. The Ki are from Haiti. My sister told me. Why are you hiding? Tell me. Have you been in this country long?"

"Yah and no," she said, licking her fingers. "Out and in."

"I've been in this country since a boy," he said. He watched her eat and nodded, remembering. "In school, all of them say to me one, 'Small Island go back.' They call me black African. They call me Small Island. And so they say, 'Go back.'"

He remembered how he had saved pennies from selling news-papers to buy a saxophone. He was only a small boy then. He saw an ad in the paper for saxophone lessons, five cents a week. He went to a building in downtown Detroit. A white man answered the door. Papa Job showed him his five cents and his saxophone, but the man shook his head. "No, you can't take your lessons here. I can't give you lessons." Behind the man, little white chil-dren sat in front of their music stands, holding their saxophones in their mouths.

He remembered walking and walking until night came down, until he got to the Detroit riverfront. Men were sleeping along the pier cradling whiskey bottles. Papa Job stood at the edge of the pier, looking down at the green water that smelled of dead fish. The handle of his saxophone case hung limp on his fingers. Slowly his fingers loosened. The case splashed.

"Ho," he sighed. His watery eyes sparkled in the candlelight. "I left this country when I reached fifteen. I went back to Nas-sau. Stayed there nine years. My mother was sick and my father had died. I reached twenty and I came back to here. America. The land of plenty. I worked in Florida picking beans. I learned to work hard.

"When we were children, my father would call us, all twelve of us children. He said, 'Now, hm, I have very very many chil-dren. I don't know how many there are of you. I can't even count you,' he said. 'But I know that all of you are not my children. Some of you just used my wife as a road to get into the world. I think there were some strangers who entered. Those of you who do wrong things and don't behave as my children, go and ask your mother whom you are. Ask her whom you belongs to.'"

The woman nodded. "Your father was rough."

"Yah. He was loving but no-nonsense."

"A'who that?" she pointed.

On the wall overlooking the four-burner stove, a nail had been ripped through the edge of a photograph of a dark-browed woman in a savanna hat.

"That's my mumma. Mumma Aba." He shook his head, closed his eyes, and clicked his tongue. He leaned back and planted his legs far apart like two strong posts just to think of his mumma. "She loooooved me. Toooo much. She would just be praising me, praising me. 'Ah, Papa Job, ah, my first son, ah, my only son, ahhh, the one who is my wealth.' I would have to tell her, no, mumma, no, to stop her from praising me because I would just be crying. Hmmmm. Mumma Aba," he said, shaking his head and clicking his tongue. "She made me to walk hard."

"A man who loves his mother," she said, "is good. There are men who take their mumma's breast and suck and never care. If they don't care for her, they won't care for any woman." She slid her bowl away. "Well, then, I got to go now. Night going to take me." She grasped the handles of her shopping bags and scraped back her chair. "Thank you."

"Where are you going?" he asked. "To your husband?"

"No. I don't have," she said.

"Do you Ki people marry?"

Umph. She laughed.

Papa Job pushed his feet back into his house slippers, scraped back his chair, and went to the mahogany bureau. He lifted his bongos off the white doily and returned with the bongos to the table.

"That your bongo drum?" she asked, letting go of the handles of her bags.

"Yah," he said, positioning the bongos between his knees. "Liza. That's what I call her."

His fingers rapped overtop Liza like a flutter of wings.

"This drum here want to be talking to you," he said.

"That right?" she replied.

"You want to hear it?" he asked.

"Mmm," she said.

He began to rap a little harder.

"Eh-hey. Can you be hearing it, now?" he asked. "Eh?"

She nodded and smiled.

He asked her again, "Can you be hearing it?"

Each time he asked her, his fingers fell harder on the drum. The veins in his arms filled with blood and leaned into his dark skin; his fingertips turned red same time. Papa Job played the bongo drum with concentrated look on his guest. He thought of what a very dark, sweet fruit she was. The tiny-boned, pipe-smoking woman listened to him and seemed contented as if she knew what he was thinking. After a while she removed her poncho and her hat. She had many thin braids that fell back off her forehead and lay limp on her shoulders. She unbuttoned her sweater and pushed the sleeves up her elbows. Soon she began to sway and her breasts swung in syncopation in the folds of the washed-out material that was her blouse. Papa Job stood up. He suspended the bongos by a strap from his neck, rapping the hollow wood. Back rounded, knees slightly bent, he glanced up at the rhythmic pendulation of her breasts.

She gave him a smile.

"Ai!" he hooted, throwing back his head. "Mumma, I die! I tell you, I swear!" And then Papa Job sang.

Hold him Joe! Hold him Joe!
Hold him Joe and don't let him go!
Hold him Joe, I say, hold him Joe!
Hold him Joe and don't let him go!
Me donkey want wah-ta. (Hold him Joe!)
You better hold your daugh-ta! (Hold him Joe!)
Me donkey wanty wah-ta. (Hold him Joe!)
Now sing a little sof-ta. (Hold him Joe!)
Me donkey wanty wah-ta. (Hold him Joe!)
Now sing a little lou-da. (Hold him Joe!)
Me donkey wanty wah-ta. (Hold him Joe!)
A kumba la-fe keemba!
Hold him Joe!

"What do the last part mean?" she asked.

"The last part?"

"Something, something, keemba," she said. "I say, what do the last part mean?"

"It is the come, woman; the come."

"Umph." The woman grunted and lit her pipe again. Papa Job played up more rhythms. He watched this woman, this rare remnant of some old tradition with origins in a people of his own. Spiritual people, yet superstitious, conjurers and healers.

At dawn, the windows smoked grey like filmy voodoo spirits on the glass. The woman had not moved from the chair all evening but puffed up rings and watched him drum through half-closed lids and contented lips.

"When will this woman tell this man, ye-e-es," he murmured, removing the bongo strap from his neck.

The woman pretended not to hear, but pulled up from the chair, which creaked beneath her, and buttoned her lint-balled sweater.

She shuffled round the table and sat cross-legged beneath the sink pipe. Her right hand began to draw ornamental designs in the dust of the floor. Her left hand held her pipe to her mouth.

"Beware, I tell myself," she said hoarsely, "for fear you follow the wrong drummer home." She eyed him thoughtfully, then looked at the floor again, at her design. "The Ki are only in Detroit for a little while," she said. "We come for Shosta. After the funeral ceremony we go back. Shosta wouldn't eat the food I borrowed from your basement. We Ki can't make a living here in the winter. We needed your food. But still she will die."

Papa Job asked, "Who is Shosta and why will she die?"

"Shosta left our community to come here to married a man like you."

He crouched on his haunches in front of her and placed the drum on the floor. She lowered her lids.

"The old people say men and women become what they've been taught," she said, "by those who make them a man or a woman. My mumma used to say, 'Gal, keep your buttocks very close together so they don't *shake* too much.' And so we been left a way of walking and eating and believing and making love and doing all the things that people do. Some of us lose our memory, however, and we live this life in the flesh. Some of us remember that we are spirit first, only flesh away from the One

Spirit. You be a man of flesh and I a woman of spirit. You and me . . . don't mix."

"Tell me of Shosta," he said.

"Shosta was taken to wife by a man who see with the eyes of the world. His name is Gorme. I will explain to you. Shosta, she marry sheself with Gorme and she bear him two children. You see, at first everything go alright. Shosta is a very, very gentle woman. But sometimes we mistake gentleness for stupidity. After a while Gorme began to mistreat Shosta. They say one who recovers from love forgets about God. He took Shosta from beside him and put her under the foot. He drank strong wine and beer and honey beer and things because . . . well, pressure drop; life be hard and pressure drop. He called her to him and he cursed her, he cursed her, and he slapped her. And he behaved this way to her."

The woman nodded and drew from her pipe.

"Gorme loved the cursing and it came back to him. It seeped into his innards like oil into the bones. If we curse some-one who hasn't harmed us, beware. It is better to tie a stone round your neck and take to the river than to curse a good per-son who has never harmed you. Shosta's spirit break run way from the body. She don't eat. She don't get out of bed. She even leave the children. She is running, running, to return to the One Spirit. She is spitting blood because she has been running for so long. She will soon die. Shosta was of spirit. Gorme was of the world. The old people say it has always been this way."

The Ki woman eyed the flawless brown skin on Papa Job and the thick wavy eyebrows and mustache. She sighed.

"I can't married with you. How can I married with you, man?"

She sat back, but Papa Job was sitting so close that their knees touched.

"Womaaaan," he said in a low voice. "I say I want you for my wife. Why? Why can't you consider me?" His hands came to rest on her knees, his palms turned up in appeal. "Consider me."

Her eyes dropped to his palms, to his fatelines etched in black. She slowly sat forward.

She remembered as a little girl dropping onto her belly and sliding like a snake through a world of thick green leaves. She saw a flutter of black behind a pile of rocks. A frightened baby black-bird flapped its wings and scuttled away from her. The bird's heart drummed at a great rate.

"Hello, Loango," she whispered. "What have you done with your mother?"

She softly clicked her tongue against the roof of her mouth and tried to befriend him. "You want to go and live with me?"

Her mumma, Manji, sat on the step of their clapboard in the Ki compound. She started out by oiling Manji's scalp, using a stick to part the thick hair, and then plaiting the teeny-tiny braids with her small fingers. Talking and talking they brought up some talk about the bird who cowered outside the camp. She asked her mumma if she could keep it. Manji shook her head. "No. The bird's mumma will come for it."

She frowned. "The bird don't have one."

"How do it get birth without one? You got nothing to do with that bird. Put me pot a'fire, now. Time for eating."

But she became full of tears.

"Stop your crying," her mumma frowned. "Birds have to get their raising from birds. They have to be with their own kind. Umph. Children have no sense."

Her lips bubbled and more tears ran down.

Late in the night, while her mumma snored in bed, she tiptoed outside with a cardboard box. She found the pile of rocks and scooped up the bird. The scratching feet, stumbling body, and flapping wings shook the box in her hands. Then she hid the box in a basket of clothing inside the clapboard house.

In the night it rained. In the morning, she pulled worms from the ground. Streams of water like a sluggish brown snake curled around her knees. She hurried past Daddy Dom, who was slumped, sleeping, on the bottom steps of the house. He had been left in the camp to care for her while her mother went with the other Ki to market to sell. She tiptoed up the stairway and into the house and was dropping worms into the box as she found them.

Manji came home wearing her black felt hat, her necklace of fishbones, and toting her jars of medicinal herbs in a kettle. She squeaked open the front door of the clapboard, smelled the dead flesh, and did not waste time in hurrying back out again, the kettle clattering against her leg. Manji made her bed on the ground in front of the house. Manji turned the iron pot upside down and slept with her head on the base.

Inside the house, emptied of her mumma, she pulled the box from its hiding place in the basket of clothes. She peeked under the lid. She shuffled out the weightless ball of feathers onto her palm. The bird's eyes had closed. The neck was like a rubber band dangling. The short black feathers on the neck were spaced apart and stuck up in points. Then she felt something cold on her palm. Lifting up the bird with a finger, she saw a brown, jelly-like substance being expelled from the bird onto her hand like a pelt of rolling mucus. She startled and dropped the bird. Her own urine began to soak her underwear, streak her legs, and water-rim her shoes.

Even after the bird was buried, her mumma refused to enter the clapboard, not for a week, because of evil smells, angry spirits, and bad omens.

Dragging her blanket down the steps and through the dirt, she cried and cried. She lay close to her mumma on the ground, licking the salt drivel running from her nose. Manji was eating nuts. She spat out the hard shell and then spat two or three more times to get rid of the tiny pieces of shell on her tongue. Finally she brushed off her blanket and said, "Stop your crying. There is nothing hidden that won't rise up. You try to hide life or death, love or a lie, and the very rocks will cry out. Hide the fire if you will-or-may, but what will you do with the smoke, hm?"

That night the sky was navy blue. Clear and cold. They sat up with blankets draped over their shoulders and she ate the nuts her mumma cracked for her. Finally Manji lay down with the back of her head on the black pot base. She folded her arms tight across her breasts. She said, "Lay down." So she lay on her side close to her mother's back but the tears kept dropping out of her eye.

Manji glanced over her shoulder at her. She said, "Stop that. Don't let people hear you doing that." When things quieted down, Manji told her, "I read the stars tonight. One day you will have a blackbird. His fatelines will be as the feet of a bird. This bird you can cover with your blanket and carry to bed. I tell you, he will lie with you and fan his tailwing with strength."

When the Ki woman focused again, she saw that Papa Job had moved beside her under the sink. His black wavy head rested against the wall and his upraised knees held Liza, his bongo drum. His eyes were closed as he tapped her tight drum-skin with his claw-like fingernails.

The Ki woman rested her head back too. She said, "Already me blackbird drum against the belly of another woman. What am I to do about that?"

Then her eyes fell on his hands, on the fatelines etched in black. She murmured, "You have beautiful hands, husband."

Papa Job took the Ki woman called Sizway on the trolley to a dusty old state office to sign marriage papers. She picked up the sheet and smiled. She eyed him curiously.

"What is this, eh?"

"It's marriage papers. We both sign."

He smoothed the sheet with both hands. He read every-thing. Then he shook his pen so the ink would flow thick, and he signed.

"Now you." He gave Sizway the pen; slid the sheet in front of her.

She stared at the sheet. "This marriage?"

"Yah."

"Umph," she said, folding her arms on the desk. "Tell me now, what happens when the building catch'a fire? What then? No more paper, no more marriage? What?"

"Sign," he pointed. "This is how we do it."

At midnight they stood together in a downtown church. Papa's midnight bride mispronounced everything the preacher told her to say, while a funeral went on outside in the snow. The mourners paraded in boots, on foot, following jazz musicians in black coats who followed a black casket on a horse-pulled junk wagon. The wagon left wheel tracks and broken rose petals like patches of blood in the snow.

After midnight Sizway blew out the red candle, took off her blouse and layers of skirts, uncovered her legs, and waded through the bedsheets. Her woven braids streaked the pillow. She renamed him Kibaba Job, the proper way of addressing her husband. As he slept, Sizway put a leg across her husband and closed her eyes.

—————————

"The Ki have a saying," the talebearer says, "Who knows all there is to know about life? And what a man doesn't know is always stronger than him. Eh-hey . . ."

—————————

Sizway moved her shopping bags of things into Papa Job's house, but she herself was rarely there. Papa Job paced the length of the tunnel of their house. He circled the bar and he circled the center of the floor. He circled the eating table and stood in front of the stove. He stared up at the picture of plump Mumma Aba hanging on the soot-colored wall. Then he went to pacing around again. The doorknob turned in on him. Sizway entered, covered from head to toe with snow.

"Where did you go this late time of night?" he asked. "I worry for you."

"Sorry you worry," she murmured. "I left you sweet rice and mushrooms in the pot."

Sizway bent over and untied her boots at the door. But twin bars of worry creased the middle of Job's brows and he stood over her with his hands in his pockets.

"Where did you go, Sizzy?"

"Hm?"

"Where did you go! Where?"

Sizway sat down on her bottom. "Come down, Kiba, and help me off me boot."

Papa Job hesitated before he came down. She leaned back on her palms as he pulled. His shirtsleeves were rolled up. She watched the muscles in his arms flex and strain. "I like your arm, man," she said. "I wish me arm could look like yours."

"And I like your leg and your eyes," he replied. "I wish me leg and eye could look like yours."

Finally he offed the boot.

"Sizzy, where did you go?"

"I am here for Shosta, Kibaba," she said. She left her foot on his knee. "Remember. We are here in Detroit because of death."

Still Papa Job's twin bars of worry went on the next night. He got home from work and Sizway was gone from there. Around 9:00 she came in making soft coughing coughs.

Papa Job clapped the door shut. He smacked the back of one hand against the palm of the other. "Eh-hey, I see now. You are sick," he accused her.

Sizway seemed listless and tired as she clumped in her boots to the closet. Slowly she removed her layers of clothing.

"Why can't the Ki come here, Sizzy? Why do you go there but you don't bring them here? Bring them here. That's the end."

Sizway began to untie her boots. "The Ki have come because of death," she said, "not because of marriage. We are here for Shosta. After the funeral ceremony they will come and we will marry."

24

Papa Job was pacing the floor when he halted. "We will marry? Is that what you said? We *are* married. How can we marry again? The church downtown, they marry us."

Sizway gazed at him curiously.

"Wait, now," Papa Job said. "Did your family tell you that? Did they tell you we shouldn't have married? Probably maybe they don't want you to marry. They want to send you out to thief for them."

Sizway yawned. "I don't thief," she said.

"You did it," he said.

Sizway sat on the floor as she pushed the toe of one foot against the heel of the other to remove her boot. Then she did the other boot. She didn't ask Job to help her. Finally she padded over to the stove and put a pot of water on the burner. She was coughing again. Papa Job turned up the flame and handed her a cup.

He stepped back, behind her, with his hands deep in his pants pockets. He was not much taller than his wife. She placed the cup on the stove, removed a pouch from her waist, and poured the contents in the cup.

"What is that?" he asked.

"Slippery elm," she answered.

"It looks like tree bark," he said.

"It is tree bark," she replied.

Papa Job remembered something and frowned. "And you thief for them. You did it," he said. "Why are you saying you didn't do it?"

"My husband," she said, "your spirit is too high."

"There is nothing wrong with my spirit," he told her.

"When your spirit is too high, there is no point in discussing anything," she said. "Your spirit is too high."

Sizway watched the water in the pot. The water was cool. It didn't start boiling up yet. She covered her mouth with the back of her hand and coughed.

"Just tell me, Sizzy," he said, "why you said a minute ago that you didn't do it? You did it for me. You remember what happened here late time of night, two weeks ago, at this same house in the cellar? You remember how you thief the tin? Eh? You remember how you *thief* the tin? And if I hadn't come back to this same house to catch you, I would just be licking me own bones at mealtime. Yah," he nodded. "You did it."

Sizway dipped a finger in the pot of water. Still cool.

"You are my husband," she said. "How can a woman thief from her own husband?"

"Don't tell me that," he replied. "We weren't married then."

Then Sizway told him what he didn't know. "Your spirit has been married to my spirit for a very long time. Ever before you found me in your cellar. Don't deceive yourself."

"And you deceive yourself," he said. "We married two weeks ago. What are you saying? The first time I met you was in the cellar."

"Don't say that," she said. "You are talking about a physical meeting. There is more to marriage than that."

The talebearer scratches her head.

"Hum, and so you have this Ki woman of twenty-one or twenty-five years, right? no one really knows her right age; and you have this Island man, twenty-five, right? and the both of them are living under the same roof. The tongue and the teeth, they live together; they sometimes fight. If you ask two people to live together, you ask them to fight. And the first year of marriage is no easy something."

When they first married they examined each other like new cloth. Papa Job had a certain way of sleeping in fetal position on his side with his knees pulled up to his navel. Sizway herself slept on her back with her hands in front of her as if she were sleeping with many people and wanted to give them room. Every feature in her face was smoothed out. She didn't sleep with her lips ajar. And her blackberry skin was flawless. When he put his nose there Papa could always find a woodsy incense smell left by her pipe tobacco.

Now you can know that they took each other in, seeming to memorize everything they were. The things they didn't like they kept it inside. You see, they were newly married. There would be time enough for that.

In the evening in this dead of winter, as was his habit, Papa Job bent over the sink and scrubbed and washed from head to toe. His earlobes were so clean they reflected light. He oiled and stocking-capped his black wavy head and combed the black eyebrows bushy and low over the eyes and then the thick mustache. His clothing Sizway washed on a scrub board. His brown shirt and trousers she ironed. Then she carefully folded them in a certain way and put them in between two pieces of newspaper, placing his heavy Bible on top of it.

Sizway's time now. She went to the facebowl. She turned on the hot water but it ran cold. She turned on the cold water but it ran colder. Papa Job smelled of soap, soap, and more soap. She washed in cold while cold wind rattled the window above the sink.

Papa Job sat at the eating table in his striped pajamas with his back to the stove. His stocking cap was snug with a small knot at the top. He switched on the table lamp and unfolded the newspaper. The President's picture was on the front page. The black-and-white photo caught him sitting at his desk. The headline read, "War Progressing Well." The President was flanked by the Secretary of the Navy and the Assistant Secretary of War. Papa opened wide the newspaper; there was more talk of war. Papa Job stroked his head in a circular fashion as he read the news.

Sizway walked naked to the bureau on the opposite side of the sink and pulled on her dressing gown. The white linen slid over her head and through her upraised arms. The hem floated around her bare feet. Then she carried a basket of small canning jars. She settled on a chair across from him. She began removing the jars from the basket. Sealed inside were medicinal herbs—pieces of bark and dried leaves. She unscrewed the lids with long slender fingers patterned with veins.

Papa turned the page. "They say the war in Korea is almost over."

"Mm," she murmured. She got up to get a mortar and pestle. She came back. She shook out a dried green leaf. Then she grinded the leaf.

She shook another leaf into the bowl, took the mortar and pestle, and grinded it down. Papa Job looked up from the newspaper. Soon the ground leaf was not one but many, like green sand.

"What is that?" he asked.

"Medicine for Shosta."

He leaned forward and lifted a jar from the basket made of branches. He unscrewed the lid and sniffed the inside. It smelled nice. He shook the herb out onto his palm. The stem was hairy and long and the leaves were somewhat hairy as well.

"What is this hairy one for?"

"For the menses. For women."

"Which menses?"

"If a woman is cramping it will bring on her blood."

Papa Job grunted. He returned the jar to the basket. He slid his feet out of his slippers and leaned folded arms on the table. He watched how she unscrewed things and shook out things. He yawned. "When will you be done with that?"

"When I have done with it."

He watched her a while longer. "Why can't Shosta go to the hospital? They have medicine at the hospital."

"The medicine they have is from our own. Only they put it in a test tube. But we, now, you see how we mix it? Now the herb won't be offended the way we mix it."

"What does mixing have to do? You don't know the doctors here might have a cure for her?"

"There is power in herbs and mooyo, the soul. We have to beg the herb to help us and the One Spirit who gave us the herbs. And then there is the head of the sick person. The herb can't work if you don't work with the head. There are many things to talk to when there is sickness. And there are many things the medicine people here don't know about."

"What are you saying, Sizzy? The doctors here have many cures for things."

Sizway listened and was quiet until he was done talking.

Finally Papa Job yawned again. "Time for sleep. You're not done yet?" He lifted another jar from the basket. "What of this one? What is it for?"

"It is for humans."

"Yes, but for what sickness?"

"When a person can't sleep, he will take it with tea."

"So this herb alone can make a person to sleep?"

"Herbs don't work alone. You have to appeal to the herb to use its power to heal. There is life in herbs and mooyo, the soul. How else could it heal people and help them? And then you have to work with the head. Do you see this mint and this stickle-wort and this one here and all of them here? They don't cure sickness alone. You have to work with the head."

"So the head and the herb, they work together. What else?"

"And so the head—so you talk to the head of the man who can't sleep. Do you know what will be there? Fear will be there. And the fear is there. In the head. If you know how to talk to it, it will come out."

"Which fear?"

"Men fear different things. How can I know until I talk to his head? Probably maybe he fears the journey of life he is on. So when I talk to his head I tell him the past is dead. I tell him the future has no life. It is also dead. So there is only this present time. Each time we speak, each word is moving fast and fast to the place of all dead things. The moment that is passing is the only one we have. If a man sees life like that, he will leave no room for fear. Talk to the head. The fear will come out. Give him the herb. He will even sleep well."

"He will sleep well."

"He will sleep *very* well."

"Humph, medicine woman," Papa muttered. "So you have power like that?"

"I don't have power. Why are you saying I do what God himself does?"

Papa Job looked at her. Then he rose from the chair. He immediately let out a moan.

"What is the matter?" she frowned.

"My heart," he said, bending over.

"What is wrong with your heart?"

"It is with you," he moaned.

Sizway continued grinding. She said, "So you don't know that if your heart was with me you would be heartless?"

"Sizzy, you don't know romance."

"Yah," she smiled. "I don't know it."

He came to her. He drew her out of the chair and sat in it himself, pulling her onto his laps. He tightened his arms around her waist and pressed his nose against her back, inhaling her woodsy incense smell. "Medicine woman. You don't see the time?"

"Shosta needs every time. Her time is running out."

The talebearer picks up a thermos beside her. Her black slender fingers unscrew the cup. She pours brown liquid into the cup. She tastes. She tastes again. She licks the sweet raisin juice from her lips.

"Love stories tell of strange things," she says. "A woman passes. . . . A man speaks to her in a friendly way. . . . They chat together. . . . They lay together. . . . They live together. They enjoy many pleasures. But with all that, they are yet strangers. In their minds they think, if I could only enter the spirit of this one and remove all this strangeness. But there is nothing left to do but to live with the strangeness. To Papa Job, this woman was quite strange. You know their eyes, they didn't see in the same way. Two people. Two different spirits. Yah. Two different worlds. When people are still immatured they don't know how to see beyond their own world. They are selfish. They don't think, if I do this will it bother the spirit of the one I live with? They only see their own side. It happens to people when they are still immatured."

She shrugs. "Love stories. Strange things. Eh?" The tale-bearer drains the remaining juice from the cup.

In this one-room house there was a rollaway bed standing upright in the closet alongside hangers of clothing. Next to the closet was a bureau and next to the bureau a window and sink. Instead of using the bed, they made their bed on the floor near the sink. Sizway's back wanted the floor, not the bed. They laid out a large blanket on the floor and took their sleep there.

This one night Sizway knelt by the light of a small lamp placed on the floor. The orange glow made a small oval on the floorboards, while large black shadows loomed on the walls. She was cutting up a white bedsheet and sewing something out of it.

"For Shosta again?" Papa Job asked.

Sizway paused. She looked at the bedsheet and then over at Papa Job.

"No," she lied. "For you."

Papa Job gave a small smile. "What?"

"Don't worry," she said. She knelt and took the measurement off of him.

"What are you making?" he asked.

"Don't worry," she said again.

Time passed.

Beside the lamp on the floor, Papa slept curled under a pile of blankets. Sizway was bent over in her underslip with her blackberry legs tucked under her and her braids hanging over her face like sheets of rain. She sewed up a square neck and big baggy arms. She embroidered intricate patterns all around the neck of the thing. Her fingers really bled from the embroidery. Finally she tapped Papa Job's shoulder and gave him to try on the thing.

"Please. Try on this something I make you, Kiba."

Papa Job turned over and examined the shirt carefully. It wasn't a dress shirt you wear with a tie; it was more of a Ki shirt. It had no collar. He didn't like it but he kept it inside. He handed it back to her. "Too big, Sizzy," he said and gave her his back. "I can see it already."

Sizway cut the thing down and shook him to try it.

"Too small," he said. "Thank you." And he returned it to her.

Each time she added more cloth or removed cloth but "this thing here would just itch me," he said, or "if I put on this shirt, this sleeve would hang down and get in the food. I'm sleeping," he said. "So you don't know I have to go to work in the morning?" until the thing she just ball up and put in a drawer.

After switching off the lamp, Sizway lay down beside him under the blankets. She closed her eyes. After a while he turned on his side, draping his arm over her waist, and he told her, "Sizzy, I don't wear that kind of shirt. I wear dressing shirt. Why won't you just go to downtown store and buy me a dressing shirt?"

"Umph," she grunted. "Okay." Her fingers were throbbing and paining her.

A few moments later his hand was stroking her arm. She didn't say anything. Her heart was against him. She covered her arm with her hand. "Something is hurting me," she told him.

Papa Job lay there for a while. Eventually his hand came moving up her leg, wanting something, and she made him feel like he was hurting something.

"Why, Sizzy? Is it because of the shirt?"

"No-no. I think my monthly—I think—umph—my arm and my leg and my belly is hurting me."

"So the shirt—"

"Not the shirt. I will even give it to one of the Ki men I know. This one I know has only one shirt. He will like it. He will even love it."

Papa Job lay there but he didn't sleep. Something new was bothering him. He lay there wondering about this Ki man who would be wearing his shirt.

Sizway woke at dawn and prepared the morning meal as usual. She took the rice. She came with it, she washed it clean and squeezed honey and oil upon it. Then she put water in the big pot. She boiled the rice and the rice swelled.

In the half-light of dawn Papa Job came and sat at the eating table.

"Bring the shirt," he said.

"The shirt?"

"So you don't know you made a shirt last night? Bring it."

Sizway brought the shirt from the bureau drawer. He took it from her and laid it across his lap.

"Maybe I will be wearing it sometime. Maybe to sleep in."

Sizway nodded. She scooped rice into his wooden bowl and placed a bottle of milk before him.

"Do you want me to be telling you story this morning?" she asked, sitting at the table across from him.

Papa Job yawned. "I like your stories."

"Won't you give me something for this story?" she asked.

Papa Job took tobacco from his shirt pocket and gave it to her. It was Sizway's ritual to tell story, but not without tobacco. Sizway packed her pipe and lit it. Then she began, while Papa Job ate his breakfast.

"Well, then, there was a husband and wife," she said, "and the husband did a bad thing by insulting the wife when she was on her blood. See, the moon had come out. He had thought she had forgotten about the insult. But when the wife gave birth to her first child, instead of burying the placenta she put the placenta in with a pot of gravy and served it to her husband. He ate it without knowing. After he ate the whole thing done, the husband's belly began to swell. His belly was just swelling larger and larger. And he thought maybe he should ease himself in the lav. He went to the lav, he wanted to shit and nothing happened. It kept on like this for nine months. He went to the lav, but nothing happened. In the ninth month he gave birth."

Job's eyes followed Sizway, who had stood up and was padding barefoot over to the stove. He saw that the backseat of her dress was brown with stain, it had soaked right through. She was rubbing her stomach that was still paining her.

"Want more rice?" she asked.

"Is that a true story?"

"Hm. It is probably not a true story but I am not the liar if it isn't. My mother told it to me and a midwife told it to her."

"I don't believe it."

She shrugged. "Believe it if you want, don't believe it if you don't want."

Papa Job glanced down at the shirt on his lap and then at the brown stain on her dress.

Hum. After winter came the month of thaw. Rain was leaking in zig-zag cracks on the ceiling, staining the paint a dull yellow. Papa Job sat on the end of the bed in the half-lit room. He listened to the drops fall from ceiling to bucket, plink-plunk. A dimly burning lamp was on the eating table. Sizway turned the knob of the front door and came in drenched. Her hat drooped down. Her eyelashes were wet and pointed like needles.

Papa Job teased her, "Didn't you tell me the witches be coming home from their meetings at this time of night?"

––––––––––

"Listen, a person should watch their talk between twelve midnight and one o'clock on a Friday night. At that time a person shouldn't discuss things relating to the spirit because the witches be coming home from their meetings at that time. And even the night has ears. There is a lot of power in the air at that time and that power could enter you. It was a Friday night. A late, late time of night I am talking about."

––––––––––

Papa Job said, "Didn't you tell me the witches be out?"

"We buried Shosta," Sizway sighed. "She journeys with the ancestors now."

Papa Job sobered. Sizway dropped off her wet cloth, one after the other.

"The Ki will go back now," she said. "Everybody will go leave me one."

She went to the lav to dry herself, then she went to the bureau for her dressing gown.

Papa Job sat quietly, polishing the silver metal of his harmonica. He watched the dressing gown drop over her head. Then he asked her, "Where will the Ki go and when?"

"They will go to the compound in Sojourner, Ohio. They will go tonight."

Now dressed, Sizway slid back the bedsheet that curtained the window. The night outside was very dark. Sizway touched her forehead against the glass. The white of the streetlamp made the raindrops running down the window look like pellets of glass. Sizway touched the pellets. But they were on the outside and she was in.

Papa Job came and stood behind her. He was tapping his harmonica in his palm to dry it.

Sizway said, "I want to go with them, Kiba. To Ohio."

"You can't. We live in Detroit now."

"But my family is in Ohio."

"I'm married with you, Sizzy."

"But you haven't yet married my family and community. When will you married with them?"

"What is the—How?—What is the meaning of what you are saying?"

"You are a man," she murmured, "yet you are asking a question that every child in the camp knows. Two people don't marry. It is two families that marry."

"I see now," he said. "Well, in time we will go."

"What time?"

"Some time," he said.

"But the time that is coming," she murmured, "we can not see, man."

Papa Job cupped his palms over the harmonica. His eyelids were two balls of wrinkles, his shoulders raised on each hard note. He slowly walked back to the eating table.

Every evening after that, Sizway asked him when is the time. Papa Job replied her, "Not the time now." Papa Job tried to play with her, tease her, distract her by trying to teach her how to play the harmonica, how to beat the drum. She pointed and asked, "When you do that, how do I do it?" And "What is the way to do that?" After a while, Papa Job just beat the drum for her. When he beat it, his drumming was powerful, filling up the room. He told her it was her own spirit in the drum that gave it power. He told her he would call his drum Black Gypsy. Still and yet Sizway listened attentively and smiled but rarely. Usually she stood alone at the window, pulling back the bedsheet covering the glass. The night's black drizzle kept coming down. She felt her head pounding, pow, pow, pow. Her ears buzzed and she knew it was her people discussing her. She stared out the window, eyes blinking like an animal lost in the bush.

One evening Papa Job pulled out the rollaway bed and propped himself up on a pillow. He was naked but for his boxer shorts. His legs were stretched out in front of him with his ankles crossed. He was reading the Bible, separating the true from the lie. That was his way. Then he looked over at Sizway who was standing by the window. "You know, Sizzy, I've been thinking about buying this house from my landlady. I'm due a raise soon at the hotel. I don't want to rent. I want to own. It will be hard but I think I can buy it."

"Mmm," she said.

He read a little more. "You know, it says here that when the Jews were in the desert, they prayed for manna. It fell, man. It fell. But the time when manna fell from heaven has passed. Now a man has got to work for whatever he gets."

He read a while longer. "Humph. You know this that I'm reading? You know this that I'm reading, Sizzy? It's talking here about the promised land. There's a guy I work with at the hotel. A bellhop. He's always saying how he can't wait to get to the promised land. He say, life down here, man, is too-too hard. He want to get to the promised land. So today he come to work sick. Real sick. His eyes all red up, you know, phlegm up in his throat, phlegm running from his eyes, you know, like he's coughing. Coughing, man, and choking and spitting phlegm in this bag, see. He said he got to go to church in the night and have the priest pray for him. By now he thinks this germ going to kill him.

"I said, 'Man, why are you troubling yourself? If you die from this you don't have to worry. Didn't you say you can't wait to get to the promised land? And now, now that you are about to die and go to the promised land, you want the priest to pray you back down here.'"

Papa Job laughed. "Heaven call him and he run come go the other way."

"Mmm. A'true," she murmured.

Papa Job lifted the Bible.

Standing by the window, Sizway's voice came to him strange. "Kiba, when is the time going to be?"

"Time for what, Sizzy?"

"You know," she answered.

"Not the time now, Sizzy. Why do you keep asking? Don't ask it again." He used his finger to follow the printed words.

Sizway came from the window and sat on the foot of the bed, with her legs tucked under her bottom. She wore a black slip. She sat very straight and still while she took all of this man in with her eyes. His thick, shiny eyebrows frowned. Soft black hair grew from his chest all the way down to the navel, where it was straight and fine as silk. His pale blue boxer shorts were neatly starched. Gentle fingers turned the page of the Bible. His fingernails, as hard as the claws of a bird, followed the print on the page, and his pastel-pink lips moved slightly, silently, as he read. Sizway sighed.

Her bare feet touched floor. She pulled up on herself skirt, then blouse, sweater, and stepped into roughly carved clogs.

Her husband looked up. "What are you doing?"

Sizway tied a long knit scarf around her head and ears, pulled on her black felt hat, and held a shopping bag over the arm.

"I'm going back to my family. To Sojourner," she answered.

In the dark one-room house she clump-slipped, clump-slipped in her clogs to the door. He heard her twist the doorknob.

He placed the Bible to one side. He stood up. "So you will go when I've asked you not to go. Are you married to me or to your family?"

"Have our families married?" she asked him. "How can I decide with authority that I will married with you when our families have not married?"

"We are married!" he said. "The church marry us! The papers are here!"

"Did you also marry my family? Did my mumma put her hand on it?"

Papa Job stood there.

"Okay," Papa said. "Do you want me to write to your mother and tell her we have married? I will write to her."

"No. She is an illiterate."

"Okay, then, I will go there and talk to her."

Papa Job went to the closet where his three pairs of brown pants and three shirts hung neatly on hangers. He pulled pants on himself and zipped them.

"Kibaba," Sizway said, "you cannot do it like that."

"I am going," Papa Job said with finality. He jerked his arms through his shirtsleeves.

"But you can't do it like that."

"Then if I stay, you will stay," he said, slapping the back of his hand against the palm of the other. "That's the end."

But Sizway continued to hold on to the doorknob.

Papa Job frowned. "Sizzy, do you want me to be addressing you like a man? You are staying here. That's the end."

"Address me as you like. I cannot stay. I want us to marry. I only followed you to the downtown church to please you. But that's not marriage in our own. I want my family to put their hand on it."

"What kind of marriage is it that you want?" Papa asked. "A black gypsy something? What? What kind of marriage something?"

The doorknob twisted.

Papa Job frowned. "If you leave now, Sizzy, don't bother coming back."

The wooden door inched open—bit by bit.

"Sizzy. If you—If you leave now—"

The door shut in the hollow room.

But that wasn't the end. The following day Papa Job got a telegram from the American government telling him to report to duty. The Americans were sending him to the war in Korea. It was 1952.

chapter two

Thunder clapped in the woods of Sojourner, then rumbled away in the night sky. ribbim-bim-bim-bim. baBoom, baBoom, ribbim-bim-bim. Arrows of rain fell all around. Thick barks of tall trees loomed in the dark. The trees shook their hair and tossed rain about in every direction. Bakatak, bakatak, bakatak, the splatter of wet muddy feet as a Ki woman runs. Stinging leaves hit against Sizway's half-slit eyes. Finally she saw the house made of jagged stone. It was not within the Ki camp but on the edge of it. Sizway splatted up the pineboard step. She shut the door on the wind and stood still inside, dripping water.

The flame of a candle on a long, narrow wooden table dipped and danced, aroused by the sudden wind. Near the table, Manji was bent over a wood-burning oven, tasting the contents of a pot.

Sizway wrung the wet from the hem of her skirt. "Hello, mumma."

"Ho. You are back now," Manji said.

Manji wore a head scarf tied in back of her head. She wore a button-down sweater. The sleeves stopped short above the bone of her skinny wrists. She wore a floor-length dress and hard shoes missing shoelaces. Finally she stepped slowly around, licking her fingers. Her dangling copper earrings made a watery tinkle. She lifted blind eyes—grey pupils smeared with a white film like mucus or clouds. Her eyes focused somewhere above Sizway's head. High cheekbones were speckled with brown raised moles. The bone of her nose was long, narrow, and pointed, then flared slightly at the nostrils.

Sizway wrung the rain from the tail of her blouse, then came and knelt before her mother with head bowed. She remembered and removed her soaked felt hat, wringing that out too. Manji patted the air with her thick working hands until she brushed the top of Sizway's braids, then she rested her hand there and continued patting Sizway's head.

"Mm. Sizway. My dear one. She who brings light into this house. She who honors a mother's womb. She who shows her womanness and keeps strong. Worthy daughter of the One Spirit. Daughter of the moon. You who are named. You who are called. You who are spirit, thinly covered with the flesh of this world. Your breath and your life be my crown. . . ."

She went on greeting Sizway with praise names, while the rain rolled from Sizway's scalp, down her long angled nose, and fell to the floor planks.

Through Manji's praises she recounted Sizway's foremothers and fathers and their foremothers and fathers who came before. She told Sizway the nature of their lives and how their spirits and their lives were all linked to hers. Sizway's spirit grew and grew with her mother's words. When her spirit swelled to its full size, she got to her feet. Though she was soaked with rain, she held the smooth line of her neck erect like a large water urn.

Manji stepped back.

"I will wash, mumma," Sizway said.

"Okay."

Sizway pulled off her blouse. She twisted her hips out of her skirt.

Manji turned around, hitting the oven with her walking stick. She lifted a metal pail of hot water off the top of the burner and placed it on the floor. "You shouldn't be out in the rain," she said.

Sizway knelt on the floor planks beside the hot water. She scrubbed her body with a soap and bristle brush.

After scrubbing, she went to a shelf of neatly folded cloth and put on a blouse and three layers of skirts, all with different patterns. Sizway met her mother at the table and sat across from her. She wrapped her wet braids in a tie-dyed scarf, which she circled numerous times like a nest around her head. As she tucked the ends of her scarf in back of her head, her mind reached out to her mother's. Sizway leaned across the table and touched her mother's forehead with the back of her hand like someone feeling for fever. Manji's hair was fluffed out of the sides of her scarf, a mixture of rust and grey.

Sizway withdrew her hand and clucked her tongue. "Mumma, don't do that. Why are you closing your head to me?"

Manji's lips seemed to hold in her laughter. "Because you like to find things you don't need to find. Cut the bread. And cut the bread."

Sizway glanced at her mother's head before she cut into the wheat bread loaf. She gave her mother her own and she cut a slice for herself. Manji bit into the bread, chewing briskly. Crumbs dotted Manji's cheeks.

Sizway poured navy beans over brown rice in a small bowl. "How have you been, mumma?"

She slid the bowl across the wood toward Manji.

"Very fine. Just too fine. And you?" Manji took up the bowl and ate with her fingers.

"Very fine," Sizway murmured. Sizway leaned over and used her hand to wipe up the spilled juice on her mother's chin. Then Sizway prepared her own serving.

"Umph," Manji grunted, then swallowed. "Ho, I make dream."

Sizway kept cool, kept down, as she dipped in her wooden spoon.

"What did you dream?"

"At night," Manji said, "when your head is at rest, hm, the spirits will come and descend to your head. And they will talk to you."

Sizway slurped from her spoon and swallowed, slurped from her spoon and swallowed. "They descended. And then?"

"And then? The spirits descended. So, you didn't know? Umph. They descended."

"What did they say?"

Manji shrugged. "They talked."

Sizway slurped. "And then?"

"Huuu. Even old women dream."

Manji ate with her fingers in silence.

"Nalajah asked of you," Manji said.

"I will go and see Nalajah," Sizway said. Nalajah was Sizway's girlhood friend.

Manji felt around for a cast-iron pot of tea on the table. Then she dipped a chipped cup of porcelain into the pot.

"Nalajah's daughter—umm." Manji winced after sipping the scalding liquid. ". . . started school." She lowered the cup to the table. "She didn't want to go to the school in town. She came. 'Mumma-agba.' She was crying. I said, 'What is the matter, why are you crying? They will teach you things at the school.' 'I don't want to learn there,' she said. 'I want to stay here in the compound and learn.' 'Oh-ho, you want to stay and learn here? There is the truth you learn here that will make you strong in the world and there is the proper truth the school has to give you. You go there to *specialize* in something. Get a skill and *specialize*.' I told Nalajah's daughter about you when you started school."

"What did you tell her?"

"Eh?"

"I say, what did you tell her? I'm remembering starting school."

"You cry-cry too much. Your father, he talked to you."

"I didn't cry for school. I cried because daddy was preparing for death."

"Yah," Manji said, remembering her dead husband. She picked up her cup and slurped. "You will talk to Nalajah's daughter," Manji said.

"Yes, I will talk to her."

"Tell her to go to school."

"Yah."

"Umph, the poor people around here say school is too expensive. But ignorance. It is more expensive."

Sizway remembered the time the schoolteacher got angry and called her a bastard. Every day the schoolteacher took up the class. She asked the children, "Who know about such-and-such?" All the children's hands were in the air. Sizway's hand, too, was always up. The schoolteacher pointed to her. Sizway would start to speak and before she could speak the teacher would point to someone else. "Next! Next!" "She gave everybody a chance but me one," Sizway thought. So one day, Sizway got very angry at the teacher. She raised her hand. The teacher pointed to her. Sizway started to speak. But the teacher shouted, "Next! Next!" So Sizway offed her shoe and threw it at the teacher. The shoe hit the chalkboard. It didn't hit the teacher. The teacher turned red same time. Her scream, "You little bastard." And Sizway said, "Oh-ho, I am a bastard? I will tell my father, then, that he is not my father. I will tell him that the teacher said I have no father, that I am a bastard. I will tell him that I don't want to live with him anymore since he is not my father. Then I will go and ask my mother who my real father is." The teacher was shaking. She was begging Sizway not to go and tell her father.

Manji's chuckles interrupted Sizway's thoughts.

"I'm remembering that too," Manji said. "But don't tell Nalajah's daughter about that. Children shouldn't throw things at their teachers."

"Ho, hunger was troubling me since I leave Detroit," Sizway sighed and placed her bowl aside. "Now I'm alright."

Done with that, Sizway began packing her pipe with tobacco. Then she pulled her leg up in the chair and rested her elbow on her knee. That pipe she smoked, a quiet it brought.

"The spirits came and talked to me when you were in Detroit," Manji said, wiping her greasy fingers into a towel on her lap. "I make dream."

Sizway sat quietly in rings of smoke.

"In this dream a man was given a drum by his dead ancestor. He was told to work the drum until eternity. This man tried to play the drum. But the drum. It wouldn't talk. A woman came. And a woman came. She sat down between the legs of the man. She turned into the drum. When the man played the drum, the drum sang. And every time the drummer played, he knew it was the spirit of this woman singing through the drum."

Sizway replied, "There is a man."

Manji scratched the side of her head, then folded her arms on the table. "Umph. And then?"

"He is in Detroit living where Shosta is buried."

Manji stared straight ahead, her elbows gouging the wood.

"This man," Sizway said. "Kibaba. He is the drummer. And he want me for his wife."

"And so he wants you," Manji shrugged. "You who never look at a man unless he is old or a wrinkled infant. This Kibaba will only suffer for it."

Manji bit into a chunk of bread.

"This man propose love to me and death do us part and so forth. Death do us part he pledge. He made such a pledge. And I pledge it."

"What else?" Manji mumbled through a mouthful.

"He said he is feeling love for me. I followed him to down-town church."

Breadcrumbs flew from Manji's mouth and stuck to the table. "He say he feeling love, eh? That what he feeling?" Manji gasped through gusts of laughter that shook her whole body. "Ho, me God," she said. "Protect us from foolishness when we are eating.

"So he think a man can really love a woman. And he think a woman can really love a man. He is a fool. A man love a woman today, he leave her and forget her tomorrow. The same tongue he use to bless her, he will use to curse her." Manji belched softly. "The feeling of love is a stupid god to follow," she said. "Forget this one." She tightened her sweater across her breasts and folded her arms on the table again.

Sizway got up from the table. She leaned her backside against the oven and stared down at her feet. The floor was gritty and cold so she stood on one foot with the other foot curled on top of it. She held her pipe slightly away from her mouth. "Love. What it is, mumma?" she asked.

"That what people calling love not love, girl. Most people, they don't know what it is. You young girls call love to mean urge. If his penis is good and he stays on for long, you think he is good. But when you find a penis that is better than the one you have, you will leave the first one. A man's penis is not a good basis for judgment."

Sizway's eyebrows came together like dark clouds. "Mumma, you should know I wouldn't marry for that. What is a penis to me?"

"Eh-hey," Manji nodded. "But is he marrying for that? Let me tell you, most men would have more power than they do if it were not for their penis. That's why women can rule them. When a man's penis stands up, hu, all their senses descend to the penis and the penis will lead them instead of the brain. They will follow a woman round like a dog. My God. You see, they put that feeling of sex in their head and not in their hand. You young girls, humph, you don't know. Ask me. I am old. I know. There are men who consult their penis on everything. Their penis will be guiding them in everything. You see, they think from their penis. Down here," she said, "not from here," she said, pointing to her scarfed head. "And this down here, girl, it will lead them in life. My God. Something you will eat forever you don't need to eat in a hurry."

"Kibaba. Hm. I don't think—I don't know if he reason like that."

"All men reason like that. Forget this one."

"Mumma, I want this one."

"And so? You are foolish. You are not smart. I try to teach you smartness and to learn from the wise people. But a smart person can throw away aaaall of their smartness on a foolish act. Then they will grovel around like the fools. You young people think you are wiser than the old.

"Yah. My own mother used to tell me a story. She say, There was a young man, see, who wanted to be wise. He sat with the old people in the camp and he listened and wrote down all the wise things the old ones said. He wrote down everything that entered his ears on little slips of paper. Then, and then, he put what he wrote in a calabash. Now after he had collected aaaall of that wisdom, he decided to hide the calabash at the top of a tree so he could keep the wisdom all for himself. He sling the thing, the uh, the handle of the calabash about his neck. The bowl at his front. He try to climb the tree but he couldn't. His arms couldn't reach around the calabash to get a grip. After time and time of trying, an old man came by. The old man told him to put the calabash on his back, not on his front, and then he can climb up the tree. When the old man left, the young man he sat down, man, and he just cry.

"You see, with all the wisdom he had collected in his one-one calabash, he still wasn't wise enough to climb up a tree. And so that's the story. You hearing me? Listen to an old person and learn. I am old. I know. You young people go to school and you like to write things down. But you don't know anything about life. You go to school to get skill. *Skill.* To specialize. *Specialize.* You go away thinking you know more than the illiterates. You go to school and think you don't need to learn again from the old people. Then you come home crying, 'Teach me again and teach me.' And the wise people never give away all of their wisdom. They always keep some of it if they are wise. And you young people discover that you may be taller than the old people but you are not their equal."

"But mumma—"

"Learn from those who are senior to you, Sizzy," Manji said. "When did you start cursing our way of life here?"

"Please, ma. Do you think I would abandon our way of life here?"

Manji frowned. "So you pick a man from the street. From Detroit. You know how the women here marry. Did they do a street marriage? Are you a street girl? Have you seen any woman like that here? Don't shame us here. If this man had come here with his family, if he had come to the family of the one he wants to marry, then he having done this—"

"So I said to him, 'You and I should come to my family.' And he said he will come. I said, 'I want my family to put their hand on it,' I said to him—"

"You said to him? Then you insult your very self. He doesn't know enough to beg the family of the woman he wants to marry? He doesn't know enough to send an intermediary? Don't shame us here."

"Mumma, he is not of the Ki."

Now Manji's eyes opened in a terrifying way. "Why should I care whom he is? What is allowing you to think like a fool? Did the witches bring you here? Eh? Did the witches put thunder in your head? . . . So you are now a fool, eh?"

Broken arrows of rain pattered the roof. Manji listened and nodded. "Even now the witches fall in the rain."

"It is the One Spirit falling in the rain. It is the One Spirit who brought me here."

"Then what do you think you are thinking when you think something like this? Didn't I say you know how the women here marry? And didn't I say they didn't do a street marriage? Did anyone tell you to do that? Come. Are you hard of hearing? Come." Manji sat sideways in her chair. "Umph," she grunted, "may I not be confronted by problems late in the night."

Sizway knelt before Manji and Manji put it to her. "If you say to someone senior to you, 'I pledge love,' and they say to you, say, 'Love is not a word and love is not a feeling'; if they say to you, say, 'A woman can't marry a feeling, you are going against our way of marriage here,' then what else are you looking for? You have to leave it like that."

All of the fight left Sizway. She knelt there like a stone in water, staring through the clear cold water of her eyes.

Manji grunted and folded her arms. "Sterility is better than a foolish daughter."

At dawn the rain lifted and patches of sun filtered through black paper leaves. Sizway left her mother's house and entered the central part of the Ki camp, carrying a large basket on her shoulder. When she walked, only her feet seemed to move; the rest of her body just skimmed along with her feet with a smooth rolling back-and-forth motion of her hips. Manji warned Sizway not to travel for one year. She was to stay in the camp. She was to keep away from any street marriage. She told her, "If you know a food is bad for you, you don't come near enough to smell it. And if you don't want to eat it, you don't smell it when it is cooking." And so Manji told her not to travel. Sizway showed her woman's strength for one year. She didn't travel. She came with her basket into the central Ki camp.

Beneath the huge trees, semipermanent clapboards were raised on stilts and sat close to one another in a circular space. The clapboards were small. Not more than two rooms in each. The front doors all faced inward toward a center space where the ground had been cleared of grass and packed down hard and smooth. Fires burned outside each doorway. Some were fires on grills, others burned inside rusty cans and others were made simply of dry branches. The Ki sat on the steps of their clapboards engaging in talk.

Females wore silver dangled earrings like a flash of fish under water. They stood with their legs spread, with their palms on their backsides.

They had fenced-in garden plots in back of their houses. They fed chickens, sprinkling the ground. Outside were wooden kitchen tables propped against trees and piled with soiled wooden dishes.

A group of men were using fibers to weave mats. The men sat on the ground, long braids down their backs and black felt hats. The children sat with the men, leaned elbows on the men's thighs, touched and talked with the men.

Women smoked pipes, this one hung a shirt on the line, that one dipped a soapy pot in clear water.

Sizway came carrying her basket of things to sell in town. Kehinde watched her approach. Kehinde was sitting on her stairway. She was clocking maybe eighty or ninety years. Her eyes were listless. She held her cheeks in her palms as if she had been sitting for long with crying children.

"How are you, ma?" Sizway called.

Kehinde frowned. "Where are you going? Sit down."

Sizway lowered her basket in the dirt. Her long skirt flapped against her ankles in the wind. She seated herself beside Kehinde.

"Give me some tobacco," Kehinde said. "Tobacco hunger is killing me."

Lighting up, Kehinde said, "So, you have come from Shosta's funeral."

"Yah."

"Humph. They say this death that is killing the ones we love is telling us of our own."

Sizway nodded, staring down at her feet.

Kehinde's eyes screwed down to slits as she drew from her pipe. "Why did you stay in Detroit for long? What else did you find there?"

Sizway swallowed hard, thinking of Papa Job. "Only death, ma. The end."

"You don't know death." Kehinde smiled. "Bring me plums from the market. Okay? And bring me plums."

Sizway hefted her basket to her shoulder.

"A person is only dead when they are forgotten."

Sizway looked to her. She nodded and smiled. Then she merged in with a larger group of Ki women who were walking the nine miles to town.

The Ki milled into an open-air marketplace. The sun was beating low down on their black felt hats. They propped up wooden canopies to shield them from the sun, then set up their wares. Sizway laid out an ancient-looking rug. It was embroidered black and red with long black fringe and tassels on all four sides. The symbols on the rug were intricate, like a tapestry. She arranged tiny brown bottles of oils, baskets of roots, and brown jars of medicinal herbs.

Soon a customer came coughing.

Sizway sat cross-legged on her rug within the cool shadows of the canopy. "Eh-hey, hello, daddy."

"How are you, Sizway?" The man seated himself on a stool in front of her rug. He came complaining of a rash and a cough. Sizway touched his throat as she murmured words to him. "What the doctor give you fi ease the pain?" The man shook his head. She touched his rash and asked him if there was someone who was irritating him these days. He nodded and said his son-in-law. She told him to settle the dispute with his son-in-law as soon as possible. "The cough comes from holding words in your throat. Because you can't speak the words, your throat chokes on them. Kuffum kuffum. Simple. You see?"

The man nodded.

She gave him a jar of ointment for the rash and a small brown jar of slippery elm bark to make a tea with. Then she told him how he must look after the tea when he boil it.

Along the long narrow aisle of the open market, the commercial farmers exchanged bags for dollars. They removed heavy crates from their trucks and berumped them down on the tables. These farmers sat on fold-out chairs with a crate in between them to place their checkerboards. They chortled in low tones and sipped from their thermoses. The Ki voices were an incessant background of bartering. Women argued and Sizway argued alongside them.

"No-no-no, Tennessee, what's wrong with you that you eat like that?" she asked. "Take the herbs here. Buy it here. Is good here. Seventy-five cents me want for it."

The Ki's vegetables were not sprayed so they wilted quicker and were eaten up in places by bugs. The farmers' vegetables were crisp, bright greens, reds, and yellows. But the Ki's tool to bargain with was to tell their customers that the farmers poisoned their food with pesticide.

Sizway dipped inside her low neckline and dabbed the wet pits of her underarms with a tissue. She wagged the tissue bye-bye to the leaving customer. Other regulars came greeting Sizway by name.

"Can't you think of something better to do on a hot day like this, Sizzy?"

Eva shielded her cat-eye glasses from the sun with her purse.

"Hello, ma. How are you?" Sizway slid her braids behind her ears and slid the brim of her hat further down over her eyes.

"Oh, I'm just fine, Sizzy. Long as I stay out the sun."

Eva was an onion-colored black woman, flat in back and flat in front. Because her legs were bowed, her shoes were miserably run down on the sides. She and her husband were farmers. Eva seated herself on the stool under the shade of the Ki canopy. She fanned herself with her purse while loose strands of hair blew back and forth like broken spiderwebs. "Jim-Walter, my husband, took in a good crop of greens this year. I got U-pick now. Lady came by the farm this morning. She say, 'You got a pound of greens?' I say, 'I got U-pick.' Shoot, I don't need to be kneeling and picking greens in that sun. Told her we got U-pick. You know, Jim-Walter want me to be out there working like him. He say, 'I was driving by today and seen some white woman out there pushing a tractor.' 'Well,' I say, 'She can keep pushing it.' Then he start talking that baby stuff, you know. I don't pay him no mind. He say, 'Baby, baby, baby, why don't you push that tractor?'

"Well, I can't stay too long today. I said to myself, 'Just go on down to the market and get some of that ointment Sizway make for this rash on your hands. Then get on back.'"

Sizway took Eva's hands and examined them. She frowned. "Mumma, the herbs won't work unless you work on the head."

Eva nodded. Sizway sighed and sorted through her jars for the ointment. She gave it to Eva. While Eva opened her change purse, Sizway turned to greet another customer. Eva paid Sizway for it, but she didn't leave right away.

By early evening, there was a bit of people still drifting about in the heat but mostly farmers were packing up, trucks backing out of the parking lot. Sizway was clearing the jars from her rug and packing them away in her basket. And Eva was still there talking.

"Round this time Ebb would've been sixty-five years old," Eva told Sizway, "but no, he had to go and put a rifle to his mouth. You know, his wife only leave him cause he told her she was getting fat. 'Just *do* something bout that *fat*,' he said. When she pack her bags, he blow his head off."

Sizway tightened a lid on a jar.

"I'm telling you," Eva sighed. Then she glanced at her watch. "Well, look at how the time fly. Let me get on." She opened her pocketbook, removing the keys to her truck. "I'll see you, now, you hear?"

"Bye-bye," Sizway called. "Greet your husband for me."

Eva giggled without turning around.

The talebearer gazes off in the direction of her makeshift shanty. The sagging roof is shaded over by trees. There is a crucifix hanging from a rusty nail in the house wall. Strung from the rafters are dried herbs, burlap sacks, and clay bowls filled with power to ward off bad spirits. The talebearer lowers her eyes where black ants run in and out between her toes.

"You know we Ki people don't live in isolation. We live in the world." She watches the ants and spreads her toes wider. "How can you know you have learnt anything unless you live among the living, eh? Sizway moved among them, the living, she listened to them, she took everything in with her eyes and her ears, and she allowed time to turn.

"Now as night fell in the Ki camp, spirited voices directed at the dark told stories and the children answered. The stories were told as lessons for the children, as lessons for the adults."

———

The next day at the open market, the brim of Sizway's hat was planted low on her forehead. Pipe smoke floated lazily from beneath the brim. Sitting on her richly embroidered rug, she had fallen into a prayer space.

Suddenly a female customer's voice jarred her to waking. "Hi, miss. You sell body oil here?"

Sizway slowly lifted her eyes.

The customer had blond hair streaked with brown that fell in crinkly waves down her back. She had blue eyes, a pug nose. Faint freckles dotted her arms and chest. Standing beside her was a little boy, maybe her son. His large ears stuck out from his whitish-blond head. The boy was licking a peppermint stick.

"My name's Billy," the woman said.

Sizway shook Billy's hand.

"I'm Sizway. Please. Sit."

In Sojourner the town was divided down the middle by a railroad track. The white people lived on one side, the other colors on the other side. But at the open market they all came together to buy each other's food.

Billy didn't sit on the stool but knelt on the back of her heels with her purse in her lap. "My sister said y'all sell honeysuckle. I smelt it on my sister and wanted to get some. Sit down, Garrett," she told the boy. "Anyway, my sister—Ohhhh, what a nice rug. How much you selling this for?" She leaned over to examine the tapestry. Her red fingernails ran along the beautiful border. "Will you take five dollars for it?"

"This rug, I don't sell it."

"You'll probably take five."

Sizway's eyes glinted through the white wafting pipe smoke. "Chuko," Sizway called.

Chuko, a Ki woman of great bulk, was sitting a few feet away from Sizway. She hefted herself up and trundled over.

"Our sister here wants honeysuckle, okay?"

Chuko left and came with a small, skinny brown bottle the size of a finger. Chuko lowered the oil toward the woman.

But Billy was lifting the rug and peering under the bottom.

"Well, it ain't like it's new but I'll give you eight dollars for it."

Sizway smiled faintly. "I don't sell it."

"Here is honeysuckle," Chuko said.

Billy dropped the edge of the rug. She took the bottle from Chuko's hand. "Thanks. Hmm. I didn't know it was gonna be so *small*. How much for this?"

"One dollar," Chuko answered.

The woman unscrewed the cap and sniffed it. "One dollar for this?"

"Yes, ma'am."

"Hey, Billy! That you?"

Billy turned. Her curious face broke into a smile. "Hey, Memsie! That you?"

"Yeah, it's me. How you doing, Billy?"

Memsie walked up with pink curlers covered with a nylon scarf. She carried an armful of brown paper bags stuffed with fruit and vegetables. "I ain't seen you in ages, Billy. How you been?"

"Real good, Memsie. I just come to buy some honeysuckle body oil my sister bought last week. Smell it and see if you like it."

Memsie knelt beside Billy, setting her grocery bags on the rug.

"Hi," she murmured to Sizway.

Sizway smiled.

Memsie sniffed the bottle. "Oh, it's real nice. What's it called again?"

"Honeysuckle," Billy replied.

"That right? I was gonna plant some honeysuckle flowers in front of my house the other day," Memsie said. "But my momma said, 'Don't do that. Honeysuckle draws snakes.'"

Billy looked at the bottle suspiciously. She handed it back to Sizway. "Well, I'll thank about it," she told Sizway.

Sizway gave it to Chuko. Chuko trundled away. Other customers came and Sizway attended to them. But as Sizway worked with the customers, Billy and Memsie continued kneeling and chatting.

"I went and got fat, Memsie. Can you tell?" Billy asked.

"Naw, I can't see it."

"I sure did."

Billy lifted her wavy blond hair from the back of her neck where a heat rash splotched the skin. In doing that, her breasts lifted up.

"Wyatt says my butt is getting fat. That's what he say."

Memsie laughed.

Billy let her hair fall back. "You see this top?" she asked, plucking her knitted pink garment away from her belly. "You like it?"

Memsie nodded. "It's real nice."

"I got it for a dollar at a yard sale."

"Yeah? Well, it sure could be brand new."

"I got a bedframe, too," Billy went on, "for ten dollars."

"What size mattress it take?"

"Queen," Billy answered. "The man selling it wanted me to give him thirty dollars for it. But I talked him down to ten. I got a big wide mirror to go along with it. I collect mirrors, you know. I got all kinds of mirrors, all shapes and sizes, all over my house."

Now Billy sighed. "I got too much stuff. I'll probably just wind up selling it all."

She plucked lipstick from her purse. She painted her lips a bright pink, then rubbed her lips together.

"Why don't you drive downtown with me, Memsie? I got to take back some of this eyeshadow I bought."

"They let you return it after you use it?"

"You just tell em it wasn't no good."

"Hm. Well, I don't know."

Memsie looked over at Billy's son, whose cheeks and mouth were stained red with peppermint. "Little Garrett's getting big, Billy. Hello, little fella," Memsie said, waggling her fingers at the boy.

Red spittle dribbled down the peppermint and onto the boy's hands. He gave Memsie a blank stare before crunching down on the tip of the candy.

"He's an awful child, Memsie. He don't mind me," Billy said.

"Aw, I bet he ain't so awful. But he sure don't look much like you."

"He look like his daddy. Speaking of which, Wyatt said he saw you selling stuff at a yard sale a while ago. I said, 'She musta got divorced.'"

Memsie's face turned a shade pinker than the color of her foam curlers.

"I'm divorced from Wyatt, you know," Billy went on. "But he's the kind that likes to linger. He come over and sit around wanting something. I'll give it once in a while. But mostly I don't."

"Hm. I guess you still love him," Memsie said, with a look of concern.

"I'll love a man three times a day," Billy said matter-of-factly. "But if it don't thrill me, I can't. Wyatt, he never did thrill me. Still he come over and bother me to death until I have to do it just to make him go home. I really want a rich man, but where you gonna find one around here?"

Suddenly a tall, stooping shadow darkened the women's faces. Even Sizway looked up. A man was bending under the wooden canopy, carrying a can of beer. He wore faded jeans and a red plaid shirt. He had a red beard and blond curling hair. The man rubbed the boy's head as he entered, but the boy clutched the man's fingers and pulled them away.

Billy looked up, eyeing the man with annoyance. "Wyatt, why don't you go home? I can't talk about nothing sexy without you comin' around."

Everyone, including the Ki women, turned to look.

Billy's ex-husband just stood there.

"Why don't you go home?" Billy frowned.

But Wyatt kept standing there, sipping his can of beer.

"You know, I had two men at my house the other day," Billy said, turning back to Memsie, "and Wyatt chased em out." She frowned up at her ex-husband. "Why don't you go home? Go on. Git. Stop following me around. He just want something. But he ain't gonna get nothing."

Billy grabbed the sticky hand of her son. "I'm going to the five-and-dime before it close. You coming, Memsie?"

Memsie scooped up her grocery bags. "Okay."

Billy pushed past her ex-husband. "I wish you just *butt* out of my business. I can't talk about nothing sexy without you coming around."

Billy's sandals slapped her heels as she worked her way past the other customers milling about in the market. Billy, Memsie, and Little Garrett hurried toward the gravel parking lot, while Billy's ex-husband slowly followed along after them.

Chuko waddled over to Sizway talking loud. "Why does this person keep following me? Do I own him that he follows me everywhere?" Chuko was very large. Chuko bumped against Sizway as she settled down beside her. Chuko laughed deep down inside herself. "Men and women in this life. What a mess, eh?" Chuko said.

Chuko's large breasts and belly shook with her laughter. Chuko wiped her eyes. "Did you hear that woman? And the man? Did you see it? Huuuu."

"Mmm," Sizway smiled.

"That's why our mothers say men would be great if it were not for their penis. To satisfy it, they will give away all of their power to a woman."

Sizway sat thinking her own still thoughts. "It is difficult for a woman to know a good man, eh?" she asked.

"Listen," Chuko replied. "A woman doesn't appreciate a good man until he is dead. That's the first thing. Now all of you are laughing. Do you think I am lying? Listen to me. The same thing for a man. His good woman will have to die first. Why are you laughing? To God who made me. We are all fools."

Sizway's eyes turned up, gazing at the sky. Clouds were rushing in, whitening the blue. "Shower of rain coming," Sizway murmured.

The season of rain came around again. During this season, Sizway fell sick. It was then that Papa Job was remembered. But first sickness came.

In the night there was a thunderclap followed by a hard patter of rain. Rainwater streamed in countless little channels. Every sort of biting and stinging thing came from the humidity and entered the screen windows of the Ki. The Ki lay on mats on the floor, restlessly sleeping, plagued by mosquitoes.

Sizway mumbled incoherently in her sleep. As the rain fell down, she felt as if the darkness was turning and she was a dead leaf floating on the surface of a puddle, turning round and round.

Thunder cracked again in the sky. It was the cracking of Death's joints as it rose up to leave.

At dawn, the humidity was too heavy to lift. Manji managed to pull herself to her feet. She swept her hair off her damp face. She slid up the strap of her slip. She called, "Sizzy?"

Sizway had not moved from her mat.

Manji began rolling up her own mat. She called again, "Sizzy?"

But Death had come and covered Sizway with its blanket. As the days passed, Death sealed Sizway's eyes shut with a sticky glue. It reached down her throat and stole her voice and stole her backbone so that she had no use of her arms and legs. It loosened her bowels, leaving a strong smell of stool. It pulled out the fat in her body and fed upon it, leaving her cheekbones jutting forward and her cheeks hollow. Her brown lips were slightly gapped with a thin crusty white ring along the inside. Frail and wizened, her breath was in her nostrils for brief periods and then retreated inside long silences.

Manji's stick clamored against the wooden planks until she hit upon the shelves that held jars and jars of medicinal herbs. She pulled down glass jars and brought them to her nose. She sniffed them or tasted them before bringing them to the kitchen table. Her stick tapped across the floor, back and forth. Manji doctored the leaves and crumbled them into a black skillet.

"Bilongo, medicines," she murmured, "and mooyo, soul. Something has come along with the power to kill."

She poured rainwater into the skillet and placed the skillet in the oven. She lifted the lid onto the skillet with tongs. She added wood on top of the skillet lid and around the edges of the pan. Done with that, she left the pan to cook.

Manji sat at the wooden table for some time. When the skillet cooled, Manji brought the skillet. She took a sponge and dipped it in there. Her fingers crept across Sizway's face until she felt her daughter's dried lips. She peeled Sizway's lips open and dropped the medicine down her throat.

The moon came, the moon went, leaving another grey sky at dawn. Manji lifted her necklace of small pebbles, seashells, cut hair, fishbones, and feathers over her head and dropped it on the table, her power of medicine exhausted. She stood on her shoetips and lifted a black felt hat from a hook on the wall. She put it on. She pulled her arms through a sweater and with stick in hand opened the door of her house. The sky was grey overhead. The woods out there was hazy with mist. Shoes missing shoelaces stepped down on the cement step. From there Manji entered the woods.

The ground was wet and cold. Her thick-soled shoes sunk into the mud, stuck to the mud, with each step. Her shoes left holes that quickly filled up with water. Her shoes dragged mud-splattered leaves along with her.

Finally she hit against a certain root growing up from the ground. The root had many sister roots and all of them looked like the grey knobby fingers of a hand and all of them belonged to a giant limb of wood. Now Manji stopped. She lifted her nose and smelled a human smell intermixed with the rain-scented air. She lowered herself and sat on the root.

"Kehinde, blessings," Manji said.

Kehinde cleared her throat and spat. "Blessings to you, old mother."

Kehinde sat cross-legged directly in front of Manji. She pulled sixteen nutshells from the small place where we put something. She held the shells in her cupped palms under Manji's lips, and she told Manji to blow her problem into them. Manji blew once on the shells. All of her problem was now in Kehinde's shells.

Kehinde went to shaking the shells. Short braids were plaited over Kehinde's eyes. Her nose was hooked like a hawk's, her eyes were black beads, her teeth were like large bones. Kehinde let the shells settle into her cupped left palm, with her right hand she quickly grabbed from the left. Three shells remained. She shook and grabbed three more times until one shell remained in the left palm. On the ground, lying in front of Kehinde's knees, was a cloth covered with white kaolin powder. On this powdered cloth Kehinde drew a number one.

Kehinde studied the number. "Something secret be buried in the house," she informed Manji. "We bury the head and show the buttocks to God. Something secret be buried in the house."

Kehinde took up the shells and repeated the shaking. She grabbed and again one shell remained in the left palm. Kehinde began chanting as she drew the number one in the white powder, "What you cannot tell the wind, tell God. Something be buried in the house. A pledge be broken in the house. A pledge be buried in the house. Now God has carried the secret and is telling the matter. . . ."

Kehinde shook the shells again. Now two shells remained in the left hand. She wrote a two in the white powder.

"Umph. This pledge you bury cannot be saved by medicine, old mother."

On the fourth try one shell remained. Kehinde wrote a number one in the powder. And so the four signs fell:

1
1
2
1

"The oracle points to your child. You have only one child. Your daughter made a pledge. This pledge she didn't fulfill. Come."

Kehinde held Manji up by the elbow and led her back through the trees. Kehinde was squat and seemed to tilt from side to side as she walked, her elbows poked out from her sides like a giant bird walking, and Manji, thin and small, appeared feeble and doddering, leaning on her walking stick and dragging the leaves with her heavy shoes. They went back to Manji's house. Inside, the two women knelt on the floorboards beside Sizway. Sizway lay there like a piece of dead driftwood on the mat. Her skin was more grey than black and it was gathering flies.

"Sizway," Kehinde called, "tell me. Did you make a pledge to someone?"

Sizway lay as still as Death.

Manji's brows furrowed. She said, "My daughter made a pledge. Till death do us part, she pledge. What sacrifice will Death take to leave my little one, Kehinde?"

Kehinde thought for a moment. She said, "Bring me a cock from your yard."

Under a full moon, Kehinde held up a cock with the head cut off, the feathers were down-dripping blood. Kehinde did a shuffle-footed dance in the leaves.

> Death would like to have you for his child,
> But you, my daughter, are my own.
> Death would like to have you for his child,
> But you, my daughter, are my own.
>
> Don't leave us to dance with your ghost,
> Don't leave us to dance with the dead.
> Don't leave us to dance with your ghost,
> Don't leave us to dance with the dead.
> Death would like to have you for his child,
> But you, my daughter, are my own.

At the same time inside the house, Manji knelt over Sizway, rubbing the boiled skull of the cock all along Sizway's body.

"In the dark we must hold to each other," she said. "In the dark we must hold to each other's hand. Death, my daughter, cannot have you for his child, for you, my life, are my own."

And so Manji called Sizway back.

Sizway heard her name being called as if from a deep, dark well. Her pupils floated upward and hid under heavy lids. Her knee slid up, trembling against the quilt. Her dried and cracked lips moved soundlessly. She tried words again and again on her tongue.

The talebearer's own knees slide up now beneath her black skirt.

"Because of Kehinde's oracle, the Ki reconsidered Papa Job," she says. "Around a fire the old-time people consulted over the marriage and they predicted any future trouble to the marriage by the letters in Papa Job's name. The letters in his name showed that he was a good man. A good man is hardworking, he will see beyond his nose. He won't eat with two hands, never thinking of the future. He will know how to save. He will have a goal. When he goes to the marketplace he will go straight for what he wants to buy and will not be diverted by the noise in the marketplace. The sellers will yell at him to buy, buy, buy, but he won't be diverted. They say a fool and water will go the way they are diverted, but Papa Job was a man with a goal. The letters in Papa Job's name showed no natural wickedness, though he could be wicked to himself. There would be times when his family would feel his wickedness. And so this Kibaba Job, he must be guided.

"All this the old people saw as their faces glowed red around the fire."

Two years were passing for Papa Job. In 1954, he returned from the war. He hadn't seen much action in Korea, though there had been many night raids. He returned with an army-green duffel bag containing black-and-white photos of little slanty-eyed children smiling beside black soldiers. He brought back a red silk kimono and black slippers. He also brought back a burlap bag of navy beans, which he boiled every evening in the emptiness of his house.

The landlady continued coming by for her rent, leaning against the doorway, sizing him up. But Papa Job wouldn't let her inside. He sat in that empty, sat alone in that empty, while the ghosts of drunken men leaned against the bar. The ghosts began to haunt him more and more. They wanted a drink. At least that is what Papa Job thought. He told himself that he was buying the whiskey for them. But it was he who drank the whole thing done and began to lean against the bar in a long line with the ghosts. One of the ghost men nudged him. "That whiskey you are drinking is going to kill you, man, like it killed us." Ghost man laughed and laughed and laughed.

When Papa Job stepped outside for air, he found a strange man standing outside his tall steel fence, peering through the holes. The man said he was Newscarrier from the Ki camp. He told Papa Job that Sizway was recovering from sickness. Papa Job slid his hand in his pants pockets; the other hand held the empty whiskey bottle. His suspenders hung down the sides of his legs. The Newscarrier told him to pack a suitcase. He would take Papa Job to the Ki camp.

Papa Job stayed for three days in the Ki compound, watching Sizway recover. Many visitors sat at the long, narrow wooden table but no one paid much attention to him. He was just another visitor come to petition the One Spirit. Visitors greeted him and went their way. When Sizway stirred on the mat on the floor, the visitors all formed a line. One by one the visitors bent a knee and murmured words to Sizway and afterward they sat again at the table.

Papa Job stood in line with the others, hat in hand. He was wedged between bodies. He wore black trousers, grey suspenders, and a starched white shirt. The collar was stiff against his clean-shaven jawbone. Without a mustache it looked like his top lip had been removed. But he looked like a younger man.

There was only one person in front of him now. She was a young woman wearing a pearl-blue shawl draped over her head and shoulders. As the woman got up from the floor to go back to the table, Papa Job saw that an earring in the shape of a half-moon pierced her nose.

It was Papa Job's turn now to talk to Sizway. He bent a knee.

The blanket was tucked around her hips and pulled up close to her chin. She gave Papa Job the gift of her eyes. It was like the sun was hidden behind her brown pupils. A golden glow circled the rims.

"Ho, Sizzy," Papa Job whispered, his eyes watering. "It's good to see you getting better. I've missed you. I would kiss you but everyone here would be looking."

Sizway kept looking at him.

He rested his hand on her thigh. Her eyelashes flickered down as if it was a stranger's hand and why should this stranger be touching her leg.

Papa Job's smile congealed. He removed his hand.

"Oh-ho, I don't have a mustache. You don't recognize me."

Sizway continued looking.

"Sizzy?"

He waited for her to talk but she didn't talk.

His voice began to crack. "Sizzy—what—what is . . ."

Bit by bit Papa Job's eyes filled with water and his nose began to run.

Sizway clucked her tongue and shook her head, a gesture that grew out of her mother in her. "Shh," she hushed him. "You should know that I know you. But I must pretend that I don't. It is our way. They all know you, but they will pretend as if they don't. Now ask the One Spirit to bless me and go your way as the others are going."

Her eyelids fell shut.

Papa Job sniffed. He blessed her. "Be well."

Papa Job got to his feet and went back to the table. He ran his palm down his face and blinked rapidly. He blew out, once, hard. The Ki faces standing in line glanced over at him and then looked away. They pretended they didn't know him.

When the sun was dropping, dropping in the sky, the Newscarrier walked Papa Job through the compound to a small clapboard house. It was the Newscarrier's own house. Papa Job treaded along in solemn silence. He scuffled up the gritty steps of the clapboard. The door squeaked open. The one-room house smelled of fresh paint. The Newscarrier was an artist. There were pencil sketches and paintings and carvings covering every inch of the floor and walls. Papa Job moved aside a sculpture and sat on the floor. It was the sculpture of a female. Her belly stuck out in front of her and her backside was high on her back. The Newscarrier had adorned the neck of the sculpture with beads. Papa Job lifted the sculpture and examined it. He put it down and mumbled, "Woman." Then he sat with his arms about his knees.

The Newscarrier brought Papa Job food but he didn't eat. The Newscarrier begged him to eat, but Papa Job wouldn't eat. The Newscarrier ate alone. The Newscarrier then offered Papa Job his best chair to sit on but Papa Job wanted to sit on the floor. The Newscarrier begged him, but Papa Job wanted something hard.

"Excuse me, but why won't you eat?" the Newscarrier asked. "Please. Eat."

"I am thinking."

"Then take my chair."

"I want the floor."

Finally the Newscarrier took the chair. It was a lazy-boy with a footrest. He lay back in it with careless ease and smoked from his pipe. Paintings leaned against the sides of the chair. Beside the chair was a table splattered with dried paint. It held aluminum trays, jars of paintbrushes, chisels, and clay wrapped in cellophane. Behind the chair was a bamboo window shade from which the red rays of the setting sun filtered through.

Because the Newscarrier had lived so long in the woods, his hair was long and hung down his back. He had a goatee that bunched in knots down his chest. He wore shorts and sandals. His fingers were short and stubby like his body. The man watched Papa Job for a time. Then he asked him, "What is wrong?"

Papa Job unfastened the first button of his stiff collar. "Is there anything wrong with wanting my wife?"

The Newscarrier blew out lazy rings of smoke. "Who is your wife? Maybe we can send for her to come here."

"My woman is here. Sizzy. I love her."

The Newscarrier's eyes crinkled at the corners and his lips smiled. "You are kidding, man."

"No. Why should I be kidding?"

"You are my friend," the Newscarrier said. "I don't want anyone here to insult you. Don't say things like that here. 'I love her.' Men don't talk like that here. And if a woman here heard you saying that she would think you were mad. Here we don't say love. We show it."

"What is wrong in saying love? Where I come from, we say it."

"Where you come from men use that to deceive women. The women here know that. They are smarter than your women there."

Papa Job frowned and the Newscarrier chuckled. "Listen. Why should you be doing this?" The Newscarrier got up from his chair and stooped over Papa Job, stroking Papa's arms, bobbing his backside up and down, and making kissing sounds.

"Ho, I love you. Ho, you are so beautiful. More beautiful than the one I had before. Ho, I love to kiss you. I would die for you. I love you."

Papa Job's lips cracked a smile. He shook his head and chuckled too.

"See, the men where you come from, they flatter their women well, fog their brain, man, and use that one for the penis to penetrate. Do you think the women here are as stupid as that? They would run from you screaming. He is mad. Stay clear of him."

Papa Job considered this. "Okay." Papa Job got up from the floor taking his plate of food with him. "I will take your chair now."

The Newscarrier jumped up. "Take my chair, man. And take my chair."

Darkness was coming down now so the Newscarrier lit a kerosene lamp. He straddled a straight-back chair, sitting backward with his arms folded on the top rung. His short legs were planted firmly on each side of the chair like the trunks of two trees.

Papa Job silently ate. He scraped the plate clean. Now he leaned back, interlacing his fingers behind his head. He licked his lips and swallowed. "I want to talk to Sizway. But I'm not supposed to talk to her."

"What do you want to talk to her about?"

Papa Job frowned. "Marriage. How can I marry her so that her family will approve?"

"Well, friend, you are asking things well now." He stroked his knotty goatee.

Papa Job nodded. "Maybe I should talk to her mother."

The Newscarrier frowned. "You can't talk to her mother."

"Wasn't it her mother who brought me here?"

"You are funny. It was the One Spirit who brought you here. You can't talk to her mother."

"Then maybe you can talk to her mother for me."

"Me? Not me."

"Listen, man. I want to marry her in your way. Help me to get her."

"You need an old person who her family will listen to. You need a woman to talk to her mother. It is better to have a woman. That way, when you and your wife have trouble, this woman can talk to her mother in the bathroom or they can lay on the mat together and talk. It is better to have a woman to talk for you. And she must be an old person."

"I don't know any old person. My own mother is dead."

"Then I can help you. I will introduce you to an old woman who can help you. Come."

The Newscarrier moved aside crates, sculptures, and paintings and made his way to the door. Papa Job followed after him then halted. "One moment," he said. He opened his suitcase and removed his bow tie. As he tied it, he gazed at himself in a broken mirror on the wall. His hair rippled in black waves down his head. He slicked down his shiny thick eyebrows. His lips were a healthy pink. He brushed the dust off his pants legs and snapped his suspenders against his shoulders. Now he was ready.

They treaded through the dark of the Ki yard toward the house of the old woman. The Newscarrier walked up the steps of a clapboard and knocked on the door. Papa Job waited below on the ground. The door opened and the Newscarrier bid greetings, though everything beyond the doorway was darkness. The Newscarrier went inside. A kerosene lamp lit up. The Newscarrier came back out and gestured for Papa Job to come in. Papa Job came face to face with Kehinde. Kehinde was sitting on hard dirt ground. There was a low fire burning in a pit in the ground, making the room smoky. Her braids were like blades of grass hanging over her forehead, her eyes like an animal peering through grass. The Newscarrier greeted her by lying prostrate on the floor. Papa Job did likewise. When she nodded they sat five feet away from her. Papa Job noticed that the Newscarrier never looked her in the eyes but kept his eyes lowered.

"Mumma, this is Kibaba Job," the Newscarrier said.

"Good evening, mumma," Papa Job said, his eyes down.

"Good evening," she murmured.

"I hope you are well," Papa Job said.

"I am good. And you?"

They danced this kind of dance together until the drumbeat changed. Then their dance changed. Papa Job said, "Excuse me, ma."

"Eh?"

"Excuse me for asking?"

"Eh?"

"There is a flower here. I want to pick it."

"You want to pick a flower here? That's good," she replied in a casual manner.

"I don't want to do the wrong thing. I want to do what is right. I want to take this flower in her own way. In your way of life here."

"How will you care for this flower? You need a house to keep your flower, man. And you need a house."

"I have a, I mean, I will rent a house in Detroit."

"Where is Detroit? This is Ohio. The mother of the flower, she won't want her daughter to live far away. You are young. Young people, they aren't mature yet. They need mature people nearby them."

Now the Newscarrier spoke. "Mumma, you are right. He is going into town tomorrow to see about renting a house there. He will live here in town so that his flower can always be near to her source. Please. I know him. He is good. He will care for this flower well."

Kehinde looked from one to the other of them. She asked Papa Job more questions. Then she pulled herself to her feet with the two men holding up each of her arms. This meant they had talked the talk done.

When morning dragged open Papa Job's eyes, he heard wooden dishes outside making a dull clapping sound. Women went about their duties, preparing the morning meal, grinding wheat and rye berries in a solemn silence. And children were sweeping the center yard clean.

The Newscarrier was already awake, eating his meal. He had a bowl of wheat cereal and fruit prepared for Papa Job.

"If you want to go to town, you can follow the ones who are going to town to sell," he told him.

Papa Job went to the door in his underwear and was peering out when he saw Kehinde walking toward the house. She seemed to tilt from side to side when she walked.

Now he was hopping in a circle to get his leg in his pants. He zipped his fly, brushed the wrinkles from his pants leg. He was buttoning his shirt collar the minute Kehinde stepped inside.

"Good morning, mum," Papa Job said, dropping his eyes.

"Good morning," she replied. "I brought you a list."

She gave him a list of things Sizway's family needed. She told him he should bring all the things on the list. When he brought all the things on the list, then she would talk to Sizway's family for him. Papa Job stared at the list with a bar of worry between his brows.

2 rocking chairs
4 rugs
1 transistor radio
5 quilts

The list went on and on.

"If you want to catch a large fish," Kehinde told him, "you must first give something to the stream."

By that time the Ki had gathered in the yard to sell in town. The Newscarrier bid him good-bye. He promised to come and visit him when he found a house to rent in town. Papa shook the Newscarrier's hand. The man had a strong grip. Papa Job was going to miss him.

They walked nine miles. But once in town, Papa Job stepped aside while the Ki passed on. He drifted down the sidewalks, looking up at the slow-breathing houses shaded by trees. White housepaint looked like skin peeling on chapped lips. Front porches with wide empty laps seemed to slump under the sun. Other porches held people who were drinking and listening to the weather report on transistor radios. They propped their elbows on the railings. They nodded and stared after Papa Job. He passed two little girls playing jump rope on the sidewalk. The little girls chanted as their rope whapped pavement:

> When I goes to marry,
> I wants a man with money.
> I wants a pretty black-eyed man,
> To kiss and call me "Honey."

> Well, when I goes to marry,
> I don't want to get no riches.
> I wants a man bout four foot high,
> So I can wear the britches.

Papa Job smiled to himself. Finally he paused in front of a house with "Room for Rent" written on cardboard and tacked to the porch posts. He wrote down the address and phone number.

There were also a few houses for sale. Their dusty glass windows peered out at him above the weeds.

He rented a room for a while. And he got a job in town. He became another bellboy in the only hotel. Soon he was able to get a house, rent-to-own. But the rent almost cleaned his pockets.

The first time he returned to the Ki camp, he came with three rugs and a straight-back chair. On that day, the camp seemed deserted. He passed the curtainless clapboards, weighed down by the things in his arms. A goat sauntered past him. Then a chicken. Papa Job continued on before he caught sight of a little girl standing at the top of a stairway. A scarf was tied in back of her head. A big dress fluttered around her. She was leaning against the door frame with one shoefoot resting on top of the other. Sizway had a habit of doing that. He walked up to her, smiling, with his armful.

The girl called over her shoulder, "Mumma, there is a stranger in the yard."

A woman's voice replied from inside the house. "See who it is."

"It is a stranger with rugs and a chair."

"A stranger with rugs and a chair? Ask for his name."

The girl asked for his name.

"Papa Job Ahdale Aba. I am bringing something for Sizway's family."

The girl ran into the house. "The name of him is . . ." she called, her voice fading away.

A few minutes later she came back and pointed to Kehinde's house. Papa Job walked backward, smiling back at her.

Kehinde came outside. She told him to bring the items inside. When all the things were placed there, she asked him, "Do you want to see Sizway?"

He smiled. "Yes."

"Okay."

Kehinde left the open compound and entered the woods where Manji's house was hidden deep within trees. When she reappeared again, Sizway was following behind her. Sizway wore a black ankle-length dress, a white head scarf, and silver bracelets on both arms. She was barefoot. Papa Job and Sizway sat on Kehinde's wooden steps with Kehinde wedged in between them. He gave Kehinde a gift of tobacco. Kehinde smoked her pipe, leaning elbows on her knees. She acted as if she didn't see nor hear them. Papa Job gave Sizway the red kimono and black slippers he had brought back from the war. Then he gave her a smaller package.

"I bought you some earrings," Papa Job said to Sizway, looking over Kehinde's back.

He handed the earrings to her.

Sizway pinned them to her earlobes. She turned her head to Papa Job. The silver earrings, they glittered.

She said, "I will bring you something to drink."

She went inside Kehinde's house. She came out with a cup of milk.

"Milk," she said, lowering the cup to him.

"Yah," he said. "I love milk."

Sizway glanced at him and smiled.

"You look very beautiful in the earrings."

"And you, too, look very beautiful," she replied.

Kehinde grunted, spitting tobacco from her tongue.

"How was it for you in the war?" Sizway asked.

He shrugged. "I sent you many letters to the house in Detroit."

Sizway nodded. She dropped her eyes.

But Papa Job brightened. "The landlady, she kept them. I think she enjoyed reading them. I think she fell in love with them."

Sizway laughed too.

And so every weekend Papa Job brought different items on the list. He gathered it all and he came with it. He packed it all in Kehinde's house. He piled them until he had completed the list.

When the list was completed, he paid Kehinde for helping him. Kehinde counted the dollar bills in her hand and then stuffed them in the bosom of her dress. Papa Job kept the remainder of the money. That money was for Sizway's family until the appointed time. More weekends passed but no word from Kehinde. Finally Papa Job came back to the camp. He asked Kehinde, "Mumma, I want to marry Sizzy. Will you talk to her family for me?"

Kehinde held an air of indecision. "You want me to beg the family on your behalf?"

"Yah."

"Hm. You want me to take this burden on myself?"

"Yes, ma."

"I guess you know that this will be a difficult something for me to do."

"Yes," he said, worried.

"Well, I will try to talk to them for you. I will take this burden on myself."

When Job left, Kehinde conferred with Sizway's family on a time to discuss the marriage. The next time Papa Job came to her, Kehinde told him to bring members of his family to Ohio in three weeks' time. He had a nephew and a brother-in-law—Buster and Jake, Claomie's husband and son. He traveled to Detroit for them and brought them back in three weeks' time.

The marriage day took a slow time coming and when it came it took a rest on a dirt road in Ohio. Grit popped beneath the tires of a truck, engine coughing to a stop. Papa Job slid down off the back of the truck, shoes sinking into the mattress of Ohio soil. His nephew and brother-in-law climbed out after him. Then the truck wobbled off on ruined springs into a cloud of dust.

The three of them were wearing suits, carrying suitcases and stuffed pillowcases in hand. Papa Job's suit jacket was safety-pinned where a button was missing. He wore an off-white bow tie that looked more like a tied sock. His hair had tight pleats of waves. His black shoes had brand-new laces.

Papa Job's nephew, Buster, was Papa's same height, only much heavier and rounded. Buster wore a pinstripe suit.

Buster's father, Jake, was a shriveled old man. He almost disappeared inside his baggy white suit. Jake wore a white hat tilted over one eye.

On both sides of the road were miles of waist-high weeds, scorched under a hot iron of sun. Papa Job led the way, slicing through the weeds that entangled his legs. Flying insects came up out of those weeds.

After trudging across the wide field, they stepped onto another road. By that time the sun was cooking the skin on their backs and their feet slow-cooked inside hard shoes. The men dropped their belongings and removed their suit jackets. Their white shirts clung to the slick sweat on their backs and dark ovals appeared under their armpits. They continued going, continued going, continued going.

After a while they trudged across another open field. In the middle of the field, they stopped to remove their ties and to unbutton their shirts, exposing white undershirts. They were forced to give themselves to any breeze that came along. The men climbed onto another road, craggy with rocks. Buster's shoes were paining him like hot needles. He removed them, tied the laces together, and slung the shoes around his neck. He hopped, wobbled, and tiptoed along in his socks.

This road ended itself with a wall of trees, thick paper leaves, black against the sky. Somewhere inside the dimness of those trees was the Ki compound.

The men heard the voices as they worked their way past trunks and moss. Underneath the trees, the shadows were falling cool. Far inside they saw the fragile little compound and clapboards arranged in a circular space.

The men stopped to arrange themselves. Finally they stepped past the trees into the camp. This was a business day. Their faces were serious as they approached this love business.

First they stopped at the house of Kehinde. They followed Kehinde into the woods that led to Manji's house. In the clearing was a house made of jagged stone. All of the items that Papa Job had bought for the family were neatly arranged in front of the house. Two rocking chairs, a transistor radio, rugs, everybody. Manji's house had a long porch with four stone pillars that held up the overhanging roof. The porch was so low to the ground that one step up led onto the porch lap. Seven old men and women, including Sizway's mother, were sitting on stools on the porch. Grey lined their hair and their skin was smooth leather. The old women held fans, moving the breeze over their faces. They wore headwraps of rich cloth and the men wore caps intricately embroidered. Their faces held an air of nobility and dignified calm. There was something in their regard that stilled return.

Kehinde introduced Papa Job and his family to Sizway's family. The old people looked slowly from Papa Job to Buster to Jake as Kehinde introduced them. Buster's belly hung low and his face was round like the moon. Papa Job and Buster greeted the elders by stretching out on the ground prostrate, face downward. Jake, who was considered an elder himself, simply bowed his head in greeting, with his hat tilted over one eye. Sizway's family nodded their heads in turn. There were four chairs waiting for them on the ground in front of Manji's porch. The three men and Kehinde seated themselves. Then Kehinde began the ritual of begging Sizway's family on Papa Job's behalf.

"I come to you on behalf of my son, Kibaba Job, to request marriage between his family and your family. I can assure you that I know his family well. I can assure you that if any trouble comes, I will be responsible."

Kehinde used every turn of phrase, every well-spoken word, to win support for Papa Job. She spoke with humble gestures and open hands.

When Kehinde was done, Manji spoke up. Manji called Sizway to come out of the house. Sizway came and sat on a chair beside her. She wore the red Korean dress and black slippers and silver earrings.

Manji told Papa Job to kneel at the middle, between his family and her own. Then Manji started telling him how she wanted her daughter to be treated. "I have heard Kehinde. She has sworn to us that she will be responsible for the safety of our daughter. She has sworn to us that you are of good report. She says you are good. But I know that nothing in life is completely good."

Papa Job swallowed hard while Sizway's family punctuated all of Manji's points with nods.

"If I give you my daughter, I want you to be respecting her. We don't want an aggressive man here. That kind of man would beat her and just kill her. We can't allow her to marry an aggressive man. She is our own. If she does something wrong, question her carefully in your own home. If she doesn't answer you well, remember that she has a family. Come to us. We will guide her back to the right path."

When Manji had finished, her brother Dom spoke up and told Papa Job what he wanted to be happening to their daughter. His unbroken stare made you want to tell any lie you were hiding.

"Sizway has told us that you love her."

"Yes, father, I do."

The old people clicked their tongues and slightly shook their heads, as if he had said something wrong. Even Kehinde glanced quickly over at him and back.

Dom told him, "Don't base your pledge to our daughter on that tradition of love you learn in the world. The only tradition of love is that love is blind. Don't base your marriage on a love feeling. A love feeling is like a reed; if you take to the river on a reed it won't carry you the whole of the way. In every decision you take, consider your wife. Consult with her and consider how the decision you make together will affect the family. Let your goal be to lift your family as you lift yourself. We old people know that it is easier to destroy than to build. Remember this what I'm telling you, as you live your life. Don't destroy your family. The oracle has warned us, there will be times when you can be wicked to yourself and your family will feel your wickedness. So we warn you. Don't destroy what you have labored to build.

"Today men like to destroy their families. We see most fathers in the world. They are dead yet breathing. They are breathing for nothing. Their children are living under a dead father. They leave their wife and they leave their children and they take no part in their children's upbringing. But the blood of their children will follow them wherever they go in life. When a man destroys his family, he destroys his own body. In destroying them, he destroys himself. Remember this and treat our daughter well."

When Sizway's family finished informing Papa Job of what he should do, Kehinde called Sizway to come and kneel between the two families. Sizway knelt on the ground in front of Papa Job, Buster, Jake, and Kehinde.

Kehinde told her, "Sizway, I want you to be respecting my son. I want you to know that there is a difference between a man and a woman. You are a woman and Kibaba himself is a man. Don't try and mix it. Just be whom you are. Care for my son in every way and consult him on important decisions. He will also consult you. Remember that he is a man, not a woman. He won't feel certain things like a woman. He can only be whom he is. When there is disagreement between you, in everything, consider the children, consider life for them without a father. Forget the minor disagreements as much as possible for the sake of the children. When two people are immatured, they say, 'I will never take that from her. I will never take that from him.' But when they gain maturity they learn to swim with most things and just live with it. Discuss the major things but the minor things just forget about it."

Jake also spoke on behalf of Papa Job. "Well, then. No infidelity," Jake said. "Can't have that. Adultery is out. Gossip is a bad thing. We don't want the man's business in the streets. Women like to talk about their men. In talking, they downgrade their men. So, uh, keep the business at home. Now . . . "

Jake spoke and then Buster spoke. After that, the items Papa Job bought were counted and checked against the list to see if all the items were there. They deliberated the business of marriage, and in doing so they tied the two families together. By nightfall, the formal marriage was finalized.

When evening fell, the camp came to life. Food was passed round—fruits, rice, chicken, goat's milk, nuts, sweet potatoes, everybody. The Ki formed a large circle in the center of the compound. Drums of various kinds were pulled between the legs of men. Papa Job himself slid his bongo drum between his own knees. The drummers' hands ran in a blur before everyone's eyes. Papa Job's red-red fingers cried out. His stinging palms said stop, but he kept going. Many people began dancing. There was the shock-shock of stones and seeds in gourds. Scattered singing. Necklaces, bracelets, and anklets went jinga, jinga, jinga. Women leaned at the waist, pricking up the cloth of their skirts between two fingers, moving their buttocks in an up-and-down something or a circular something. Men leaned over and rubbed their stomachs, moving in the same suggestive way.

Sizway sat on a stool taking it all in. She held her head high on her slender neck. Indeed, she was very, very beautiful. Many people sat gifts and money at her feet while Papa Job drummed. Cords of veins pulsed on his rigid neck. He shut his eyes and felt Sizway's strong spirit infill the drum and the drummer.

With all this talk of marriage and dancing, the talebearer appears noticeably cool. Her face is shadowed over by the brim of her hat, but beneath the brim her eyes are cool.

"It is one thing to dance," she mutters. "It's another thing to maintain the dancing. After a marriage dance, the celebrants go home. There are no married people who will die dancing."

She grunts.

"Do you see my eyes? These old, watery black things? They see how people today marry. They marry any way any how of nowadays. Seeing that, I don't talk. They exchange rings, they enjoy sexing themselves until the skin wears off their backs, until the mat underneath them begins wearing away, yes. And their world becomes two and only two. Too, too small. Two feels fine during times of pleasure; but times of trouble? What of that? Life. At the end of crying there will be laughing. And at the end of laughing people will cry. Surely as they laugh they will cry."

chapter three

Sizway wiped her hands on her backside before bending at the waist and pouring on the dirt road a few drops of cool water and raisin juice from a thermos. Then she shuffled over to the side of the road and knotted burnt grass together.

"Eshu-Elegba, make me walk well," she murmured. Then she screwed on the cap to her thermos.

Papa Job put on his hat and stepped over to the knotted grass, lowering himself on his haunches.

"What is this?" he pointed.

"Is a grass," she said.

"Is a knot, Sizzy."

"Humph," she said. "Let me look it."

Sizway crouched next to him and pulled back the weeds.

A farmer's truck sped by like a madman running on tiptoe. Sizway and Papa Job watched the truck disappear into the haze of heat. Then they turned back to the grass.

"Well, I spread out the grass to examine it and now I recognize it," she said. "I ask Legba of the crossroads to make we walk well. I ask Legba to keep the road to my family and community open."

Papa nodded. But suddenly his eyes shifted away from her, past her.

Sizway followed his gaze down the road, down the dry landscape, where the farmer's truck had melted in a haze of heat. Far down the road was the legs of a cardtable and men in black suits were sitting around that cardtable. Above their head was a sign pointing in four directions, the crossroads. The men's faces were wet and burnt black by the sun. These men were seriously drinking and debating it looked like. Papa Job saw their kinky heads turn to him, a lifted palm from one man, and a brief wave.

Papa shielded his eyes. Papa waved back.

"Who they? I've never seen them before."

"Men of the town," Sizway answered. "Forces of the road."

Sizway gathered up her thermos and her shopping bags. Papa Job stood up with her.

Under the shade of his hand, Papa narrowed his eyes. He saw the men in black suits with hunched broad shoulders. Men of importance it looked like.

"What you mean forces of the road?" Papa asked. "What they got to talk about, discussing like that?"

Sizway shrugged. "Umph. Can I know? I am only a poor black woman."

Papa Job grinned at her reply but he kept watching the men. And Sizway watched him watch the men. Then she held Papa's hand. "Sit again," she said, pulling him down. "I will tell you a story about Eshu-Elegba."

"What?"

Sizway and Papa Job squatted down on the ground, facing each other. There was a bar of seriousness between Sizway's brows.

"Eshu-Elegba is owner of the crossroads. Some say he is a mischief-maker, a deceiver, a very, very bad devil. He comes out when the sun is hot and waits at the crossroads. I've heard many stories of Legba. Now the story is coming. I will break it open so you can see what's inside.

"There was a time when two friends were like this," she said, lifting two fingers and intertwining them. "Whether they were together or apart, they had a perfect friendship and they agreed on everything. But Legba wanted to test this so-called perfect friendship, right? So he passed by them one day at the crossroads. The two friends were talking and laughing together. Legba passed straight between them. One of the friends thought he saw a bald-headed black man pass by. The other friend thought he saw a bearded white man pass by. You see, Legba had cleanly shaven his head on one side and painted his skin black. On the other side he had left a long white beard and had painted his body skin white. So he looked very different for each friend.

"Eh-heey. Now, for the first time, the friends began to disagree. Did you see that black man? No, he was a white man! I'm talking of the bald-headed one. No, he was bearded! They continued going, continued going, on and on like that. Soon they started shouting on each other. By the time Legba disappeared in the sunset, the friends were beating each other and rolling around in the middle of the road."

Papa Job slid his hat back off his forehead, nodded and smiled. "Yah. He is bad, this Legba."

But Sizway didn't smile. "No. Legba isn't bad. Isn't good. He is Eshu-Elegba, owner of the crossroads."

"Humph."

"You see?" Sizway drew a cross in the dirt and placed her finger at the middle. "Here, here is Legba. Legba is the point where doors open or shut, man, the point where a man must make decisions that will forever affect his life."

Now Sizway knotted two more blades of grass together.

"Legba of the crossroads, make we walk well. You can ask. Ask."

Papa Job glanced down at the knotted burnt grass.

"What is Legba? Man or spirit?"

"Legba is orisha."

"What is orisha?" he asked. "Man or spirit?"

"And you?" she replied. "What are you? Man? Or spirit?"

She gazed at him thoughtfully.

Papa stared at her and then smiled. "How should I know?" he answered. "I am only a poor black man."

Sizway took his hand and pulled him to his feet again. Papa Job turned to take another look at the black men in black suits but they had gone, even the cardtable had gone. Only the post with four signs pointing in four directions remained. The road before them now was clean and open.

Finally they arrived at the crossroads and took a left where one of the four signs pointed toward town. The sun beat down and burned them as they proceeded along the shoulder of the road. Their feet were a constant whispering shuffle.

Finally they entered town. The dirt road concretized into cement. They walked the pathway of many sidewalks until they came to a standstill in front of their little clapboard that seemed fragile beneath the expanse of sky. It was surrounded by tall grass and sparse trees. They pulled their legs through the waist-high weeds toward the dusty glass windows.

Sizway climbed the two wooden steps and scraped open the front door. She stepped into a musty narrow hallway, long and dark like a tunnel. There was a bedroom on her right and a bedroom on her left, a bathroom on her right and a linen closet on her left. Then the tunnel opened up onto a large kitchen filling the back of the house.

"The navel," Sizway said, smiling back at Papa Job.

"The navel? You mean the kitchen?"

"Yah. The kitchen be the navel," she replied, pointing to her navel. "And a child will move from the navel onward, out of the womb and into the world."

The back door of the kitchen led onto the wide lap of a back porch with tall wooden posts. The back door was locked.

Sizway said, "Please. Open it, Kiba."

Papa Job drew keys from his pocket and unlocked the door. He then shook open the screen door. The screen rattled and vibrated from top to bottom. The porch was long and deep, running from one end of the house to the other end, shaded overhead by a wooden beamed ceiling.

"Ahh," Sizway said. The porch. "We will call the evening stories here and so we will call the One Spirit. Your talking drum will call him and you will teach the children to call him."

Papa Job slid his hat back off his forehead and a red ring was left in the skin.

Sizway descended the porch steps to the far left of the porch. Papa Job slid his hands in his pants pockets and followed her.

The backyard was a cleanly swept expanse of ground, dusty and parched. Job gripped the well-maintained metal fencing and gave it a shake.

"Good and strong, Sizzy. This fence won't be falling apart soon."

"Mmm. Fence good . . . keep out forces of the road."

Papa Job flipped up the metal tong. He stepped outside of the fence. He closed it and watched Sizway walk the yard as if she were in a shrine. Along all three sides of the fence were tall pine trees. Sizway tightened her white scarf in back of her head. She secured her pipe between her teeth and slowly treaded along the three sides of the fence. As she walked the yard, her ankle-length skirt created a powder-puff of dust.

Three times she came back to the center of the yard, her face turned toward the ground, wetting the pipe handle by sliding it between tongue and lip. Her eyelids were rings of red burned by tobacco fumes. There was a rhythm in the pressing of her lips against pipe stem, in the way one finger tapped the side of the bowl, offering the first smoke to the One Spirit.

Papa Job remained outside the fence, arms propped on the pointed wire.

Sizway turned to him. "Bring come."

"Hm. I think I stay out here for now." Then he smiled. "Like the forces of the road."

Sizway slowly lowered herself on her haunches, pipe in one hand held to her lips, the other wrist hanging limp over her knee. She looked up and eyed him thoughtfully.

At midnight, Sizway walked the empty rooms of the house. She prayed that peace come and live in their home and that no thief should find their home appealing. She prayed that thieves go their own way. The candlelight she held flickered, making large shadows on the walls. She returned to the kitchen, where Job was sitting on a wooden crate in the dark. Sizway knelt on the floor in front of him, placing the candle beside her.

"Are you done praying?" he asked.

"For now," she said.

Late in the night, Sizway and Papa Job lay damp on their backs after a time of wrestling and she told him what she knew.

"When women are pregnant they develop strange longing. It was said of a pregnant woman that she desired to eat nothing but rats."

But before she could finish, Sizway pulled up the blanket.

Papa Job sensed that someone else was in the bedroom.

"Ibeji," Sizway said.

"What?"

"In the room corner there."

Papa Job's fractured eyes looked around the dark room. The patches of spackling on the wall seemed to glow in the dark. And then a patch slowly lifted up, transparent and pulsating. The pulsating faded and appeared on other areas of the wall. Finally the patch split in two and ran down like spilled paint, taking on two human forms. Papa Job slowly stood up, his sex limp. Sizway sat up. Her breasts swung down.

"My children," she said. "Two children will struggle together within me. They are there."

Papa Job hurried as he sliced through the weeds of the front yard and sometimes his shoe got pulled off and he had to stop to stick his foot back in there. He was zipping his pants and his pajama shirt was flapping loose around him. He was headed back to the Ki compound.

After nine miles of walking he arrived at the camp. His shoelaces slapped dust and the backs of his shoes slipped away from his heels. After passing through the center yard, he entered the woods. He stumbled over knotted roots in the dark. Tree leaves pricked him with their pointed tips. Finally he found the clearing and Manji's stone and mud house. He turned the knob of the front door and entered.

Manji was sitting with many guests at her wooden table. She was carefully slicing chunks of pineapple and licking the juice from her fingers. She rubbed her hands into her skirt and continued slicing, her blind eyes staring straight ahead.

Papa Job took a step past the doorway. No one paid attention to his open pajama shirt or how he slid his hands deep in his pants pockets and exposed the waist of his striped pajama pants. Eyes remained concentrated on whoever was talking at the table. Papa walked toward them. A woman uptilted her chin as he passed and her teeth were whiter than the pipe smoke seeping through them. Papa glanced back at her over his shoulder and then paused, hesitant, behind Manji's chair.

Papa's lips peeled apart to speak but his words were lost in the onrush of Manji's voice.

"Yeah-heh! I'm glad you know!" Manji laughed. She bit into a syrupy pineapple. "Ohh God! You know how to choose it. Taste it! Is all right? Sure!"

"Is good," Dom, her brother, mumbled. He was sitting next to her. "I have, I give you; you have, you give me. It's all the same."

Manji's grey pupils didn't flicker. She chewed briskly, fixing her eyes straight ahead. Brown wires of hair shook on her head. Her shoulders were angled bones.

Dom sat so close to Manji that his knee pressed against her own. He rose from the chair and pulled some crushed-leaf tobacco from his back pocket, also an old wooden pipe with only the bowl intact. He lit the bowl and inhaled deeply four or five times before he sat down again. Then he grasped Manji's fingers and put the bowl in her palm. Manji smoked the same way.

"Manji!" someone shouted. "What of my son, eh?"

"You would like to see your son carry home his life?" Manji replied. "And what do you think I would like! I tell that boy, if a man want to fight, say, 'Man, go on and pass, and go if you come to fight!' Yah. The boys these days be getting on rude. Yesterday at the market, one go tell me, 'I need medicine, ma. I make bad dream. I dream my brother get up from his bed to use the lav. He sit down on a pistol. Pistol let go, boom boom!' Ohh God!"

Manji felt for another chunk of pineapple, which she slid between her lips.

There followed an overlapping of shouting. Now Papa Job shouted to be heard. "Mommy, I got to have a word with you! Mommy! Mo—"

At that moment the room fell silent and caught Papa Job shouting.

"A' who that?" Manji asked.

"Excuse me, ma."

She heard that the voice was the voice of her son-in-law. "Why are you shouting?"

"I worry for your daughter," he said. "Like a woman with child at the time of delivery got her pain and writhes and cries out, your daughter seems to be with child. She writhes and cries out, but how can she be with child? We are just married. She can't bring forth anything."

Manji continued chewing with her head cocked. Finally she said, "Come." She turned sideways in her chair. "Come." Papa Job bent a knee before her.

"Did your wife place a pan of water by your sleeping mat and ask God to get to work on her children?"

"Yes, ma."

Manji grunted and nodded.

Papa Job waited for Manji to say more but no more words were forthcoming. So Papa went on. "So she place the pan, you know, the pan, then she call upon me, say, 'Me husband-man, do me good and go away from me. I got to pray for a little while.' And for that reason she say, 'Go away.' When she start to pray, she start speaking—it isn't a language I know, ma. And as she was speaking this language, she was shaking. And sometimes she be panting as if she were laboring with child. I leave from my wife to go. And just as I am, I leave."

The old woman next to Manji now commented. "Prayer is hard work for a woman, hm? You go buy her shoes and a hat."

Manji agreed. "He can even just leave her. When she is praying like that, just leave her. Umph."

And that was all Manji said about that. She turned back around. "Eat pineapple, Kibaba," she said. "Join us."

Papa Job's pockets bulged knuckles. "But, mumma, before that, something come to our bedroom. There be two . . . two . . . Human features, all those features a parent give one, they were finished. I saw it."

"Eh-heey," Manji nodded. "You saw spirits, eh? And they were two. The spirits of your children, no doubt. After many births you will have twins. The power of Ibeji. May you bring forth *tall* children."

The talebearer's eyes glitter, a small smile on her lips.

She was born Ibeji woman,
By the sun and by the moon,
By a star come late in winter,
One was born and then came two.

"Everyone has a star," the talebearer says, "and when you die, your own star it dies. It blinks out in the night."

With her black eyes glittering wet, she slowly spreads open the plaid woolen blanket around her shoulders. Underneath is a long, ornamented string at her neck. Numerous small objects are fastened along the length of the string. She holds one end, the beginning, between two fingers. The first object is a silver bead. She turns it this way and that and it glitters like her eyes.

"This represents the Ibeji star," she says.

Next she points to the second object, which is really three objects hanging one below the other by a continuous string. The first object is a piece of wire with a zig-zag shape like the peaks of three mountains. Hanging from this by a string is a black smooth stone and hanging from the stone is another piece of wire in the shape of the small cursive letter "m," with three humps. Her brown lips twitch at the corners.

"The first one represents the moon, the next one the planet, and then the sun. See . . ."

The moon was in Aquarius,
Pluto rising the goat's sun
Fate be born in this triangle
Ibeji woman. Timeless one.

The third object on the necklace is a tiny clay face. One side of the face painted white, the other side black.

"A new birth, an old soul," she murmurs.

The old ones say around the fire,
She wears the mask of Life and Death
They say her other half is sleeping,
They say her own half never rests.

She was born Ibeji woman,
By the sun and by the moon,
By a star come late in winter,
One was born and then came two.

With that she covers herself with the blanket again, slipping
the necklace back into hiding.
"Hmm. That was after many earlier births."
She lifts her pipe to her lips.

———————————————

chapter four

Soon after their marriage Sizway gave birth to a son whom they called Toomi. Then she gave birth to another son, Balinga. And then her youngest child was born, her youngest child who survived, and she was named Taiyewo.

When Sizway was pregnant with Toomi, the first one, she squatted in the kitchen on her black-and-red embroidered rug to give birth. The rug was laid out in the kitchen. As Toomi was emerging from her body, her black skirt was hiked over her knees and her braids fell around her damp face. Two women held her arms up on either side as she strained. Nalajah, Sizway's childhood friend, and Chu, a widow in her early fifties, were sweating like women in labor themselves because when Sizway bore down, she put all her strength into her back; she strained with her arms heavy on their shoulders and they had to use all their strength to hold her up. Sometimes Sizway's face would screw up tightly. At other times she would drop her head on Chu's or Nalajah's shoulder like a limp and wounded thing. Her labor pain was like a wrench pulling apart two tightly linked muscles. And the pain that gnawed at her inner parts took no rest.

The kitchen table was pushed back against the sink. The sink had two white enamel bowls and a window above it with bamboo blinds. The blinds were rolled down now, so slithers of shadow and light crisscrossed the women's faces. There were cupboards and handmade shelves that climbed from floor to ceiling, crammed with canning jars, bottles, cloth bundles, and wide gourd bowls. Opposite the window, facing the sink, was a wood-burning stove. Sizway's rug had been laid in front of it. A black pipe rose from the back of the stove through the ceiling like an elephant's trunk. The four black burners held pots of boiling water, sterilizing the midwife's tools. Three elderly women from the compound sat on the rug alongside Manji and Kehinde. They surrounded the mother, whose knees trembled as she gave birth. After a while, Kehinde, the midwife, laid a wrinkled hand on Sizway's belly and chanted close to the navel.

> Child of the great earth
> Head emerging from the warm earth
> I take out the child
> I blow out the child

Then she blew. Sizway strained, she strained, she strained, and soon her first child was born into Kehinde's hand. Kehinde scooped up the child.

> O Still Small who has come to this life!
> O Still Small, welcome!

You will be strong-carrying legs,

strong arms,

clear eyes!

One Spirit, your ways he shall see!

Kehinde blew around the baby's head and the baby boy wailed. Sizway held the baby's hand with a finger. It was so small.

Soon after, her labor pains came again. She clung to Nalajah and Chu. She strained, she strained, she strained, and the afterbirth came down. One of the old women took up the afterbirth and put it in an earthen pot while the young women washed the blood from Sizway's thighs and genitals as she lay back on the rug. Other old mothers cleaned the child, who was covered with a slippery white coating. The blind mother Manji listened intently to everything going on. Her lips began to move silently as she prayed that any bad fate or spirit that had come with the baby be removed. She prayed that whatever came with the boy should be washed away, disappeared, flowing away in the pan of water which the women used to clean him.

Wrapping him in cloth, Kehinde placed the boy in Sizway's arms. He was cutting the air with his arms and legs in slow motion. He frowned up at Sizway through squinting grey eyes.

"Hello, husband," Sizway murmured to him.

Manji had been sitting quietly through it all, staring through her milky grey eyes. Now she frowned. "Where is the afterbirth? Bring it."

Kehinde set the earthen pot in front of Manji.

"Take the pouch from my waist," Manji said.

In the pouch were certain herbs. Kehinde held Manji's hand over the earthen pot while Manji sprinkled the herbs onto the placenta.

Papa Job entered the kitchen as the lid clamped down. He wore black pants and suspenders. His white T-shirt was sleeveless but still a line of sweat ran down his back. He squatted in front of his wife and his newborn. Sizway was sitting up, though her insides were still sore. She placed the boy gently in his father's arms. Papa Job rocked the baby while he praised him. His thick mustache hid his small smile. "I have a son," he said. "Yes, a boy. And a strong boy."

Kehinde slid the earthen pot close to Papa Job's feet. She waited.

"Husband," Sizway said, "take up the pot there. Dig up the ground in front of the house in a spot where rain falls from the rafters. Bury the placenta there. Mark it. And see that no one steals it."

Papa Job looked from Sizway to the ancient female faces staring back at him, and then to the pot.

"Why would someone want to steal this?" he asked.

"They will want to steal it," Sizway said. "Sometimes people want to bring the good fortune of the child to themselves. Sometimes they just want to harm the child. With the child's placenta they can do it. Bury it well and see that no one steals what belongs to the child."

The rains had not yet begun. The first great downpour came on the day of the naming ceremony. The Ki came like the storm clouds stampeding across the sky to celebrate the naming of the newborn. They hurried through the yard. They clumped up the rickety porch steps. On the landing, they rapped at the wobbly screen. Some brought gifts, but they all brought praises for the newborn. They crowded into the skinny hallway, filled the kitchen, and overflowed onto the back porch. Their mouths were filled with laughter, their tongues with talk. Huge pots of food cooked on every burner to feed the guests. The child was passed from hand to hand. Then the time for naming came. Lightning flashed and frightful bolts of thunder shook the tiny clapboard. Rain pounded the roof, leaking into buckets. The child was named Toomi. It means the Son-of-Thunder. It was the same name of Sizway's father who died. You see, a name is important, it carries the family.

A little girl led Manji by the hand into the yard. Manji wore a blanket over her shoulders to keep dry in the rain. But it didn't quite conceal her thin arms and legs. She wore a black felt hat, a necklace of fishbones, a shapeless dress, and a broken pair of men's shoes.

"Mumma? How are you?" Sizway called.

Manji was led up the porch steps where Sizway and Papa Job were waiting.

"Is your husband here?" Manji asked.

"Yes, he is here."

"Bring him out if he isn't here."

"I am here, mumma," Papa Job said.

Water dropped off the leaves of the trees in front of the porch railing where Manji stood. Her high cheekbones, sunken cheeks, and pointed nose resembled Sizway. She said she would come and stay with them as long as they behaved themselves and didn't involve her in arguments. But if they behaved badly, she would run from them. She wouldn't want people saying that she stayed too long and got blamed for the fights that went on.

"Now, where is my grandson? Let me see him."

The little girl took the blind woman by the hand and led her inside.

Even after the naming ceremony many of the Ki came often to visit. They bounced Toomi on their knee while Sizway sat close by. Papa Job took Toomi and bounced him as well, but when Toomi began to cry he handed him back to Sizway. Ki men, however, knew how to soothe a crying boy. The Ki men often carried babies in their laps or had older children leaning against their thighs.

Whenever Toomi wanted to nurse he could nurse. He slept beside Sizway at night and was carried in a sling, skin to skin, during the day. And Manji taught Sizway many things.

The first time the child nursed, Manji showed her what to do. Manji waited a few minutes and then she told Sizway to give her the baby. She placed the baby over her own shoulder. She patted the baby's back to bring up the gas. Then she returned the baby to Sizway. After a while of nursing, Manji again told Sizway to hand her the baby, and she laid Toomi over her own shoulder and patted his back. Milk dribbled from Toomi's mouth as he burped.

"One day," Manji told her, "I will go back to my house and your child will be your own. So just watch what I am doing so you will know what to do."

Manji showed her how to prepare certain herbs for the child to drink to make him strong, and she prepared herbs for Sizway to drink to bring on more milk. Sizway's breast milk was just flowing. Then Manji kneaded Sizway's belly to remove the old blood that was still inside.

"Umph," Sizway grunted. "Hurts, mumma."

"This is the way we do it," Manji told her.

Sizway winced. Her mother was tiny, bony, but strong.

Manji also exercised the baby. Laying him on Sizway's embroidered rug, she said, "Show me where his legs are."

Sizway placed Manji's hands there.

Manji gripped the child's ankles and shook him upside down a few times. Then she laid him on his back and pulled his arms and legs away from the joints. She let the child grip her fingers and pulled him gently up and down.

"Now bring me the cup of herbs."

Sizway brought it and guided the blind woman's fingers to the baby's lips. Manji tipped the cup and let the liquid fall into the baby's mouth. The baby immediately began choking.

"Pick him. Pick him," she said hurriedly.

Sizway picked up the baby and patted his back.

"Pat his back," Manji said.

They waited until his coughs died down.

"Okay," Manji said. "Now take the flat tin from my sweater. In the pocket there. Open it."

Sizway opened it and Manji rubbed her fingers in the greasy ointment. Then she rubbed the ointment on the baby's gums.

"He'll have strong white teeth," she said smiling.

Manji showed Sizway many many things about caring for a child. And the child grew and grew and became strong.

Manji's chickens took over the backyard, clucking and scuttering here and there. The backyard grew a small patch of tomatoes, cabbage, cucumbers, lettuce, various herbs and wildflowers on one side and a patch of red dirt on the other. The red dirt area held four rows of clotheslines. Manji was sprinkling the red dirt area with chicken feed from a burlap sack. Her chickens were squawking and scurrying about her legs. Manji called to them.

"Chick-chick-a-dee," she screeched. "Come here and eat. And come if you want to eat. Now who that cackling, trying to

push? Onye, that you? Last time I'm speaking to you, not again.
You heard me? The last time."

Manji pointed her thick finger as she spoke, spraying the
ground with meal. The veins in her hands were like the gnarled
bark of a tree. After feeding the chickens, she sat on the bottom
porch step, listening contentedly to her chickens.

Sizway's vegetable garden was growing. With Toomi in a
sling in front of her, she had hoed a small patch of ground and
fenced it in with chicken wire a foot high to keep out Manji's
chickens. She had planted tomato seeds and lettuce seeds. As
the ground grew damp, the vegetables grew, the leaves began
spreading out, the vines inched up toward the sun. In time the
red and green food ripened.

Sizway now knelt in the dirt of her garden with Toomi in
her wrapper. Before digging up the food by the root, she spoke to
it. "Don't think I will harm you," she said. "I will do good for
you. I will put ginger and sweet-smelling anise on your back.
Your body will be a part of my own so that you, and I, and my
husband can continue to live."

Toomi watched what she did. When he was able to walk
and talk, he would eventually help her in the garden by picking
weeds and talking to the vegetables.

Papa Job had taken up his own pastime. He repaired and refinished used furniture on the back porch, furniture that the
people of the town had thrown out. There were bureaus, bed-
posts, side tables, coffee tables, and other items stacked in one
corner of the porch. Cardboard boxes hid away smaller items
like lamps without shades and broken radios. The boxes smelled
of mold, dampness, and decaying time.

Newspaper was spread out on the floorboards and Papa Job
was sanding the old finish off a drop-leaf table, bringing it to a
fine, silky condition.

Sizway climbed the steps with Toomi. She settled in a chair with her back facing all the junk Papa Job had collected, but watching him. Papa Job stepped back, examining the table.

Sizway slid her feet out of her house slippers. She began to fan herself and the baby with folded newspaper.

Papa Job shook a dust cloth from his back pocket and rubbed the table with it.

Sizway smiled faintly. She was contented. She had a good husband, a son, and a long extended family.

Papa Job smiled faintly as he worked on the table. He was contented. He had a good wife, a healthy son, and good in-laws. He glanced up at the sky. "Maybe rain," he said.

Sizway sniffed the air but smelled no rain on it.

"I don't smell rain on it."

"It will rain," Papa Job insisted.

Sizway clicked her tongue against the roof of her mouth. "I think you are right. It will rain."

She didn't care to be fighting about rain. She didn't marry him for that. She married him for companionship. Her mother used to say, trouble starts when people are too happy or too sad. Their mouths begin to run when they're too happy or too sad and they blurt out whatever their mouths want to say. A person should be most careful when they are happy.

At the sound of Manji's voice, Sizway lifted Toomi in her arms.

"Bring me my son," Manji called.

Sizway came down the steps where Manji sat at the bottom. She gave the baby to her. Then Sizway turned and climbed up the steps and went inside the house and came out with a wash-basin of wet clothing. Manji had washed the clothing in the kitchen sink. Sizway had even told her, "Mumma, you don't have to do washing."

"Umph. Let me wash it," Manji mumbled.

Sizway was careful not to let her mother do too much work because she didn't want her mother to insult her. It is said that a new mother tends to overburden the grandmother until the grandmother has to tell her, "Don't kill me with work. I only came here to help."

Sizway came down the stairway with the basin of laundry. In the red dirt area she began clipping the wet clothing to the line. Manji's chickens ran away from the dripping wet things. Sizway could hear Toomi begin to fret for his milk. At the sound of his cries, her breasts began to swell up. The milk began to drip from the nipples onto her blouse. She looked over her shoulder and saw that Manji had already unbuttoned the front of her own dress and removed her own dried breast. She gave it to Toomi to suckle until Sizway could bring her own. Sizway turned back around and continued clipping the laundry to the line. She stooped over the basin. She straightened her back and wrung the water from a shirt. Wet pellets splattered in the red dirt. She side-stepped, inching her way down the clothesline.

These days she felt like a different woman altogether, no longer The-Daughter-of-Her-Mother but The-Mother-of-A-Child and The-Wife-of-a-Husband. She felt like a part of herself had been buried with her son's placenta and the boundaries of her own body and her own life were merging with that of her child and her husband.

It was evening and Sizway was preparing dinner over the wood-burning stove. Manji and her group of old women friends sat around the table in black felt hats. Their thick working hands stirred bowls of cornmeal and other foodstuffs, flavored with quarreling conversation.

A thick black pipe curved up from the back of the wood-burning stove through the ceiling. All four burners were cooking things. A pot of boiling pigeon peas made for steam like wisps of vanishing spirits, drawing out beads of sweat on the walls. Sizway's body was slightly angled toward her right to balance Toomi on the left side of her full hips. She started stirring the pot of pigeon peas while Toomi slept against her shoulder. Toomi was two years old now. His black soft hair stood on end, his belly was full and round, and his little penis dangled down like a worm. As he slept he sucked rhythmically on two small fingers.

The kitchen door was open. On the back porch were the voices of men laughing and arguing together. It had been raining off and on all day. The sky was darkening and the forest-green trees surrounding the yard were all dripping water from the tips of their leaves. Two pine trees were close to the porch railing and cooled the air considerably. On the porch Ki men sat on wooden chairs with their legs propped far apart and their elbows resting on their knees. There were seven or eight men, including Abel, the Newscarrier, and Sinsi, who was a cousin of Sizway's. A few small children sat on the laps of old men, listening to Sinsi talk. Sinsi was tall with the same sunken cheeks and angled nose as Sizway's family. Like most of the Ki men, he wore a black hat and a long braid down his back. He had a thin black mustache that drooped on either side of his lips. Draped over the shoulder of his regular shirt, he wore what looked like a long sash that was knotted near his waist.

"I say own your own business," Sinsi said. "Be your own boss."

Papa Job grunted. "Easier said than done."

Sinsi turned to Papa Job. "Brother, what would you say to coming to work with me in the compound? We can own our own business together."

Papa Job smoothed his mustache with his finger. "Doing what?"

"Farming. I'm considering commercial farming."

Papa Job looked down at the floorboards. He shook his head. "Hm, Sinsi. Let me stay with my job in town for now."

"What do you do here in town, brother?"

"I work at the hotel."

"Doing . . . ?"

"Bellboy."

"Excuse me? Bell . . . what? Boy, you said?"

Papa Job shrugged. "I work for a living, Sinsi. What else?"

Sinsi laughed. He moved his chair closer to Papa Job and rested his hand on Papa's thigh. "I asked you what you do, man. Why do you try and defend it? The best thing you could have said was, 'Sinsi, why are you asking me what I do here in town?'"

Papa Job smiled. Sinsi smiled after him.

"What I'm trying to tell you, Sinsi, is that I'm not a farmer. I'm a city man."

And Sinsi said, "Don't try and tell me, just tell me. You are my brother. Tell me. Do you think city work is better than farm work?"

Papa Job shrugged. "Your work is superior to you and my own is superior to me. Why are you asking?"

Sinsi lifted his head and laughed. "Then you are superior to me? How can you be superior to me, man? How much did you make in town today?"

Papa Job straightened. He drew his billfold from his pants pocket and flipped it open. "You see this money, Sinsi? How much did you make at a market selling your farm goods today? Can you make these money that I'm showing you by your one-one self?"

Sinsi's expression was solemn. "No, sir."

"You can't?"

"No, sir."

"Then why are you talking to me?"

"Sorry, sir."

Papa Job smiled wryly. He removed Sinsi's hand from his thigh and leaned back in his chair until the front legs were lifted off the ground. "Sir? Why? Why are you addressing me as 'sir,' Sinsi?"

Sinsi leaned forward, resting his elbows on his knees. He peered over at Papa Job with a faint smile. "Is there anything wrong in calling you 'sir'? Isn't that the way you address some-one who is superior to you? You are superior to me. So I address you as 'sir.' All the men here, we should address you as 'sir.' They are all farmers here like me."

Papa Job glanced at Abel, who was staring at his feet. He glanced at all the other men, who were purposefully not look-ing at him. The small children were the only ones to meet his gaze. Papa Job turned back to Sinsi. "Just call me by my name."

"Excuse me, but if you are superior to us here, why are you trying to prevent us from resenting you? A man who is superior to other men doesn't try to prevent them from resenting him."

"Am I preventing you from resenting me?"

"You certainly are trying to prevent us. No? Okay then, why did you look at all the men here and feel bad? Why did you say, 'Don't worry, Sinsi. Address me by my name?'"

"Humph, I don't know what you're thinking of," Papa Job said.

"Then let us look at it in another way," Sinsi went on. "If you are superior to me, you are federal, right? and I am local."

"What?"

"Federal. Local. The federal government, man. Isn't the federal government superior to the local? The federal is the branches of a tree. It branches out from the local. You are the federal—the branches. I am the root—the local. So I ask you: Which is greater? The branches of a tree or the root?"

Papa Job said nothing. Sinsi always wanted to be proving something. Papa Job knew him.

"Which is greater?" Sinsi asked all the men. "The branches of a tree or the root?"

The other men chuckled softly and looked off at the pine trees.

Sinsi turned back to Papa Job. "How can the branches be superior to the root, eh? How can you be superior to me? Without the local, there could be no federal. Without the root, you got no branch. I am the root that feeds you."

"So, Sinsi, what is your point?" Papa Job asked.

Sinsi opened his palms and sat back in his chair. "No point, man, if you don't see one."

Now that the talk was done, the men laughed, the children laughed. But Papa Job smiled only faintly. Sinsi's humor was not to his liking.

An old man stood up. "The night is coming. I am going home."

Then two other men tapped the ashes from their pipes and rose up, lifting small children in their arms.

Sinsi and his brother, Ashe, also began to take their leave.

"Abel, give me some tobacco," Ashe said. "Tobacco hunger is killing me."

Abel gave Ashe some of his tobacco from the pouch at his waist. As the men descended the porch steps, Abel called after Sinsi.

"Sinsi, when you start your commercial farming business, plant tobacco first, okay? for all of us."

Sinsi laughed and waved bye-bye.

Only Papa Job and Abel remained. They sat still, listening to the crickets and the rain drip off the leaves of trees.

"So my brother Sinsi had a good laugh on my behalf," Papa Job remarked.

Abel stroked his long, knotty goatee. "I will tell you a story that I heard from your wife," he said.

Papa Job glanced over at him. "Okay. Sizzy tells good stories."

"The story starts here. A young boy's father is killed. The boy goes out looking for his father's killer. He wants to kill him. When he finds him, he can't even raise his cutlass to strike. The cutlass is too heavy and he is too small, he can't lift it to strike. So his father's killer ends up killing him as well. Can you see the meaning?"

"No."

"See, the boy wasn't smart. If the boy had been smart, he would have waited until he was grown matured and strong enough to lift the cutlass. Only then would he have gone looking for the killer of his father. When you are working at a job that is under you, you don't try and defend your position. You keep shut and wait and grow strong. You and I know that this bellboy's job you have is beneath you. Are you a bellboy? A bellhop? Do you answer to bells and hop to it when they call? No, you are not a bellboy, you are a man. You are using that job to grow strong so that you can eventually kill it off. Once you are strong enough to raise the cutlass, then strike. Kill it off. Go for a job that will lift you. In doing that, you will kill off the mockers as well."

Papa Job stood at attention in the hotel lobby. A plastic-brimmed cap and a red jacket with gold tassels on the shoulders was his uniform. His bellboy's smile had not changed over the years. He pulled open the door and beamed, "Yes sir." He grasped the handles of luggage and shouted, "Yes sir." He stepped soundlessly down fettered Persian carpeting. He turned a crystal doorknob. He placed the suitcases on carpet. His other hand closed around a small coin. He beamed, "Thank you, sir."

At five o'clock, Papa Job turned the wooden knob of the employees' bathroom. The door hit against the toilet. He relieved himself and washed his hands under a faucet that trickled rust. He closed the lid of the toilet. He sat down. His fingers hung limp between his legs, his shoulders heavy, and a piece of lint wiggled on his thick mustache each time he exhaled.

At five forty-five, Sizway was up to her elbows in flour. She wrung the dough and flopped it over on the table. She pressed down on the dough and a whiff of white blew up. A wagon wheel hung from the ceiling, strung with pots and pans. All were lightly powdered with flour.

She looked over her shoulder at the sound of the screen door rattling from top to bottom. It was always sticking, so it rattled when pushed.

"How are you?" she asked as Papa Job stepped into the kitchen.

Papa Job came with his red jacket slung over his back. He greeted her and went to the stove. He pointed to one of the pots cooking. "What is this?"

But before she could glance over her shoulder to find out, Papa Job had already dipped in a finger and tasted the soup.

"Acch!"

He ran in the other direction and held his tongue under the tap of the sink. The water dribbled down his chin. "Why did you put pep-pey in the food, Sizzy?" His tongue was throbbing, pow . . . pow . . . pow.

"Shh," she whispered, "Toomi is sleeping."

"Eh-hey, and so? What is preventing Toomi from sleeping? Why are you shushing me? And why is pep-pey in this?"

Sizway continued kneading the dough. "Mumma likes pep-pey in her soup," she said. "That pot is for her. I make another pot without pep-pey for you."

"You make it or you are making it?" he asked.

"I am making it," she replied.

"Are you kidding me?" he demanded.

Sizway stopped kneading at the sound of his voice. She straightened her back and cupped one floured hand in the other. She was standing on one foot with the other foot curled on top of it.

"You are yet making it?" he demanded.

Sizway said nothing. Even a mad person knows fire.

"What else have you cooked?" he asked.

And she counted, "Red bean, potato, wheat bread—"

"But that isn't the kind I wanted," he said. "Why aren't you making the kind I wanted?"

His wife's face was dusted with flour, her braids speckled with dough. But in her mouth were no arguments nor replies.

Papa Job entered the dim hallway that led to the two bedrooms. He paced back and forth and he thought. He shook his
head and he thought. Then he left through the front door, taking
the bus downtown to eat at the deli.

Beyond the fenced yard, tree leaves were black against the
sky. It was getting late and Papa Job had not returned from another night of eating at the deli.

Sizway sat on the porch with her pipe between her teeth
and her elbows on her knees. She puffed up white whiffs of
smoke and listened to the tree leaves rustle like rice paper and
she listened to the other lost sounds of the night.

Sizway wore a purple dress painted with orange birds that
drooped like a hammock between her legs, where her son slept
curled in a ball. Bracelets circled her arms to the elbows. Her
plaits swung easily and the glint of her long gold earrings appeared through the plaits.

Manji sat beside her, doing her own hair.

"Mumma, I can do your hair for you," Sizway said.

"Let me do my own hair. I am not so blind like that."

After that there came an uproar. Manji's chickens started
cackling inside a wooden crate beside her feet.

"Ah-ah-ah, no-no-no," Manji scolded. "There ain't no reason why you go and peck him. Well, it sound like you trying to
hurt him to me. Well, I been out here a long time, I know what
I'm talking about."

Manji's skirt stretched taut across her knobby kneecaps. In
her laps was a jar of hair grease. She dipped in her middle finger,
rubbed the grease into a parted section of her hair, and then
braided the hair.

But then came another uproar. Manji's chickens screeched and screeched.

"Aii! What sort of chicken is this? What is she doing? I'm sure I didn't tell her to go and peck that one. Those two. They're jealous of each other. They would kill each other over the rooster and he's out in the yard with another one. The rooster, he's just worn out from those two. If he goes to one, the other one will say, 'What's the matter with your heart? Is it too cold to care?'" Manji started laughing. Her laughter shook the jar of hair grease from her laps. She had to lean over and swish her palm over the floorboards until she hit upon the jar. She then scooped it up and placed it back on her laps. "Huuuuu," Manji sighed, her eyes wet from laughing. "Those chickens make me laugh like a white person."

Sizway puffed slow streams of pale white smoke. She gently swung her sleeping child in the hammock of her skirt. A line of worry creased her brow. At her back, the smell of burning sage wafted through the wire mesh screen.

Manji knew Sizway was worried for something, still she waited. She sniffed the air. "Sizzy, is that you burning sage?"

"Mm," Sizway answered.

Sizway shifted in her chair. Her earrings tinkled like chimes, stirred by the evening wind. She unbuttoned the front of her dress and slid her feet out of her matted slippers. "Ho, me God, I ready to meet you," she sighed.

"Please. Don't talk of Death tonight."

Sizway's eyes fastened on her house slippers and she spoke in a small, quiet voice. "Mumma, my husband leave another man in the house. But he himself is gone."

Manji sat very still, one side of her head plaited, the other side thick bush. She said, "I don't know what you're thinking of."

"He is not himself. He himself has gone."

Manji pulled a tattered ball of tissue from the pocket of her shift. She wiped the hair grease from her face and neck, leaving tiny dots of tissue crumbs on the skin.

Burning sage drifted out to them.

"Mumma, maybe you can prepare some sacred herb for me. Some power to drive out the bad ones."

"Some . . . power? Some bad ones? So that is why you are burning sage and killing me with sage? To drive out evil spirits? You are a child. You don't know anything. Why can't you find out what is pursuing you before you start running? Maybe your husband is bothered by the outside and want to bring it inside. Maybe his penis is worrying him. Maybe like most men he just want to come home and start beating his chest a little like an ape in the forest to let everyone know he is still in charge. Find out what is pursuing you before you start running. I told you before when I came to live in the house of your husband that I wouldn't get involved in disagreements, neither will I use my power. But words, too, have power and if you are wise you will be patient and keep this," she said, pointing at her tongue, "inside. Keep it faaar back inside. All you need is the power of patience."

At that moment, Papa Job lifted the metal tong of the gate. The gate squeaked open. Sizway moved Toomi from the hammock of her skirt and brought the baby close with an affectionate gesture.

Manji's blind eyes probed the dark. "Kibaba, is that you? Why are you wandering about in the night? Are you one of the spirits with no ground to walk on? Why must you wander in the night?"

The next evening, Sizway cooked Papa Job's favorite: black-eyed peas, wild rice, yam, and cornbread. She worked quickly. The wagon wheel strung with pots and pans was spinning and spinning above her head. While she was stirring this one, that one would be steeping, that one would be frying, that one would be baking, and that one would be salted.

By the time Papa Job came from work, the ashes in the oven were cold. Sizway's cooking was done. The screen door vibrated from top to bottom. Papa Job had entered. His plastic-brimmed cap was pushed back off his forehead. His sleeves were rolled over the muscles of his forearms. He had his jacket slung over his shoulder, hooked by a finger.

Papa Job smelled the air.

Sizway said, "I cooked your favorite."

"I know," he replied.

She hesitated. "How was your work?"

Papa Job smiled with his lips but not with his heart. "What can I tell you that you want to hear, Sizzy? I dress in a red monkey suit every day. Bellboy. That's what I am. You can find something like this," he said, lifting his jacket with the gold tassels, "at the circus. I carry luggage up and down the elevator. They tip me in this little cup of a hand. They send me off. I leave from work. I take the bus because I don't own a truck. I come home and as soon as I enter the door, my wife asks me, 'How was your work?' What do you want to hear, Sizzy? Why are you asking me?"

"Sorry."

"Don't worry," he said. At that, he brushed past her and went to the lav to wash. Now Sizway knew. She grunted and looked up as Abel pushed open the screen door and entered the kitchen. His stubby legs were in shorts. His wild, unkempt hair grew like twisted tree branches, while his knotty goatee lay against his chest. He came carrying with him a canvas under his arm and a suitcase of paint and paintbrushes.

"My wife! How are you?" he greeted her.

"Good evening," she smiled. "He is washing."

"Did I ask for my brother? I asked for my wife."

He set his canvas and suitcase in a chair. "What did you cook for me?" he asked. He placed his hand on his belly and peered into the pots.

Often Abel would come by in his truck to visit Papa Job. Usually he found him in the dry cellar. The dry cellar was outside, in back of the house. You had to lift a latch door in the ground and climb down moss-covered steps to get to the dry cellar. Papa Job repaired most of his furniture down there now. There were no windows nor floors, just dirt. The ceiling was low even for short men. For months, Papa Job and Abel had nailed plyboard to the walls. They had also hired an electrician to put in wiring. They put up hooks which held hammers, hatchets, and mallets. They built shelves to hold smaller tools such as brads, screws, staples, and nails in jelly jars. Against the wall was a workbench. Papa Job measured and sawed things on the bench but mostly he was on his feet repairing or refinishing a piece.

Sizway ladled soup into a bowl. She placed the wooden bowl on the table, set water in a cup, and laid a spoon nearby. Then she lowered herself into a chair across from Abel. She folded her arms.

Abel had a wide, kind face. He said, "Tell me one of your stories, Sizzy."

"I know many stories," she replied. "But first give me tobacco. My pipe has gone out."

He gave her tobacco. She lit the black long-stemmed pipe and puffed . . . puffed . . . until it was smoking. Then she lowered her eyes and spoke thoughtfully.

"I will tell of an old woman who owned a farmstead and seven chickens. One day she sent out her chickens to wander around the wooded area and when they returned home one chicken was miss. You see now, a thief had run off with it. And then you see now, the woman had faith. She believed the One Spirit would find the thief who took her chicken and punish him. So she quietly took patience and waited. Eventually the One Spirit did revenge on the thief. He cursed the thief and made chicken feathers to start growing all over his body.

"So now, since the thief was cursed like that, he said to himself, 'Why shouldn't I just go back to the old woman and take the rest of her chickens? My life is cursed. What else? Does life matter to me?' So the next day when the old woman sent out her chickens to wander, the thief was waiting. He grabbed the rest of them, all six of them that were left. When he reached home he started growing chicken feet, chicken wings, chicken beak. He grew everybody. The One Spirit was cursing him.

"So now, the woman saw that all her chickens were miss now. 'So if the One Spirit is not going to revenge for me,' she said, 'I will just revenge for myself. I will show that thief what he doesn't know.' She started cursing the thief. She was walking up and down, shaking her fist, and crying and screaming and shouting. And do you know what happened same time? The thief started turning back into a man. Each time she cursed him, well, he just turned back. He lost the chicken feathers and got his own skin back. He lost the chicken beak and got his own nose back. He lost the clawed feet and got his own back. And he walked away from her farmstead a complete man.

"Now what lesson is there in that, brother? What lesson?"

"Tell me," Abel replied.

"The thief's life had been cursed, man. The One Spirit did the job. But the woman's faith in the One Spirit didn't last. In losing patience, in taking revenge for herself, she destroyed everything that the One Spirit was already doing to help her. So I'm telling you: What point is it in being patient for a year and destroying everything you were waiting for in an hour? The woman didn't have patience enough to wait to see the end of her problem. Her patience ran out. Patience is never too long. Patience never has enough of patience."

"Hum," Abel nodded. "That was a good story." He kept his eyes on the bowl. "The story you told, it reminds me of a similar story," Abel said. "In the compound the other day a woman was extremely angry at her husband. She told him why she was angry in the privacy of their own house. Her husband wouldn't listen. I talked to the woman. I told her she should wait until her anger cooled. But she wouldn't listen. She followed her husband out of the house and into the middle of the compound. She was cursing him before everyone."

"Mmm," Sizway murmured.

"And she was cursing him."

Abel stood up. He put his hands on his hips and started stamping his leg. "Here. This is what she did. And she was shouting. And the people they said, 'What is this? Why is this woman shouting and stamping her leg?'"

A shout of laughter came from Abel's mouth. He reseated himself.

"Now, even if the husband had been wrong, her problem had doubled. On top of her being angry at her husband was now shame. Shame for public disgrace. And now people will even believe she curses her husband all the time in the private. They will say he is a good husband but she is a bad wife. Even if it isn't true, that is what people will think." He scraped the bottom of his bowl with his spoon. He slid the bowl away. He lifted the cup and drank the icy cold water. He drank it all down. Then he placed the cup on the table. "Thank you." Leaning back in his chair, he placed interlaced fingers on his full belly. He studied Sizway with a small smile on his lips.

"Woman," he said. "There is a mystery in them. A woman will be shouting and cursing and stamping her leg and when she comes back to herself she will cry. She may have completely destroyed her home. And then she will cry. Humph. It is too late to cry after the head is off."

Sizway smiled. "That is what my mother used to say—too late to cry after the head is cut off."

Abel studied her again. His chair legs hit the floor.

"Sizzy. Forgive me. You are a woman," he said, folding his hands on the table. "But a woman has one-one problem. Her feelings control her too-too much. Especially during her monthly something. She doesn't know that feelings will pass. She doesn't know that it is not worth destroying her home over a feeling that will pass."

"Mm," Sizway murmured, cupping her cheeks in both palms. "And there are men, too, who behave like women on their menses."

A shout of laughter again escaped Abel's belly. But Sizway remained silent.

"You are right, my wife."

Now Abel pushed back his chair. He left the kitchen and entered the hallway. He knocked on the door of the lav. "Hey, man," he called. Abel opened the door and closed it behind him. Loud, playful voices were heard from inside.

Often Abel and Papa Job would go off in Abel's truck to collect furniture. Sometimes they found whole pieces of furniture or at least old wood that Papa Job could use to repair things with. Sometimes one of Papa Job's neighbors would ask that he come and remove what they didn't want. So Papa Job and Abel went to the neighbors' basements where furniture pieces were tucked away in dark corners. Papa Job used a strong flashlight to see. He wiped off as much of the dust and dirt from the furniture that he could. He would check the furniture for loose joints by wobbling it. He checked for warps, cracks, bruises, small holes, dents, and for dry rot. He checked for missing parts or parts that were damaged or broken. He slid the furniture out from its corner and placed it on a level spot to see if it was in balance. Finally he would spit on his fingertip and wet the wood to see if it would take a fine color when refinished. Satisfied, he and Abel hauled the piece out and onto Abel's truck.

Now Papa Job and Abel emerged from the bathroom. Sizway could overhear Abel asking, "Are you eating here?"

"No," Papa Job answered. "The deli in town."

"Let us go, then," Abel said. He collected his things and headed for the door.

Sizway stood over the sink, washing dishes. Papa Job glanced at her back and paused. He started feeling bad. How long can a man be wicked? Sizway washed and washed but didn't turn around. "Wait, Abel," he said. "We are eating here tonight. Sit down, man."

Abel had already gotten onto the porch.

"Abel," Papa Job called, "where are you going? So. You can't stay here and eat my wife's food?"

Abel complained through the wire mesh at Papa Job. "At first you refused to eat your wife's food and now when I almost finished most of the food myself, you say, 'Let us eat my wife's food.' Well, go ahead and eat it if you must."

Abel came back inside laughing and pulled out a chair. He sat in it backward, his arms folded on the top rung. He smiled at Sizway's back.

"I've been thinking about something, Abel," Papa Job said.

"Mm," Abel responded.

"I've been thinking about opening my own business in town."

"What kind of business?" Abel asked.

"Used furniture."

He looked at Abel.

"So you don't think people will want to buy the furniture I have? Antiques like this? The poor people will buy it because it is cheaper than the new. And the rich people will buy it because it is old, antique."

The lines near Abel's eyes danced. "And here I thought you were still the small boy who couldn't lift the cutlass to strike. So you can lift it now? Then strike out on your own, man, start your own business."

The two men put their heads together and began discussing this business idea in earnest. The voices of the men rose and fell in pitch, circling the kitchen like the pots and pans spinning above their heads. Sizway came and stood beside Papa Job's chair. With pot in hand, she filled his bowl. Papa Job kept his eyes on Abel, listening, but his arm came up and encircled Sizway's waist. That is where Sizway remained, piling on food and more food and more food. . . .

―――――――――――――――

The talebearer's lips curl into a half-moon around her pipe. After a moment, she removes the pipe, spitting the tobacco off her tongue.

"Every woman has trouble with her husband," she says. "Every woman. If a man comes home wanting trouble, the whole house will be shaking. But most women fight with the wrong weapon. They think they have two . . . two power: their mouth and their vagina. They force all of one and hold back the other. But a mouth will just answer to mouth and the fighting will rise. As for the vagina, my mother used to say, 'What even a slave can buy in the marketplace is not something a woman should withhold.' You see, a man can even buy a vagina. That is why a woman's weapon must be patience. She must be able to roll back her tongue, far back inside, and keep patience. At the height of provocation she must keep down and know that the end of a thing is more important than the beginning. My mother used to say, 'With patience you can see the legs of an ant; with patience you can cook a stone.'"

―――――――――――――――

Papa Job now had enough furniture to open a store but he didn't have the money to lease building space in town. Then one evening Sizway entered Papa Job's dry cellar with three Ki women. These women didn't come to look, they came to buy from Papa Job. The Ki were his first customers. Papa Job pulled out this item and that item to show them and he pulled out more things to show them. Soon more of the Ki were scratching on the cellar door and they came with dollars to buy. Soon a few poor blacks in town began to buy. Papa Job didn't make much money, but saving a little at a time he was building toward owning his own business.

He started keeping a small notebook. Each page was set aside for each piece of furniture he worked on and he gave each piece a job number. He wrote down when work was started on the piece, he wrote a description of the piece, and he listed the work he would have to do on it. When he finished the job, he entered the number of hours he had worked on it. He listed the materials he used to get the furniture repaired. And he gave himself an hourly rate of $3.00. He added the cost of materials by the total hours spent working on the job, and from that he came up with a price.

After filling his tin with the day's earnings, he leaned back in the kitchen chair. He had taken to wearing a pair of gold-rimmed spectacles. They were perfectly round and the handles hooked around his earlobes. He smiled contentedly and called Sizway onto his laps. His eyes followed the feline outline of her cheekbones.

He said, "What do you think I should buy with our first big money?"

Sizway wore a buttoned-down sweater and held a pile of diapers on her laps.

"A house we can own."

"That's good. But which house—one you build or one that's built for you?"

"One we must build."

"Hm. It's good to build your own, but in this country a man can't own his own land. The government owns it. You buy land and the government forces you to pay taxes on it. And if you don't pay your taxes they take away your land. If we were in Nassau we could buy land and build and no one could ever take away the land. We would own it and our children and their children."

Sizway shrugged. "Then we will buy a ticket on a boat and go back to Nassau."

Papa Job laughed. Sizway laughed too.

"No, Nassau is very poor."

He sighed. He thought about the Island. His thoughts lingered there. When his mind returned to the present, Sizway was gone from his laps. He took out his harmonica from his pocket. He placed the cool metal between his lips, his hands cupped over the instrument. He closed his eyes.

Ki women don't start sharing blankets again with their husbands until after their child is done nursing. When Toomi turned three he stopped nursing. And Sizway's mother returned to the compound. That was when Sizway moved back into the bedroom with Papa Job. For many moons soft moans like a woman complaining kissed the darkness. But then one moon passed Sizway by and another came and went. Then another and another. The moons kept passing her by. When Sizway went back to selling at the marketplace her stomach was big again with her second child.

Wearing Papa Job's big brown shirt, Sizway could feel more comfortable with her large breasts and her tight belly that pushed away from her. She pulled her braids behind her ears and lowered her black hat on her forehead. She felt miserably hot. She sat on her embroidered rug in the open market with her knees upraised, her bare toes spread out like small fingers on the rug, and the hem of her black skirt brushing the top of her feet.

Occasionally the women would touch her belly and caress the child inside.

She sat in a long line of Ki women beneath a makeshift canopy. They all sweated misery in the heat. They didn't even bother to shoo off the flies. There were many canopies attached from end to end, propped up by wooden posts. Within the hot dimness, the women sold handmade rugs, tie-dyed cloth, and blankets. They sold jewelry and oils and herbal remedies in brown jars. And Ki children played in between the women's warm bodies.

"Mommy," Toomi said. "Mommy, tell me a story."

Toomi at three years was still in diapers. He was naked but for a diaper, which hung like a bowl around his curved belly. And he knelt in his buckled sandals.

"Mommy," he said, patting her arm. "Tell me a story."

Sizway sighed. "I know many stories. How should I know which one you want to hear today?"

Toomi laid his arms on top of his head where the hair was black and soft and sticking straight up. "The finger story," he said, wagging the fingers of one hand.

Sizway was stringing a necklace of eggshells.

"What will you give me for this story?"

"Tobacco," Toomi said automatically.

"Then bring it," she said. Sizway took her pipe from her shirt pocket.

His mother's small leather pouch had been placed between two piles of folded tie-dyed cloth. He brought the pouch to her. When she had lit her pipe, she began her story. She touched Toomi's short finger. "This boy was hungry," she said.

She shooed away a fly from her eyes and touched his next finger: "This boy said, 'Mumma's not at home.'"

She touched the middle finger: "This boy said, 'Let us steal.'"

She touched the pointer: "This one said, 'What if we are caught?'"

She touched the thumb: "This one said, 'Then I'm going to separate myself from all of you.'"

Toomi pulled his thumb away from the other fingers and chanted, "I'll separate myself from all of you."

"That's right. So the thumb separated. He didn't want to steal. That is why everyone's thumb is separated. But remember, we tell stories to teach lessons. You must separate yourself from any bad thing."

"I'll separate from all of you," Toomi shouted. He stood up and slowly turned round and round in a circle to make himself dizzy. "I'll separate from all of you, I'll separate from all of you, I'll separate . . ."

"Kosi has a new lover," Tickney informed everyone.

Everyone peered down the line beneath the wooden canopy at Kosi. The back of a wooden chair was facing Kosi, who sat cross-legged in front of it. She leaned forward, peering into a mirror hung by a string on the arms of the chair. She widened her eyes and lined the rims with black kohl. Her hair was braided in thin cornrowed spirals around her skull and at the center of the spiral a single braid hung down, strung with tiny wooden beads. Heavy jewelry covered both of her arms. Anklets covered each foot. Kosi was twenty-two and very beautiful. Even men looked at her and were embarrassed. When Kosi walked, her rounded hips took on a smooth rolling motion and her breasts stood up ripe and full.

"Who is your new lover, Kosi?" Ayana asked.

Kosi smiled but didn't answer. Kosi's dimples were like deep holes in her cheeks.

"Tell us. Why don't you want to tell us?"

"She wants to tell it but she is afraid."

Kosi wasn't afraid of that. Kosi whose house was more fanciful than anyone there, Kosi who spread her couch with handspun rugs and intricately woven cushions, with sheets of fine linen, Kosi whose bed was perfumed with imported oil, wasn't afraid of that.

"You are talking of sex," Kosi said, replacing the lid on her eye pencil. Her eyes were perfectly round and beautiful. "Sex is a private thing. But this one I have, he is good. His penis never tires. When he gets on you, you just want to be crying."

Laughter moved down the line.

Sizway's face was shadowed by the brim of her hat. Sweat trickled down her nose as she smoked her pipe.

"I took my first lover after my first child was born. A man can forget his woman when she is pregnant and when her children are still small, so his woman begins to dream. A woman can dream, let me tell you."

"But you are doing more than dreaming, Kosi," someone said.

"Listen, my husband is always concerned with business. He is always away. But this lover I have, he is good. He has lots of money, too."

"If you think a man is good when he brings you lots of money, you are mistaken. A rich man only thinks of making more money. Even when he is on you in bed he will be thinking of how to make more money."

"Maybe Kosi's lover sees her like new cloth rather than old," someone else said. "Maybe he is still trying to win her. My mother used to say, the best time for a woman is when a man is trying to win her. At that time, a man will do anything to please her, he will be anything she likes him to be and wear anything she likes him to wear just to win her. But things for a woman changes after she marries. All the things a man did to win her, he doesn't do again."

"Listen, Kosi. What will you do when your lover begins to treat you like old cloth, not new?"

Kosi clucked her tongue in annoyance and stretched out her arms to Toomi. "Leave me," she said, "and let my son come to me in peace." Toomi waddled over and was soon swallowed up in her warm, scented flesh.

Papa Job was more busy now than ever trying to build his business. He rented some building space in town and moved all the finished furniture there in five truckloads. He worked days and evenings. Eventually his business did so well that he hired an assistant. Often Sizway and Toomi were by themselves. One evening a new child cried inside their home. Their second child, Balinga, had come. This birth, like the first one, was fire.

"Whose seed is this?" Kehinde chanted, lifting the child. "This one belongs to the Great One."

> I give you this our son for your blessing
> Give him the strength of the ancient ones
> Let him run boldly with his life.

Each of the midwives laid hands on his soft belly and prayed for him. At the naming ceremony, he was given the name Balinga, which means The-Beautiful-One.

When Balinga was born, Toomi had to give up his favored sleeping place in between Sizway and Papa Job. Toomi had to sleep at his mother's back while Balinga himself slept in between their parents. Toomi had to walk beside Sizway on their way to the marketplace while Balinga was carried in a sling. At first Toomi resented the new baby. He bit him and pinched him, but eventually he began to like him. He would hold Balinga's tiny finger as he nursed and put his nose near the baby's mouth to smell his sweet, milky breath. But later on, when Balinga began to walk and talk and behave like a human, they began to fight again every day and every time.

The screen door opened and Toomi stepped onto the porch planks, carrying Balinga on his back. He held up Balinga's legs while Balinga wound his arms around Toomi's neck. Toomi was seven years old now and Balinga was four. They were naked except for their white briefs and undershirts.

"Good evening, daddy," Toomi said.

"Good evening, daddy," Balinga said.

Toomi bent his knees and allowed Balinga to slide down off his back.

Papa Job knelt on a pile of newspapers. The night was lit by a single lightbulb from the porch rafters. Papa Job was using a dull putty knife to scrape old finish off a dresser. From time to time, he wiped the knife on the newspaper. He wore his gold spectacles and workpants that were stiff as a board and splattered with paint. His big clunky shoes held no laces and he had on one of Sizway's old head scarves tied in back of his head.

"Daddy, what are you doing?" the youngest child, Balinga, asked.

"Removing paint."

"Why?" he asked, squatting near his father.

"To change the color of the wood."

Balinga watched his father peel up the finish with his putty knife. "Why do you want to change it?" Balinga asked.

"To make it beautiful," Papa Job answered.

Balinga rested his hand on his father's thigh. "What color will you use to make it beautiful?"

"Mahogany."

"Ohh, mahogany. What's mahogany?"

"Brown."

"And what's in that can?" he pointed.

"Mahogany stain."

"What's stain?"

Toomi had stepped back against the porch railing and was bumping the vertical bars with his bottom. Now he slapped his forehead with the heel of his palm.

"The child has no sense. He doesn't know what a stain is."

"Don't tell me that. I know a stain," Balinga said.

"No, you have no sense," Toomi said.

"I have sense as much as you," Balinga said.

"Then how many sense do you have?"

Balinga stood up, resting his small hand on his father's scarfed head. "I have so many sense I can't count them to you, for them they're all over me body."

"Ho-ho," Toomi laughed, bumping his bottom against the vertical bars again. "I only have two. One for me and one for you."

Now Balinga turned his back to his brother and patted his father's shoulder. "Daddy? Daddy?"

Papa Job was rolling some newspaper into a ball.

Balinga squatted next to him. "And what are you doing with that newspaper, daddy?" Balinga asked.

"I'm going to wipe the paint off of this putty knife. Step back, Balinga."

Balinga straightened his legs again and backed up against the vertical bars. Then he and his brother sat down on the floorboards. They silently watched their father work. Finally, Toomi turned to his little brother, sliding his arm around his shoulder. "I am your father, too, Balinga. I am senior to you."

The little boy just looked at him, unblinking.

Toomi tore off a bit of old newspaper and balled it. "Look. I've come home from work and I've brought you food. Here is some food."

He told Balinga to eat the paper. But the little boy carefully slid his hands underneath his buttocks and sat on them. Toomi put the paper aside. He tugged at his little brother's arm.

"Bring out your hand, Balinga. Bring it. Look. I brought you food. Bring out your hand."

After a while he stopped tugging at Balinga's arm and began pressing the balled newspaper against the boy's lips. Balinga turned his face this way and that, still sitting on his hands.

"Oh, you are stubborn," Toomi said.

This struggle went on for quite a while until Toomi commanded him. "Eat your food!"

And Balinga shouted, "Make me!"

Toomi held his little brother by the neck and pushed his face down toward the balled paper on the floor.

"No!" Balinga screamed. "Don't make me do it!"

Toomi released him. Balinga sat up and stared boldly at Toomi. "Make me," he said.

Toomi forced his neck down again.

"Don't make me do it!" Balinga screamed.

Then . . .

"Make me."

Then . . .

"Don't make me do it!"

In no time, the boys heard the screen door clattering and vibrating shut. Sizway padded across the porch. Her stomach was slightly rounded, three months with child, and she had one hand raised to strike. You couldn't judge her by her size.

"Have you ever heard of my left hand?" she asked them.

Balinga burst out crying. "Brother killed me!"

And Toomi began crying too. "I didn't. He is lying."

"No, *he* is lying."

"Since when have I been telling lies? I am telling the truth today."

"Go to bed," Sizway said, pointing at the door with her pipe. "You are brothers. You are the same. Stop fighting."

Papa Job was standing, cleaning his hands on a rag. He gestured to Sizway. "Bring them." Papa Job seated himself sideways on the edge of the landing that led onto the first step. He rested his back against the wall of the house. Sizway took each small hand and brought the children to him. The boys knelt on the landing near their father and Sizway settled on the step directly below Papa Job. Papa Job told Sizway to tell them again the story that teaches a lesson. The story that teaches that brothers are one.

The night all around them was dark. Moths danced in a frenzy around the porch light, clinking against the lightbulb. Sizway took her pipe out of her mouth and examined it with an air of indecision. She said, "My pipe is cold. Give me tobacco and I will tell you that story."

Toomi and Balinga both ran into the house, bumping into each other so that one brother would beat the other brother to their mother's tobacco. Toomi returned first with Sizway's leather pouch, while Balinga followed behind, crying. Papa Job placed Balinga on his laps. Sizway lit her pipe and started.

"There were two crows and they were brothers—Sola and Kumsa. Sola was the eldest crow and Kumsa was the youngest crow. When they flew together in the woods they usually played at fighting games. They spent long hours leaping off the branches and diving toward each other, clacking their beaks together, and frightening each other with their powerful wings.

"One day while they were fighting, clacking beaks and such, Kumsa asked his senior brother, 'Why do you always want to fight me?'

"And Sola replied, 'Because I want to be the first and only son. I don't want to be the first of two sons.'

"They continued fighting, driving each other back and forth with their flapping wings, and littering the woods with their loose feathers. Eventually Sola stopped and asked his junior brother, 'But Kumsa, why do you always want to fight me?'

"Kumsa replied, 'Because I want to be first. I don't want to be the second of the first.'

"Daily Sola asked his heart, 'When will Sola be the first and only son?' And daily Kumsa asked his heart, 'When will Kumsa be first, and not the second of the first?' By day when they flew at each other and drove each other away with their wings, they thought only of conquering a small space on a branch. By night, when they settled down with the evening on branches with the crow elders, Sola would hear how the elders praised Kumsa and he wondered when he would be the first and only son. As for Kumsa, who listened to the elders praise Sola, he himself wondered when he would be first.

"Daily the crows fought against each other. They fought every day and every time. Never was there an end to the fighting. One day there came to the woods a war between their clan of crows and another clan of crows. All the men crows of the clan prepared to do battle with their enemy. Sola and Kumsa's father called them. 'My sons, today we go to battle. I pray that you and I will live on and endure. Stay behind me and protect my rear.'

"The enemy leaped off the branches and flew at them. Father and sons flew at them. They fought bravely. The enemy pressed them hard. Then the sons started arguing about who should be protecting their father's rear. Sola said, 'Look here. I should do it because I am the firstborn,' and Kumsa said he should do it because he came last, which means behind. While they were arguing, one of the enemy crows thrust his beak into the back of their father's head and death entered him. Their father fell from the branch, dead. Now the boys flew at each other and began fighting each other. Each brother blamed the other for allowing their father to be killed. As they beat each other with their wings, every crow of their clan was struck down, one by one. The woods was soon littered with the bodies of dead crows. Eventually the enemy crows triumphed over the clan entirely.

"Only Sola and Kumsa were left, pecking at each other with their beaks. The enemy swooped down. They pecked out Sola's eyes and broke the wing of Kumsa. Sola and Kumsa lay helpless. Sola took Kumsa on his back and escaped through a path in the woods. Sola, who couldn't see, depended on Kumsa's eyes. And Kumsa, who couldn't fly, depended on Sola's wings to carry him. Before, they refused to live as one. Now life forced them. For the remainder of their lives they had no family, no clan. The Ki say they are wandering still . . . and alone. And their crow cries can be heard deep in the woods. They make repetitive call, like the rhythmic crying of a child. Now you can see how brothers should know that they are one. Let it become your way as it is the way now of Sola and Kumsa."

The boys got up and held hands. They went to bed silently.
Papa Job turned to Sizway. "That was a good story."

She emptied the ash from the bowl of her pipe. She said,
"Will you bring me a pack of tobacco from town tomorrow?"

Papa Job smiled. "I will bring you two packs. It was a good
story."

And so Toomi and Balinga ate together, slept together, went
out together, and wore clothing cut from the same cloth. Eventually they came to think of themselves as one. They learned
every day to be cultured. And out of the lessons of their parents,
their grandparents, and their extended family, the strength of
the two boys grew.

The trees are alive with many black crows. As the talebearer peers up at them the leaves make large, trembling shadows on her face. Her head is cocked slightly, like the crows', listening. The crows' black eyes are beady and still. She begins to
speak to them in their own language, using unintelligible words.
A crow leaps off a branch and hops a little as he lands on the
dry dirt ground. He is so tall and heavy that his tailwing dips as
he walks toward her. His black feathers glisten. He walks right
up to her as she continues talking to him. After some time she is
silent and turns away from the crow. She rests her cheek in her
palm, her eyes lowered.

"My mother who died knew the language of crows and the
language of all the animals and plants in the forest. This crow
is the elder of his clan. He says women, too, can be clannish like
crows. Women will sit together for long just talking. Often their
talk will turn to men. But if a woman is wise she won't talk
about her own man."

The talebearer picks up a stick near her feet and idly taps it against the ground.

"The crow gives a bit of advice," she says. "He says, 'A bird doesn't appreciate his tailwing until it is cut off.' That is good advice. I would give it to women."

The talebearer continues idly tapping the stick, she picks at rocks, pokes at dirt. She lets out a breath and tosses the stick aside. She dusts the dirt off her hands.

"Don't throw out what I say right away. Just listen."

chapter five

"Kosi, why are you not talking today?" Ayana asked at the open market.

All the young women turned and looked down the line at Kosi. It was true. Kosi's lively spirit was down.

"What is wrong, Kosi?"

"My lover is traveling," Kosi sighed.

"Ah, but you know rich men, they like to travel," Ayana giggled. "You must be missing him."

Kosi nodded.

"But what of the one that lives in the house with you? You used to complain of him traveling too much as well. You said that is why you took a lover. Now your lover is traveling."

"Yes," Kosi sighed.

Laughter passed down the line.

Kosi's eyes widened with hurt. "What?"

Bimbi, who was a widow and who had borne eleven children, said, "Some women have to taste two men to learn. If a woman doesn't taste two men she will never know the best man for her. If a man is really good she will say he is boring. Perhaps he is not one to talk but keeps his words one or two and then says no more. Perhaps he stays home while other men drink beer and laugh loud in the town. Perhaps he doesn't flatter her too-too much. He doesn't tell her she is beautiful so much. She will leave him to find one who will flatter her well. But when she tastes the second one she will know. When she sees the other side of life, she will balance her judgment."

Kosi ignored Bimbi. "I know of many women in the compound who have lovers."

Bimbi laughed bitterly. "They lie for you. They want to see you destroy your home."

"Ho, ho. Look, Sizzy," Ayana whispered. "Your customer is coming. The one who always smells of beer."

Everyone forgot about Kosi and turned to look. He was a young man in cowboy boots and Levis, making his way through the crowd toward the Ki women's canopy. He started coming to the market some months ago. He would drive to the lot at midday in his pickup, turn off the engine, click open a can of beer, and drink it down. All the while he drank, his eyes never moved from Sizway. His spirit was very strong and was felt by all the Ki women, making them restless.

When he finished his beer he would swing open the door of his truck, climb down, and slowly approach the Ki women's canopy. As soon as his truck door opened, all the women would watch him approach and feel their own spirit retreating. He always went directly to Sizway.

The first time he came to her, he bent under the canopy, looked Sizway in the eye, and said, "Sizzy, do you remember me?"

She searched his face. Shook her head. No.

He stepped back from the canopy, stuffed his hands in his jean pockets, and gave a small smile.

"Now you will."

After the first meeting, he always came to Sizway. He said, "I'd like this herb and that herb." After paying for it, he'd say, "Thank you, ma'am," and move off.

Now as the man approached, Ayana said, "Sizzy, I think this one smells of drink because of you."

The other women giggled.

But Sizway clucked her tongue. "Umph, why should I care if he is smelling, Ayana? He may be smelling, but his money isn't. Allow me to take his money and light my incense after he leaves."

Sizway looked up and smiled. "Hello. How are you? What can I do for you today?"

He stooped under the canopy. He took off his heavy Western-style hat and held it in two sweating hands.

"You can call me Michael."

All the women, even Sizway, fell silent.

The open market was practically deserted now. The sun was going down and many of the farmers' trucks were backing out of the parking lot. The Ki's wooden canopy had been taken down and most of the Ki were gone, either taking to the road on foot or riding on the backs of pickups. Sizway knelt on her embroidered rug, screwing jar lids tight and stacking them neatly in a basket made of branches. The last Ki truck waited for her in the lot. Suddenly a long, thin shadow fell over her body.

Standing behind her, he watched her kneeling there. He
gazed at her sky-blue shirt, a man's shirt, probably her husband's;
her long black skirt; and her bare feet turned up so that he could
see the flat soles of her sandals. Her toothpick-thin braids lay
limp and damp on her back and her black felt hat was pulled
down low over her eyes. She wore earrings that reached her
shoulders and they were made of wooden beads and turquoise.
He came up beside her and squatted down. She raised her
golden-brown eyes to his. His eyes rested there. He gazed at the
crow's feet that lined her blackberry skin from squinting for so
many years in the sun.

"Hello, Michael."

Michael removed his large Western-style hat. He was a
warm brown–colored black man with blue-black hair plastered
silky and wet against his skull. He was a farm worker with thick,
callused hands and fingernails lined with dirt.

"I was driving by in my truck," he said. "I seen you packing
up. You need some help?"

Sizway shook her head, No. But he glanced around and noticed a pile of tie-dyed cloth that had been picked through all
day by customers. He came down on one knee and began folding
the cloth.

In the parking lot, a few Ki women sat on the back of their
truck chatting. A young Ki girl was sweeping the ground. And
old farmers from the town lolled around near their own trucks
chatting.

Michael glanced over at Sizway every now and then. He
glanced at the sleeves of her shirt that were rolled to the elbows
and her arms ringed with copper bracelets. She held the jar in
one hand and twisted the lid with the other, which caused a
gentle movement of soft flesh beneath her shirt. Finally her

buttocks sat back on her heels. She removed her hat and fanned herself.

"Where should I put this?" he asked, lifting the folded cloth in his hands.

"In the basket."

He gently placed the cloth in another basket made of branches. Sizway continued fanning herself. Though she was only three months pregnant and not sticking out too far, the baby felt very heavy.

Michael knelt on one knee, the other upraised and his elbow resting there. He pulled a handkerchief from his back pocket and offered it to her.

"It's clean," he smiled. "You are sweating. Use it. I took it off the clothesline on my way out."

"No. Thank you," she said. She breathed through slightly parted lips; the heat seemed even heavier now.

"How are you doing? I mean, you and the babies," he asked.

He watched her thin brown lips form words. Her teeth were like the white flesh of pecans. He started to ask her something else to keep her talking, to keep her for a brief, fleeting moment, but suddenly she was standing. She had put on her hat and stooped to lift the basket on her head.

"Whoa, now. Let me do that," he said. He stood up, putting on his hat. He took the basket from her. "I got my truck parked over there. I can give you a ride."

She lifted the lighter basket of cloth on her head. "I am riding with the Ki."

With one hand balancing the basket on her head and the other hand resting on her belly she headed toward the parking lot. Michael followed behind her. Her skirt swayed gently from side to side and her anklet made a soft watery tinkle with each footfall.

They slid the baskets onto the back of the truck. Sizway turned to him and smiled. "Thank you, Michael. Bye-bye."

The women who were sitting, swinging their legs, stopped chattering and watched. Michael touched the brim of his hat and nodded to Sizway and to the two other women.

"Well, have a nice evening, ladies," he said.

He looked at Sizway again. Her eyes were as cool as a stream in the evening sun, deep, serene, tranquil. He turned on his heels and headed toward the farmers who were parked further down the lot.

Sizway told the young women, "Come. Help me."

She went back to her rug and rolled it up, while the women collected any loose items lying about. They returned for the last time. But down a ways, an old farmer called out to Sizway as he stood beside his own pickup. He said, "How'd y'all do today?"

Sizway replied, "Good."

"Come on over here, Sizway. I got something for you," the farmer said. He climbed inside the cab of his truck to get it.

Sizway slid her hat further down over her eyes and walked the tar-paved lot. The tar slow-cooked her sandaled feet. She placed a hand on her small, pregnant belly. As she neared the farmer she saw that another truck was parked on the opposite side of his. She came. The old man climbed down. He handed her a bag of plums.

"Thank you," she smiled.

"You're welcome, Sizway. That poultice you give me for my back was like a gift from God. It wiped out all the pain. I had carried that pain for forty-some-odd years. I figure I owe you a lot more'n plums."

She thanked him.

"Hell, I don't know how to stop thanking you. Take care of that new one you're carrying, too," he said, nodding at her belly. Then he slammed the door and started the motor. He backed out of the lot. That's when Sizway took closer notice of the truck that was parked beside it. Michael was sitting with one foot against the dashboard, gazing out the windshield at the trees beyond.

Sizway turned on her heels to go back, but Michael's voice came out to her as if he were talking to himself.

"I'm not leaving without you, Sizzy."

The door of the truck swung open. He dropped down.

Sizway started walking.

"Sizzy, wait," he called. "Sizzy . . . If I have to, I'll follow you over there. But it'd be better to say what I have to say right here."

Sizway's footfalls slowed. Michael came up behind her. His boot heels slowly crunched down on loose tar and gravel. Soon his shadow fell across her body. She could feel the heat of him close against her back. Sizway placed a hand on the top button of her shirt.

He glanced down at her hand. He said, "Why do you want to protect yourself from me? Why?"

Her eyebrows frowned, her brown lips sealed. She was protected. She had put on the amulet that morning; it hung from her neck, hidden beneath her shirt. And he knew it was there.

He said, "I know many things about you, Sizzy. I know you have the same dream all the time. You see a child floating around the moon. . . ."

Sizway's tongue came out to wet her lips.

"You see this child laughing and floating around the—"

Sizway started walking.

"When you were a little girl you used to play in the fields where the grass was as tall as your head. You were running and the grass was like a million fingers, tickling your legs and your face. Suddenly you stopped running and looked up at the sun. . . ."

Sizway's footfalls slowed again.

"You were alone, but when you looked at the sun a warm mouth touched yours. Your mouth, when I kissed it, was like sweating wildflowers." He had come up behind her. His hand came around and rested on her belly, his fingers spread out to hold its fullness.

"You're gonna have twins," he murmured in her ear.

Sizway slid his hand off and slowly turned to face him.

His eyes held her. "I know the black gypsies say I drink because of you. Tell them it's true. I do drink. Because of you."

She said, "I don't know why you drink. But I am married. I have a husband and children."

Michael slid his hands in his pants pockets. He glanced at the red ball of sun setting behind her. He frowned. "I leave Sojourner tomorrow. I don't want to leave without you. You're my wife." He stood silent for a while. He said, "I sold the farm. I sold everything. It's time. The moon child you dreamt of is here." And his eyes fell on her belly.

Sweat shivered in beads above her top lip. She stood very still.

Now he pulled his hands out of the pockets of his Levis and came up with two stones. One was amethyst and the other onyx. "These are for the twins," he said.

Sizway glanced at the stones but kept her arms at her sides.

Slowly he slid the stones back in his pocket.

"Okay. I'll keep them for you. I don't want to leave without you, Sizzy. Come with me. Please."

"No," she said. "My husband is here. My children are here. I don't know who—you know many things, but—" She shook her head. "But I don't know you."

"Don't say you don't know me. We're the same. I'm the husband you found that warm day in the sun when you were a little girl, the husband you didn't choose."

She spoke to him quietly and gazed at him curiously. "And now I have chosen again. I have a husband. He is the one I have."

His eyes darkened. He nodded. He slowly walked backward toward his truck. Then he wheeled around and walked quickly to his truck. He climbed in. At the sound of the motor starting, Sizway lowered the brim of her hat over her eyes and made her way back down the tar-paved lot.

Early morning at the market Sizway was scolding her two sons.

"Don't come near the fire, Toomi. And take your brother from here."

The Ki women were selling only tie-dyed cloth today and they made the cloth right there in the market for their customers to see. The customers sat beneath the length of the canopy. They had come from all the surrounding counties to buy the cloth and to watch the Ki make it. Behind the canopy many fires had been built upon which sat huge black pots for tie-dying fabric. Sizway was dipping a cloth in and out of the boiling pot of water with a long stick. She lifted a cobalt-blue-and-orange-patterned cloth that was steaming with filmy heat. She dropped the cloth in cold water; she wrung it out and hung it over a clothesline behind her.

Many of the Ki women exclaimed, "Sizzy, how is it that you are making such beautiful cloth?"

Murmurs passed around and black felt hats nodded. "It is the hands of the twin spirits."

Everyone knew now that Sizway carried twins. She was in her sixth month and she began making cloth more beautifully than she had ever done before. She tie-dyed the cloth in intricately patterned designs. She sold many, many cloth that day, even selling to the other Ki women. Now, even today, when the Ki see beautiful tie-dyed cloth, they say it is as beautiful as the hands of the twin spirits.

The twin spirits hovered over Sizway's belly every day, never fully entering. Instead, they entered in and out of the two shells inside her that were to be their own bodies. That is why the ghosts of the future are as real as the ghosts of the past. Even at birth, when an infant sleeps it will leave its own body and travel. Finally the skull closes and the spirit is imprisoned in the body forever. At least until the point of death.

The Ki held the day of tie-dying in autumn. Brown leaves were pushed along the ground by the wind. The Ki women's children sat under the canopy in a large circle eating with their hands from the same communal bowl. It was dim and cool beneath the canopy. Suddenly Toomi and Balinga left the circle and ran to Sizway who stood over a boiling pot on the fire. Toomi was seven and Balinga was four. Toomi's head reached Sizway's breast. He had partly curly and partly straight black hair and a large black mole on his deep, chocolate-brown cheek. He patted her skirt and told her that a boy over there from the town was calling all of them black gypsies.

Sizway slowly stirred the cloth in the pot and said, "If some-one calls 'witch' and you are not a witch, will you turn around?"

Toomi shook his head.

"Then why are you answering to black gypsy? They are only calling you what their parents are calling you because they don't know whom you are. In this country we have no identity, we are called black gypsies, but we know whom we are. We are the Ki. And so must you."

Now Balinga was patting her skirt and complaining because no one left him any juice to drink in the children's circle. Balinga had perfectly round eyes and bright black pupils. His long lashes brushed his cheeks. Sizway left the boiling pot and stooped under the canopy. She stepped over her embroidered rug. She sat cross-legged and unscrewed the cap on a thermos. She poured the cool apple juice into a plastic cup. There were many people milling about them talking loudly and laughing and children ran in between the close bodies.

Balinga scooted onto Sizway's lap and took the cup in two hands. He began to drink. Sizway waited but Balinga said noth-ing. Sizway plucked the cup from his hands and held it away from him.

"Say good-bye to this juice," she told him. "If you are so un-grateful that you don't know how to say 'Thank you,' then you don't deserve to drink this. Now you will know the difference between have and have not. Say good-bye to it. And tell the juice why you must throw it out."

"Mommy, I forgot to say thank you."

"You always forget. But today you are throwing it out."

Balinga took the cup and spoke to the juice inside the cup. He told it that he didn't say thank you and now he must throw it out.

"Now, throw it out," Sizway commanded him. Balinga scooted off her lap and ran across the rug to pour the juice on the ground. Two Ki women were sitting near Sizway. Balinga ran to one of them, burying his face in her chest and spilling precious eye water.

"Acch, why is Balinga crying?" she asked.

"Balinga is crying because he doesn't have good manner," Sizway replied.

"Ah, but he is such a beautiful child."

Sizway stood up. "Umph. What good is beauty without good manner?"

She walked back behind the canopy to the boiling pot. Three Ki women were hanging tie-dyed cloth on the clothesline, whispering.

"Kosi is pregnant again," Tickney said.

Kosi was not with them today.

Ayana sucked in her breath. "Is it her husband's or her lover's?"

"Who knows," Tickney shrugged.

"So she has a lover again," Ayana giggled. "I thought she was tired of that."

Then Unus, who was in her early twenties, spoke. She said, "Well, I see nothing wrong if Kosi takes a lover. Men take lovers, don't they? How many of your husbands in the compound have done it?"

Bimbi, the old widow, was adding wood to Sizway's fire. She straightened her back, wiping her hands on her skirt. She turned to the young women. She said, "You should know that this is not our world. It is a man's world. We women may not like it but it is true. It is their world. If your husband sexed every woman here in the compound no one would condemn him. They would just say he was being a man. But if a woman did the same thing they would condemn her and cast her out. This isn't our world. In this strange land we women take pleasure like that and lose the father of our children.

"I know that none of you who support Kosi love children. Kosi is more concerned with oiling her vagina than with her children. If she is caught with her lover her children will be fatherless. When a man and a woman marry, they may not always get along but they must remember that children are important. If you ruin a marriage you can marry again. But once you ruin a child's life it is forever."

After Bimbi spoke, the women sobered. The women stopped chattering and began busying themselves with their work, while the peeling trees dropped leaves upon the ground.

Soon Sizway was in her ninth month with her twins. Between the rainy fall and winter season, the people of the Ki compound were unable to sell at the open market. But Sizway, who lived in town, would often peddle door to door to her neighbors. Sometimes a few women from the compound would come in a pickup truck to Sizway's house and together they would go peddling door to door. Afterward everyone went back to Sizway's house, rain-soaked and shivering. They kept close to the fire of the wood-burning stove and talked.

Today the kitchen was as dull as the cloudy sky outside. Sizway and Nalajah sat cross-legged on Sizway's beautifully embroidered rug in front of the oven. Sizway filled her pipe and lit it with a glowing ember brought to her by her child on a clay plate. Nalajah was the same age as Sizway. They had grown up together in the compound. Nalajah was a head shorter than Sizway. Her neck was ribbed like the sides of a can. White disks of earrings weighed heavy on each earlobe. And her woolen hair was closely cropped to her scalp.

"How is Mommy?" Sizway asked Lajah. She was speaking on Manji now.

"Mommy? Ho-ho, Mommy is really starting to act blind, Sizway. You know how she doesn't want certain things done for her and she doesn't want to be treated in certain ways like a blind person? Well, now she is behaving like a blind person. I came to her house bearing food, see. And do you know what she did? She take me arm here and sniff me cloth. 'Yah, this is the smell of Lajah.' Then she take the fingers so, and she go so feeeel cross me face. 'Mmm,' she say, 'this is the face of Lajah. Come in.' Umph. Mumma," Lajah giggled.

Sizway's eyes pleated at the corners. "You think mumma is starting to act blind?"

Nalajah nodded. "Hm. Yah. She do."

"You are funny. She is starting to see."

"Her starting to see? You don't mean it?"

Papa Job paused at the kitchen doorway with a folded newspaper under his arm.

Nalajah looked up. "Hello, Kiba."

"How are you?" he asked.

"Fine."

Papa Job had returned from his furniture business in town. He had taken his bath in the claw-footed tub and came out smelling like soap and talc and more soap. He wore a yellow shirt and neatly starched yellow pants and leather house slippers that flapped at the heels. His skin shone from oil and his mustache was cut neatly over his brown upper lip. With his newspaper under his arm and his gold wire-rimmed spectacles circling his eyes, he stood over the stove, pouring hot water from a kettle into a teacup.

The women sat at his feet.

"Oh, Kibaba, I see some tiredness there," Nalajah said, looking up at him. "Is Sizway keeping you running up and down with this pregnancy?"

Papa Job nodded. "Yes, that. And apart from that there is not a day she won't involve me in arguments."

Nalajah's eyes widened. Papa Job held the tag of a teabag and bobbed it around in the cup of water. Sizway tapped the back of Nalajah's hand and murmured, "Don't mind him."

But Papa Job told their guest, "You see, a husband knows that when his wife is pregnant he is not fighting with one but two, and in Sizzy's case, three."

Sizway smiled faintly as she drew from her pipe. Her eyes glittered.

"But do you know how I handle her? this one that I keep in my house?" he said, nodding at Sizway. "I don't argue with her. I reply her, 'Yes, ma.' I just laugh, 'Ho-ho, ma.' And I keep piling her offenses one on top of the other, one on top of the other, until the day she delivers."

"Aiii!" Nalajah exclaimed. "You are bad!"

Papa Job shrugged. "What's bad in that?"

Nalajah giggled and warned Sizway, "You'd better watch."

Papa Job stepped around the edge of the rug, around the women, and seated himself at the table. He crossed his leg, one over the other, and opened his newspaper.

Sizway's eyes now fixed on her toes folded beneath her dress. "I will tell you this," she said to Nalajah, her gold earrings swinging. "Mumma's blindness wasn't the work of nature, my sister. It was the work of a witch."

"A witch?" Nalajah gasped. "Yah?"

"A witch," Sizway nodded.

"In the compound?" Nalajah asked.

"This witch is no more in the compound," Sizway said. "She died the day mumma turned blind."

Papa Job's house shoe slipped down and dangled on the end of his toes. He peered up from his newspaper. Witches, it was said, could be male or female and could put bad spirits in people. Witches had the power to make a pregnant woman give birth to bats, they had the power to talk over the grave of a dead person and make the dead person reply, they had the power to disappear and reappear somewhere else. And there were witches living in the Ki camp. Most witches were bad but there were some who were good. Manji had been warring with a witch and was turned blind by the witch. But the blindness, it was said, would be removed after ten years. Now Manji's ten years were up.

Papa Job lifted the cup to his lips and nearly choked on the tea when it was said that his own mother-in-law, Manji, was a witch.

Sizway turned around at her husband's choking. "You'd better watch, Kiba. Mind you don't choke yourself."

After his coughs died down, Sizway turned back to Nalajah.

Other Ki women began entering the kitchen through the back screen door. They carried large baskets on their shoulders, which they placed upon the floor. They removed their coats, ponchos, or blankets and shook off the rain. Papa Job looked closely at the strange amulets and articles worn about their necks, wrists, and waists. Some of the amulets were worn for protection, others for healing, and others for luck.

He murmured greetings and nodded. They draped their garments over the table and the backs of chairs. They sat around the embroidered rug, warming themselves by the fire. Though Papa Job had lived amongst the Ki for many years and behaved now in many ways like a traditional Ki male, there was still a lot he did not understand about them.

With all these women in the kitchen, Papa Job folded his newspaper and prepared to leave.

"I have a story," Kosi called.

"Good. Tell us your story."

Everyone loved Kosi's stories.

"It is the story of a woman who fell in love with a spirit."

Papa Job frowned. "How is it possible to fall in love with a spirit?"

All the women looked at him and asked all at once, "Why can't a woman fall in love with a spirit?"

"There was a young woman," Kosi continued, "who had no husband. One day . . ."

Sizway was peddling door to door on her own today. But the weight of the twins wouldn't allow her to go peddling too far. Snow clouds loomed overhead. She wore a woolen head scarf beneath her black felt hat, a heavy woolen poncho ballooned over her pregnant belly. She wore gloves without fingers and laced boots. Her next stop was Eva and Jim-Walter's farmstead on a hill. Sizway had to enter a gate and walk up a long dirt driveway to reach the farmhouse. On either side of the driveway

were apple trees. Unpicked apples lay rotting on the ground. A
pickup was parked in front of the house. Behind the house were
acres and acres of land for growing produce, but barren now.
With the cold season, no one was farming. Sizway paused. She
listened to the silence. Listened to the winter wind.

Eva was inside the farmhouse, on the telephone.

"Well," Eva whispered, dusting the telephone table with her
palm, "between you, me, and the gatepost, they don't speak to
each other now. . . ."

Eva crossed her legs in her cool, dark kitchen. She cradled
the receiver against her ear. Eva was about sixty-five years old.
Tiny, arrow-like wrinkles marked the corners of her eyes and
pale blue cat-eye glasses balanced on her nose. A cake-box
string held her grey silky hair in a bun.

"See, Edna's on Reba's land," she said to the telephone. "I
feel for Reba cause they done her so bad. Dr. Frank say Edna
need to die on that land. Uhn-huhn. Well, he's South. You
know, they got names like Frankie and Janie. Uhn-huhn. Well,
he say, 'Edna need to die on that land.' I say, 'You ain't got no
right to that land, Edna. It's Reba's.' I let Edna know. I didn't
worry. Well, Edna, say such'n'such. But she don't come by here
to see me no more. I tell Jim-Walter, 'I guess you know Reba
don't speak to Edna.' Jim-Walter say he ain't got time to hear
about it. He ain't interested in other folks' business. Never heard
of family being other folks. Have you? Well, we drove by to see
Reba the other day. Here come Edna flying out the house across
the way. Jim-Walter stopped to talk to her about some weed
killer or something. I didn't say nothing to her."

Eva switched the phone to her other ear and recrossed her
legs. She had tiny ankles and wore loose-fitting stockings dotted
with snag balls.

"'How long you been married to Jim?' folks ask me. 'Ohh, too long,' I say. Then I count. Uhn-huhn, that's right. My children say, 'I wish you had'a worked them years instead of staying at home.' I don't say nothing. I let em go on. My oldest daughter say, 'When I have some kids, I'm gonna work and put some *new* clothes on em once in a while.' You see what she saying, now, don't you? Uhn-huhn."

Eva bit into a long hangnail and spat a few times before it flew off her tongue and onto her laps. "Jim-Walter ask me, 'Who's such'n'such?' He don't know but one name anywheres he go. I tell him, 'Oh, he's such'n'such.' Tell him anything, you know. Uhn-huhn. He ask me, 'Did your children write you yet?' I say, 'I told em not to write. They busy. And I ain't got no time to be writing to people myself.' . . . Who? Jim-Walter? No, he ain't quit the cigarette habit. Soon as my brother Timothy come by for a visit, he go over to him, whisper, 'Say, Tim, you got eighty cents to get me some, you know.'—Yeah, Tim's fine. He and his wife should've stayed together. But nooo, they had to separate. I see his wife once in a while. She remember I used to sell apples. She ask me, 'What you got today, Eva?' I say, 'I ain't got nothing.'"

Eva's husband scuffled into the cold kitchen, yawning in his dirty thermal undershirt. He pulled up his suspenders, hiking up his blue woolen pants at the same time. Pieces of wood chips trembled like crushed leaves along his leggings.

Eva's eyes darted over to the doorway and back. She immediately lowered her voice, her lips brushing the receiver. "Lawd, Lawd, Lawd," she smiled crookedly, staring at her laps. "Jesus, Holy Mary, what a day . . ."

Sizway blew on her fingers before she rang the front doorbell. She could see the house was dark inside through the white lace curtains. She waited a while. She rang the doorbell again.

Jim-Walter opened the front door. He was a coffee-and-cream-colored black man like his wife and stoop-shouldered. White whiskers covered his head and white whiskers covered his chin. But his arms and chest were muscular and strong from farm work.

"Hello, daddy," she smiled. "How are you?"

"Fair to middling," he replied in a gravelly voice. "Come on in, Sizway."

Their house was cold and seemed full of old memories, old keepsakes. The fabric on the couches and chairs was fading. Above the couch a cuckoo clock with two long chains chimed the hour. The bird flew out as the chains rattled down, then the bird was yanked back inside, the door clapping behind it. There were mahogany tables displaying catalog-ordered items like little porcelain figures of Dutch boys. On the carpet was stacked old newspapers and copies of *Reader's Digest*. The tables held pictures of the children Eva and Jim-Walter had raised, photos of relatives now dead, pictures almost frightening they were so old.

Sizway sat down in a straight-back armchair, placing her small basket on the fettered rug at her feet. At her elbow, a white Jesus was framed in oval glass with metal curlicues bordering the frame. It was placed on a small side table.

Jim-Walter took a seat on the couch.

"How you, Sizway?"

"Just fine. And you?"

He took a gulp of no-brand cola from a can that clinked against his wire-rimmed glasses. His wife muttered from the kitchen. "No, we ain't got no wood in the stove. Old and cheap. That's all. He's old and cheap."

"I don't know," Jim-Walter said to the cola can. "I thank she got a lil . . . lil hatred towards me."

Sizway was removing her head scarf when Eva poked her head around the kitchen doorway. "Who you talking to, Jim-Walter? Is that Sizway? How you doing, Sizway?"

"Just fine, mumma," Sizway smiled, folding her scarf.

"Did you bring me that ointment for my hands?"

Eva's hands constantly itched. The skin was cracked, red, and peeling. She was scratching her hands as she seated herself on the couch next to her husband. In front of them was a coffee table and then Sizway's armchair. Sizway lifted the lid of her basket on her lap.

Jim-Walter snorted and said, "I hope you can give her something that works this time. She scratches like a cat with fleas." Saying that, he got up and slowly made his way to the kitchen.

Eva was still scratching but kept her eyes and her smile on the two jars of ointment Sizway was placing on the coffee table.

"I don't mind him," Eva said. "He's the same thang he's always been—senile. It's his age that's against him."

Sizway explained to Eva what was in the ointment to help her itching. She had mixed herbs with hot petroleum jelly, water, olive oil, and beeswax.

Eva lifted one of the jars and began unscrewing the cap. Then she rubbed the ointment on her hands. She lifted her hands to her nose and sniffed. "Got a nice smell to it."

"You know we don't just give herbs," Sizway said, her eyes serious. "The herbs won't cure if we don't cure the head."

Eva nodded. "Yeah. Like you used to say, it's probably my itching to get out, to get away from something. I guess I'm a hopeless case. I had this rash for years."

Sizway closed the lid on her basket. "Well, mumma, I must be going."

"Well, I know you gotta get going. You look like you about ready to deliver. You shouldn't even be out in this cold kind of weather bringing me thangs."

"I don't sell too much today."

"You know, during this cold kind of weather I do my indoors puttering. Then around four o'clock, I watch my two TV shows. Bob Brown's guest today spent fifty years writing a cookbook. You know, my sister met Bob Brown once? She took her Winnebago to Sandusky for vacation. I don't know why, but it seems to me she'd want to go to Florida or California or something. But no, she just prefer to go around the block. Little old Sandusky. Well, this last time she got on the Bob Brown talk show. She told him her son, Eli, was manager of the supermarket in Sojourner. Told him her son's market had the cleanest floors this year. I guess she want Eli to get on that talk show."

Jim-Walter called out from his bedroom. "Eva? Where's my lunch?"

Sizway began covering her head with her woolen scarf, then she put on her felt hat, preparing to leave.

"Hold on, Sizway. I got to pay you for this."

Eva scurried into the kitchen. The refrigerator squeaked open and shut, the silverware drawer jingled, a plate clattered on the table. Eva hurried down a long, deep hallway. Outside Jim-Walter's open bedroom door the television set brought the soft, drowsy voice of a female talk-show host.

"Where would men be without a woman?" the host asked her guest.

"In the Garden of Eden," Jim-Walter muttered. The cushions sighed as he sat forward to flick the channel. Then he sat back on the daisy-splattered armchair.

After a while Eva returned to the living room, opening her change purse.

"He wanted them corn pops," Eva said, settling onto the couch again, "but there weren't none. I used to buy him them corn thangs. I stopped doing that. He said, 'I sure like them corn thangs.' I thought to myself, Well, if you like em you get em yourself."

The sound of Jim-Walter's footsteps were heard coming down the hall.

"Well, this ointment sure works nice," Eva said, raising her voice. "How much I owe you for this?"

"Three dollars," Sizway said.

Eva picked through the change in her purse. She counted out three dollars in change. Sizway thanked her and stood up.

"Probably maybe you watch Bob Brown," Sizway said.

"Oh, Bob Brown is off. I suppose I'll doze off. Jim-Walter'll doze off. It'll be just like Sleepy Hollow around here."

Eva wobbled on bowed legs, following behind Sizway to the door.

"You about due to deliver looks to me."

"Yes, ma."

"I always tell young women your age not to marry too fast. No need to marry right away. And don't just start having babies neither. Some women just have one baby after another. I tell em, 'Hold off with all that.' Before I met Jim-Walter I was a secretary at the Air Force base. Now I don't do nothing."

Sizway nodded. "Mm."

The sky was cold and grey. The wind whirled snowflakes around like moths in the sky. Sizway's boots crunched down on snow as she entered the Ki compound. The camp was clean and open, the center yard deserted. Sizway went to Nalajah's clapboard and knocked, but no answer; so she walked to the edge of the camp and sat in the woods under the barren trees. All the trees were naked and exposed to the cold and to the sky. Sizway built a fire with dry twigs and prayed for the twins she was carrying and for her family. Eventually Nalajah came. Within this woodland sanctuary, the two women sat close to the fire, put their heads together, and talked.

The fire crackled. At the same time the two women heard the crunch of snow under boot and twigs breaking underfoot. They looked up and noticed Kosi pulling her feet through the underbrush that was coated with a thin layer of snow. Finally Kosi met up with Sizway and Nalajah. Together they huddled around the fire.

Kosi touched Sizway's large belly. "You are carrying the twins high. It will probably be two girls."

Sizway smiled. "Maybe."

Snowflakes fell lightly on the tops of their black hats pulled down over woolen scarves. Kosi clucked her tongue and sighed. "Women. Do we not have babies all our lives and all of our lives take orders from our husbands? What else?" When Kosi spoke, she blew out frigid clouds of air.

Sizway smiled inside but she didn't say anything.

"I just left my lover in the woods," Kosi went on. "Do you know what I said to him? I said, 'If my husband finds you here he will surely kill you.' Do you know what he said? He said, 'If your husband is going to kill me, let him. It doesn't matter to me. Because you are so beautiful that I just want to stay a while longer with you.'"

Nalajah giggled. Sizway's eyes were lowered. She seemed almost to be sleeping.

Kosi glanced at Sizway. "What, Sizzy?"

Sizway looked at her coolly. "I love lovers, Kosi. I am even jealous. I even want many lovers myself."

Nalajah's eyes widened as she looked at Sizway. But Kosi giggled and looked up at the darkening sky. "I must get home and cook my husband's food. My mother has been watching my daughter all day."

Kosi waved bye-bye and left.

Nalajah wrapped her woolen scarf tighter around her neck and mouth. "Lovers, Sizzy? Why did you tell her you want lovers?"

Sizway shrugged. "I do."

Nalajah giggled. "You lie."

"Umph," Sizway said as if she couldn't please anyone.

Nalajah said, "Why is it that women are never satisfied with the men that they marry? Why is it that we always think our former lover was better than the lover we married?"

Sizway sighed, "How should I know, Lajah? I am a woman myself."

"Has a man ever asked you to be his lover?" Nalajah asked her.

"Yes."

"And did you?"

"I asked him a question," Sizway said. "I said, If he were selling the most expensive cloth in the world at the market, would he allow me to be wearing it whenever I wanted. You know, if I wear it I might dirty it. And the more I wear it, the more the value is going to go down. So I asked him, will you allow me to wear your most expensive cloth whenever I wanted? He said,

'No.' He wouldn't be able to sell it that way. So I said, 'I see my-self as cloth like that. I don't want you to be using it. I don't want my value to go down.' Before I married, I had a lover. I re-member the good things about my past lover. I also remember the bad things. But more than that I remember my children and the father of my children. I don't want my children to wander in the fields of the fatherless. Family is important. Husbands, wives, children; they are all important."

Nalajah nodded. They stared at the tiny red sparks of fire.

Suddenly Nalajah giggled again. "You told Kosi you wanted many lovers like her."

Sizway shrugged. "I told Kosi what she wanted to hear. If the truth isn't what a person wants, then you sing the music they want. If you sing what they don't want, they will insult you. I don't want Kosi to insult me."

At the sound of a truck, Sizway and Nalajah turned their heads. Papa Job rode into the center of the camp in a truck. He was the new, proud owner. With the money he had saved from his furniture selling, he had bought the pickup and he had taken Toomi and Balinga for a ride in it. Nalajah and Sizway came up to it. The truck had sideboards and a black leather interior, a red exterior. Papa Job sat inside the warm dark. It was dark outside, too, night time. Snow was falling from the moon. And the moon set the snow on the ground aglow. The boys climbed out and jumped up and down in front of their mother.

Sizway knelt in the sparkling snow to greet both of them.

"How is the truck, hm?"

Toomi replied, "Daddy says she's big so she takes her time getting started, but she's got a good engine."

"Mmm. You sound like you know a lot about trucks."

Toomi nodded.

Then Balinga complained of a button he had lost on his coat.

"But we are going inside," she told him.

"But I don't want to go in without a button," Balinga said.

Sizway unclipped a safety pin from her poncho and held the safety pin between her lips. Then she sandwiched Balinga's coat lapels together and pinned them. Snow fell lightly on them. Papa Job had been standing and talking to Nalajah. Now he told Sizway, "Nalajah is going to take the boys tonight. There is an empty house over there. The owner has allowed us to sleep there."

Sizway said, "Thank you, Lajah."

Nalajah took both of the boys' hands.

"Come," she told them. "There is sweet meat inside for both of you."

In the night, Sizway and Papa Job unrolled a mat and lay down on it. As was his habit, Papa Job gently polished Sizway's belly with coconut to ward off the death marks. Then they intertwined their bodies and talked in low voices until the flame in the stove became a tiny red ember.

Suddenly there came the sound of a dog barking outside and a knock at the door. Sizway dressed hurriedly and went to the door. A woman with a baby was there.

"Why are you crying, Kosi?" Sizway asked.

"I am not crying. I have smoke in my eyes."

"Yes, you are crying. Have you quarreled with your husband?"

Sizway pulled on her poncho and boots and softly closed the door behind her.

The two women sat outside on the steps and talked in low voices.

Suddenly Papa Job heard shouting. He got up, found his pants and shirt, and opened the door. Slowly his eyes adjusted to the dark. He made out Sizway sitting on the top step with Kosi's child in her arms. Kosi's back was to Papa Job as she stood facing her husband. Kosi removed her coat. She undid her shirt and drew it off her back. She unbuttoned her skirt and let it fall to the snow. She stepped out of the puddle her clothing made and knelt naked before the man. She began to beg him. The man told her not to beg him, nor to kneel before him, but to tell him why he should come back from traveling and find her sexing another man. He had a stick in his hand. He wanted to kill her.

"Brother," Sizway murmured. "Drop the stick. Please."

He stood there, trembling and weeping.

"Your hand has power in it tonight," Sizway said. "If you hit her with it you could kill her."

Finally Kosi's husband dropped the stick in the snow and disappeared into the dark.

Kosi was shivering as she put on her clothing.

"He wanted to kill me."

Sizway replied her nothing, holding the infant in her arms.

"He says he doesn't want our child. He says he doesn't know if the child is his. But the child is his."

They sat for a while in silence. Sizway held her cheek in her palm. They continued sitting in the falling snow.

Papa Job closed the door and lay down again.

After a few minutes, both women came inside. Kosi put her baby in a basket. Then Sizway and Kosi lay together on a mat and went to sleep.

On the following night of snow a Ki procession headed for Manji's house in the woods. There was to be a celebration of

Manji's return to the seeing world. The celebration went on all day and into the night. Ki from far, far away, from other states, came. The white woods surrounding Manji's house was alive. The houselights lit up the snow outside. The night of celebrating had left the compound deserted.

But in the silent dead of the woods, beyond Manji's house, five old women sat around another ceremonial fire. Snow was falling in the darkness and it popped as it hit the flames. The fire burned in a shallow pit. The women were hunched over the fire, draped in blankets. The light of the fire reflected in Kehinde's small black eyes. She looked up and gazed past the barren trees in the direction of Manji's house. It was a long, steady gaze.

Manji's house lights were hidden deep inside trees. The Ki were dancing the whole length of the one-room house, filling it with noise. Even the cobwebs that hung from the stone and mud ceiling were dancing.

> Hear this song
> passing through my lips.
> You are a fortunate woman,
> You have recovered.

> Hear this song
> O Eyes That Can Never Close.
> I know why you took blindness
> to save the life of another
> But The Ever Present

Ever Near
has cured you.

The Ki shook rattles, Clack, schlick, clack schlick, *clack-clack*. Clack, schlick, clack schlick, *clack-clack*. And the drum-mers scraped and whapped against hollow drums, whapping first with the palms, then with the knuckles, now with the side of the hands, and then with the elbows.

Manji leaned on her walking stick. Her hair had faded from grey to wispy white. She was old in skin and old in voice. Her eyes were wrinkled into slits, trying to make out all the figures in the room who were celebrating the return of her sight.

She walked over to the moon-washed windowsill. A moth fluttered against the pane. Winter raved and howled outside. Manji leaned her stick against the wall and cupped the vibrating wings in her hand. She left her walking stick there and slowly shuffled to the door. Her shoes crunched down on snow. The wind flipped off her shawl, flapped her skirt against her legs. Her thin, frail body wavered before she pulled herself through the blowing flakes. Soon she met up with the woods where the night swallowed her completely.

> If I am dreaming, let me never awake
> If I am awake, let me never sleep
> Hear this song
> and believe it mother
> though you are hidden
> though you are weeping
> this night shall be a part
> of all your children's dancing

Deep in the woods the wind howled around the aged and grey-haired by the fire, then died down. There was now only the soft sound of crackling branches. Kehinde opened her divining bag and blew sacred herbs into the flames. She looked long at the fire before she spoke.

"It is done. She has left for the woods. Her daughter will soon deliver. The one she delivers shall belong to us."

"And the moon child?"

Kehinde grunted and closed her eyes as if she were sleeping.

Back in Manji's house, Papa Job sat in a corner chair with Abel, the Newscarrier, watching the dancing. After a while Papa Job asked, "How is it possible?"

"Now you are asking a child's question, Kiba."

"But witches. Power," Papa Job said, confused. "Manji's sight has come back. How?"

"We don't discuss that," Abel said. "We just accept."

"I don't believe in any of it."

"Am I asking you to believe anything? Believe it if you want. Don't believe it if you don't want."

Papa Job grunted and turned back to the dancing. "I don't believe any of it."

While the celebration went on, a kerosene flame flickered in the window of a clapboard in the compound. The wind howled and blew against the glass panes. Inside, a coarse woolen blanket and a pile of newspaper were placed next to a wood-burning stove. Sizway squatted on the blanket and bled through her genitals. She gave birth to twins—a boy and a girl. The female twin took hold to this life but her twin brother entered this life, took a breath, and refused to take another. Sizway covered his mouth with her own and blew into him the life he wanted to refuse. When she smacked the bottoms of his feet, he cried out. His spindly, wrinkled and red fingers grasped at the air. Sizway used the white cloth of her slip to clean both the twins well. Then she wrapped them in a cocoon of white linen. Finally she laid them on a pile of newspaper near the wood-burning stove and began to light the stove. The Ki would later get together for the naming ceremony. And they would name the first one, the female twin, Taiyewo, Come-to-Taste-Life. The second one, the male twin, they would name Kehinde, The-One-Who-Came-Behind. The twins were the last of Sizway's children.

The infants lay on the newspaper, moving their arms about, trying to suck on her fingers. Sizway squatted with her insides still sore and blood on her legs. She whispered, "Mtucktu . . . Shushana," greeting them with praise names.

Papa Job and Abel stomped up the steps of the clapboard and shook the snow from their boots. Abel followed behind Papa Job. He said, "There is a full moon tonight."

Papa Job looked over his shoulder. "Yah," he murmured. He swung open the door. Sizway turned to look, squatting with two infants in her arms. Papa Job smiled. "And look at what the moon has brought us," Papa said.

Sizway's eyes lifted. She saw the cold moon shining behind the two men through the open door. She remembered something. A dream. A boy child laughing and floating around the moon. She looked down at Kehinde, the boy twin, and was suddenly frightened.

Dusk is falling and the moon, an ancient dream, is coming out. The talebearer's eyes lower from it and then narrow. There is a brooding darkness in her eyes. After a while she picks a stick from the ground. She spreads her legs, hiking her long black skirt over her knees, and begins to draw in the dirt, in the falling dark.

"Hm, now the matter turns badly," she says. "The bad spirits came as the heavy rain that waters the earth. They moved like a river of melting snow through the woods and the streets of Sojourner. The bad spirits came and even stayed for three long years. Spirits are not always seen, you see, but are usually faint as air and only make indentations on things when they sit. The bad ones run up beside you and stick out a foot so that you trip. And they keep up this way, running alongside you, sticking out a foot. I will tell it to you. . . . And so it is I telling you."

Bowing her head, the talebearer completes her drawing scratched out in the dirt, the signature of Elegba at her feet, the crossroads.

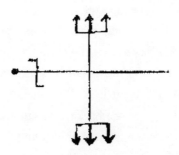

chapter six

A scream broke the silence of the night, frightening the Ki camp into wakefulness. A second scream came, then a third. Women sat up on their mats. Dark shadows emerged from houses, hurrying toward the source of the screams.

"A child died," someone said.

Eventually all the compound had assembled under the moon. Someone murmured that the child had been taken to the hospital in town because the father had insisted on taking the child there. Everyone went home and put on the ceremonial black. They climbed onto the backs of pickup trucks. The trucks whirred slowly, one by one, out of the camp.

At dawn the Ki stepped through the rubble of a bulldozed building that surrounded the town's hospital. The area was desolate as if a bomb had dropped, leaving a mass of rubble, rock, and shattered cement. Men and women wore black felt hats and black garments. They entered the hospital in a quiet, dignified procession. They laid a hand on the walls of the elevator that lifted them up into the sky. They proceeded down long green hallways and shielded their noses from the foul ammonia smells. Some stood but most sat against the wall outside the dead child's hospital room. They smoked their pipes and sprinkled the sacred ash on the floor.

Sizway and Papa Job came out of the hospital room, followed by Toomi and Balinga and their sister, Taiyewo, who was five years old now. Toomi lifted Taiyewo by the armpits and slid her to one side of his hips. He was eleven. He clasped interlaced fingers beneath the girl's bottom, bending one knee for balance. Then he listened as the hospital official questioned his parents.

The official was a hunched man of timid eyes, scratching on a clipboard, while his pants sagged limp at his backside.

"Um, it says here he died of respiratory failure. Sorry to hear that . . . and only five. Is the name right?—K-e-h-i-n-d-e?" he asked, peering up at Papa Job and Sizway.

Papa Job nodded.

"Very good. Then, uh . . ." The official asked more questions.

Sizway looked down at her hands.

"Well, uh . . ." The official asked more questions.

The man and woman shook thier heads.

"Okay, then, will you sign here, please?"

Sizway and Job stared up at him unseeing.

"We don't sign," the old woman, Kehinde, said. She sat on the floor in a huddle of other old women. "We just want to take the child, take our own."

"Oh," the official said, straightening his eyeglasses, "we can't release the body like that. You gotta call a certified funeral home."

Kehinde grunted and half-closed her eyes. "We don't bury our own like that."

The official insisted and Kehinde nodded, realizing the official would only listen to the rules of his own world. She placed her fingertips to the side of her forehead. She pressed them there. Then she removed her hand and looked up at him. "Bring him," she said.

The official no more hesitated. He went into the bedroom and came out again with the boy wrapped in a sheet. "Give the child to his father," Kehinde said. The official handed the boy to Papa Job. Then he led the Ki procession out of the hospital, through the rubble outside. There the Ki piled into the parked trucks. The official stood in the heat of the trucks that were pulling out all around him.

The trucks proceeded down the road. They parked three and four in a row on the street in front of Papa Job and Sizway's small clapboard, which stood now like a tombstone in tall weeds.

The clapboard was so full of people that it was almost impossible for anyone to move. Women cooked meat, cornmeal, sweet potatoes, brown bread, brown rice, and coffee. The women who cooked also ate freely from the pots. Many Ki sat around the kitchen table or on the floor. They uttered concilia-tory words to entreat the One Spirit to become generous and concerned at this time. Throughout the day, weeping was inter-woven with prayers. People in black dress moved from the child's bedroom, where the body lay, to the kitchen, and then back to the bedroom. Kehinde was laid out on his sleeping mat. His limbs had been pulled through small soft garments—a buttoned shirt, khaki shorts, knee-high stockings, and brown polished shoes. They smoothed his forehead with their hands. Kehinde's half-straight, half-curly black hair had been cut. His long lashes swept his dark cheeks. He seemed only asleep.

By midafternoon the time for sending Kehinde off had arrived. The boy's body was rolled in his sleeping mat. Four men hoisted the body to their shoulders. Then the procession formed and started toward the pickup trucks. Sizway didn't go with them. No parent would want to see their child die before they themselves die, to bury their child before they themselves are buried. She went into her bedroom and shut the door. Papa Job took Toomi and Balinga into the bedroom that Kehinde once occupied and shut the door. The boys wouldn't attend the burial either. No brother would want to see his junior brother die before he dies, nor a junior brother be buried before he himself is buried.

It was Taiyewo who left with the Ki to attend the burial. She was a tiny girl, short for five. Her black dress fell to her calves. She wore black tights and sandals. Her hair was plaited neatly in numerous braids and her ears were pierced with copper earrings. A Ki male held Taiyewo close to him as they stood on the back of a pickup truck. Tai seemed dazed. The procession of trucks was so long that she couldn't see the end of it. The sun beat down, then a summer shower fell, sprinkling their black garments. When the shower stopped it left a thick layer of mugginess in the air.

The gravesite was marked not by tombstones but by objects that encircled each grave. In the center of each grave was a thick stick pushed into the dirt and the tip of the stick held the last thing the dead had touched: a pipe, an iron pot, or a black hat last worn by the dead.

At Kehinde's grave, beneath a knotty old tree, a hole had been dug. The sun glared through the knobby arms of the tree and beat down on them.

Taiyewo remembered a verse from the Bible, which her father often read: "More fortunate are those who have been long dead, than the living who are still alive. But better than them both is he who has not yet been born, who has not seen. . . ." Taiyewo watched the body of her twin brother lowering, lowering into the earth. She felt the tears tickling her face and rubbed them with both fists back into her eyes. When the grave was filled with dirt, white stones were placed around it in an oval shape, and a strong stick was stuck in the center. There, Tai hung her twin's pajama shirt and pants, the last things he had touched.

After the funeral, the Ki slowly left the gravesite. Abel and the old woman, Kehinde, came toward Tai. Kehinde knelt at Tai's feet. The twin's hair had been cut and plaited into a bracelet which Kehinde now tied around Tai's wrist. The Ki believe that if one twin is lost, one must use means to separate their spirits because they've been living together for a while. The bracelet was put on Tai's wrist so that she wouldn't see her twin's spirit. Then Abel handed Tai something heavy wrapped in burlap. Abel had sat up for long hours chipping away at a narrow block of wood which he had carved into a hand-size ibeji doll, the full figure of the dead twin, Kehinde. The ibeji doll was meant to be the home for her twin's spirit. As Tai grew she would make cloth for the ibeji and drape it with beads. She would wash the ibeji until the features were gradually worn away. She would sleep with the ibeji beside her on a mat. And when she fed herself, she would also lift the spoon to the wooden mouth of the ibeji doll.

It was midnight. Tai had returned from the funeral and was squatting at her mother's feet in the backyard. She held the ibeji doll in her arms. Sizway sat on the last step of the porch near the ground. Her black skirt draped over her upraised knees like a tablecloth and brushed her bare feet. She folded her arms on her knees. Tears flowed steadily down her face and dripped from the edges of her chin.

"Brother has been buried," Tai said. "He is with the living dead now."

Sizway's voice was leaden. "Brother is traveling, journeying with the ancestors. No one is dead until he is forgotten."

Tai looked down at the ibeji doll in her arms. The doll's eyes were wide and his wooden chin hung low against his neck. His wooden belly extended out, coming to a point at the belly button. His knees were slightly bent on two stout legs.

"Brother's house is in here now. When he returns from traveling he will live here."

Then Tai looked up at the night, a night full of shifting breezes. A breeze slid across her face like a black nylon scarf. Sizway, too, felt the breath of the passing wind.

"There are more than two of us here," Sizway said. "When you think yourself alone, you are not alone, for the living dead, unseen, will be there, passing through the night."

"Look," Tai said, pointing at a shooting star.

Sizway peered up. Dark circles ringed her tired, watery eyes. She nodded. "They say shooting stars are spirits darting cross the sky."

"Where are they going?"

Sizway shrugged. "How should I know the ways of spirits? I am only a woman."

Another breeze blew gently across their faces.

"Are the living dead like the wind, mumma?"

"Yes. Like Yansan."

"Who name Yansan?"

"God of the wind. She must be sleeping. When death comes, she sleeps."

"Why does she sleep?"

Sizway's tears flowed warm.

"Sleep is needed to dream; dreams are needed to go on."

The moon died in the dawn and for days after there was nothing but heat and rain, heat and rain, and the air just got muggier and muggier. Taiyewo became sick. Like Kehinde, who bled through his nose before he died, Tai bled from her genitals onto her underwear.

Sizway and Papa Job argued. Sizway wanted to take Tai to the compound for traditional medicine and Papa Job wanted to take Tai to the hospital in town. Sizway brought many of the Ki to the house to beg Papa Job. The Ki stood around him in the kitchen.

"We don't bring our own to the hospital in town," they said. "There are medicine people in the camp."

Papa Job listened with his lips sealed and with Taiyewo on his laps. When they had talked their talk done, Papa Job hefted Taiyewo up in his arms and stood up.

"I believe you have good medicine, but I want the hospital for Tai, the hospital in town."

He wouldn't listen to any of them.

The following day, Papa Job held Taiyewo's hand and led her through the rubble of a bulldozed building that surrounded the town's hospital. It was the same hospital her twin had died in.

In the hospital room Tai undressed and put on a limp gown, while her father stood listening to the white doctor. Papa Job was much shorter than the doctor, he had to look up at him. His white shirt was buttoned to the neck and his black shiny mustache drooped thick around his lips. His eyes were big, black, and wet behind his gold-wired spectacles. His face was solemn. He held his worn hat in two hands and glanced every so often at Tai sitting on the examination table. She was still very small.

Taiyewo was wheeled down hallways and into elevators. In the basement of the hospital she was wheeled down a brick tunnel with no doors on either side. Her daddy walked alongside her. Suddenly another elevator reared up to the left and she was pushed inside. The door slid shut. The door slid open.

Beds with metal bars lined the walls on either side. There were little children behind the bars and the little children were crying.

Taiyewo climbed onto her appointed bed, a black-and-white-striped mattress, no sheet. The bars were pulled up, clanging locked around her. Her daddy left.

Taiyewo sat cross-legged on the bed, watching the door, waiting for her daddy to come back and get her. Slowly the doorway filled up with white men doctors in white coats. They came toward her. A plastic curtain was yanked closed all around. The doctors lowered the bars and told her to lie down. They pushed up her limp gown. Hard fingers entered her. Whispering passed down the line, "Collapsed urethra." A clipboard was scribbled on. The bars clanged, locked in place; and the clipboard was hung at the end of the bed. Curtains whisked open. Tai pulled down her gown and sat up. She waited for her daddy to come get her.

A nurse in white told Tai to follow her. Barefoot, Taiyewo followed the nurse out of the room. They walked down hallways and around many corners. In a white room, her finger was jabbed with a pin. Tai blinked rapidly, watching her blood being squeezed into a clear tube. Then she was told to go back to her mattress.

Hours later the room had darkened; it was dusk. Tai sat in the middle of the striped mattress, watching the empty doorway, waiting for her daddy to come get her. Her eyelids flickered when suddenly Sizway framed the entrance. She wore a felt hat over her braided hair. She wore a shawl around her shoulders. Taiyewo saw her mumma's lips, like the edge of a wheat sandwich, moving but she didn't hear any sound. Then her mumma turned to leave, turned to wave, turned to smile. The doorway was empty again. Tai slowly shut her eyes. And her spirit left her body.

When Taiyewo returned from the hospital after the operation she was always crying. She would cry all night, cry and cry until dawn broke. Some mornings she just stayed around and her tears fell and she cried and refused all food.

When dawn broke, Papa Job, Toomi, and Balinga left to go to work at the used furniture store in town. Taiyewo watched them. Then she got up and ran after them. But when Balinga saw her, he pushed her back inside the fenced yard. "Go back and stay with mumma."

Sizway was in the kitchen preparing a basket. Taiyewo followed Sizway around the kitchen crying. Then Sizway took her hand and they left the house.

After many miles of walking, they arrived at the Ki cemetery. The graves there all looked run down. The sticks in the mounds leaned every which way. The mounds were enclosed by broken clay pots or broken glass bottles. The gravesite was also full of twisted, knotty old trees and the grass was overgrown with weeds. The gleam of white stones surrounded Kehinde's fresh mound. Above the grave were the arms of another old twisted tree with a tortured trunk. Kehinde's pajamas hung limp on a stick. Sizway stood facing the east and puffed from her pipe, then she turned to the north, the west, and the south; the four directions.

Finally she lowered the brim of her hat over her head and knelt on the grave. She took from her basket a clay bowl and arranged fruit inside the bowl. Kehinde had loved every kind of fruit. Then she rested the back of her hands on her knees, palms upward. In the ancient Ki language she appealed to the spirits to guide Kehinde's spirit to the other world and to prevent him from wandering. She chanted for his safe journey, that he wouldn't feel loneliness nor the weight of darkness.

Slowly by slowly the sun began coming out. And Taiyewo began crying. Even though she wore a black felt hat like her mother's to keep out the sun, she still cried from the heat. She even drowned out Sizway's prayers with her crying. Finally there was nothing to do but return home.

Every day the same thing. Taiyewo would watch Papa Job, Toomi, and Balinga leave the fenced yard and walk to the front of the house. She climbed the stairway and went into the kitchen where Sizway was preparing things. Taiyewo thought, "My twin is no more here. Who am I going to play with now?" Carrying her ibeji doll, she hurried out the screen door, down the steps, and started to run after her father and brothers. She ran and ran, crying out to them. She kept running and calling out. Finally Balinga turned on the sidewalk to see who it was. He stood waiting for Tai to catch up. When she was beside him, he held her hand and they climbed inside their father's truck. Papa drove around the block three times to let her feel like she was going somewhere. Then he parked in front of the house. Balinga held her hand, walking her back to the house, back to their mother.

Taiyewo cried in the day and in the night, following Sizway everywhere. When twilight filled their clapboard, Papa Job, Toomi, and Balinga returned from work. Sizway was holding Taiyewo on her laps, offering her a biscuit and milk. Tai ate and ate and ate. But when she was finished she started to cry all over again.

Sizway told Papa Job, "We don't take our children to the hospital in town. Taiyewo is still a little child. But I allowed you to take her. Now she won't stop crying. Her body is full of crying."

Papa Job nodded. He said the home would soon be as it was before. The boys would stay home and watch Tai and Sizway would return to work.

Each dawn before going to work Sizway visited the grave of the one who had died at an early age. She was gone before the children awoke. Papa Job would prepare the children's breakfast and leave for work himself. While their parents were at work, eleven-year-old Toomi was in charge. Toomi liked reading. He would lie out on the porch and read all day. Eight-year-old Balinga and five-year-old Taiyewo were on their own. They ran in and out of the house, letting in mosquitoes and flies. Taiyewo used to play with her twin constantly, now she followed Balinga around wherever he went. Balinga was wiry, tough, and strong. And he was very beautiful to look at. His hair and eyes were black like their father's and his nose and chin sharp and angled like their mother's. And he looked the most like the dead twin.

Balinga himself preferred the company of his senior brother, Toomi. And Balinga's beauty even charmed Toomi. Toomi would put his book away. They played all kinds of card games on the porch planks while Tai knelt outside the circle watching. All afternoon the boys talked and laughed about things. One day they played with a kind of firecracker—it was strips of paper with tiny white circles of carbon lining each strip. By rubbing the carbon with a rock the carbon would pop and smoke. Toomi and Balinga enjoyed rubbing and popping the firecrackers. Taiyewo wanted to do it but when she tried she burnt her finger. After that she was afraid of the firecrackers and wouldn't touch them. When the boys popped them, she just knelt outside their circle and watched.

By early afternoon sweat and dirt ran down all their faces. They wiped it off and immediately sweat and dirt returned. Toomi began reading again only to fall asleep on the porch with his book opened on his chest. Two pine trees stood against the railing of the porch. But in this humidity they seemed to be leaning. Balinga sat on the porch against the chipped wall of the house. Taiyewo sat close by, scratching her legs. They were pocked red from mosquito bites and she was scratching them. Balinga watched her for a while. Finally he said, "Don't scratch them."

But she was overcome with itching. She just wanted to scratch. Soon some of the mosquito bites began to bleed.

"Didn't I tell you not to scratch them?"

Taiyewo just looked at him, scratching some more. "Are you my father? No. You are only my brother."

Balinga rubbed his stomach. He said, "I am hungry."

He opened the screen door with Tai following. He opened the refrigerator door and they stood there for a while cooling off. Sizway had left the children's lunch wrapped in wax paper—cucumber, lettuce, and mayonnaise on black bread. But Balinga looked past the sandwiches at something else he liked. There was a clay bowl of strawberries on the rack of the refrigerator. Sizway always brought fruit to Kehinde's grave. Balinga said, "I'm going to eat some." He took the biggest strawberries. Then he went and sat somewhere to eat.

The rattan shades in the kitchen were always drawn and only let in slithers of light. The shades kept the kitchen somewhat cool. Balinga and Taiyewo sat underneath the kitchen table. Taiyewo was eating her sandwich but watching Balinga eat strawberries.

"Balinga, give me some. You're not going to refuse me, are you?"

Balinga gave her some. The rest he ate himself.

When Sizway returned home from work at the market, she said, "Umph, the children were in here and ate all the strawberries." She called Toomi, Balinga, and Taiyewo into the kitchen. She held the empty bowl that was once full of strawberries in her hand.

Sizway frowned. "I left something in this bowl. Have you eaten anything that belongs to me?"

"No," the children answered.

Sizway's frown deepened.

But day after day whatever fruit Sizway left in the refrigerator, Balinga would wait until midday, open the fridge, and eat it. Other times he ate meat marinating in sauce. Or sweet rice with lemon. There was one time when Sizway returned home early and caught Balinga with his fingers in the bowl of stew in the refrigerator. It was for Kehinde's grave. She grabbed at him to hit him. But Balinga darted away and crawled underneath the kitchen table.

"Balinga! Stop taking things!"

Another time Sizway left cranberries. Balinga ate them all. He wiped his red fingers down his white T-shirt and his teeth and tongue were stained a bright red. Sizway came back from the market. She went to the refrigerator. She saw that the bowl of cranberries was empty. She turned and called the children to her. At the sight of Balinga, she knew who had eaten them.

"Balinga, you ate the cranberries! What do you have to say for yourself?"

He said, "I didn't eat them."

She said, "You *ate* them. You certainly did. Now don't do that again! Do you want me to beat you?"

"If you want to kill me, go ahead. It means nothing to me to be killed."

Taiyewo was frightened at the thought of Balinga being killed. Hadn't she already lost a brother? She stepped closer to him. They both knew that their mother had power. Sizway knew their mind before they could speak it. She would tell them who was driving up to the house before the engine stopped. She answered their unspoken questions and finished their sentences. And when they were sick she would prepare ritual and herbs, she'd chant, drawing the sickness out of their body. They could feel the sickness draining out through their head. If Sizway had the power to read minds and heal, couldn't she also have the power to kill?

Sizway frowned. "Did I say I would kill you? I said you are stealing. Don't steal."

"I didn't steal," Balinga repeated. "And if you keep saying I steal, I won't want to live with you anymore, I will go and live with mama-agba."

"Balinga, stealing is stealing. You *ate* the cranberries. You certainly did."

The talebearer laughs. "Children. They really do things when they are small. Eventually what children do around their mother they will forget and do around their father. Up to now, Papa Job didn't know that this stealing was getting out of hand."

It was Saturday. Cleaning day. The children were under their father's rule on Saturdays. There was a little of the military still in their father and he commanded them. They scrubbed the kitchen floors and grimy windows, the bathroom tile, the floors and walls of the two bedrooms, and the hallway. Then they dumped the dirty water on the back porch and scrubbed down the floorboards. Papa Job scrubbed alongside the children, his sleeves rolled up to the elbows.

Next came clothes washing and ironing. Papa Job washed the clothing in the bathtub. Toomi, who was eleven, ironed the clothing; Balinga, eight, went outside and hung the wet clothes on the line; and Taiyewo, five, helped both brothers.

Toomi was in the bedroom putting away the neatly folded cloth. Tai knelt on a chair at the kitchen table to complete Toomi's ironing. There were a few shorts left to be ironed. She spat on the iron until the saliva sizzled. She sprinkled her father's boxer shorts by dipping her hand in a bowl of water and shaking the drops on the shorts. Then she pressed down on the cloth with the iron. Next she turned over the boxer shorts to press the other side. She dipped her hand in the bowl of water again, but her arm touched the flat of the iron and she bruised up her skin. She blew on the burn and watched it puff up like a burnt omelet. She blew on her arm with a loud whistling breath to get her father's attention. Papa Job was lifting a pail of water from the sink and setting it on the floor. He looked over at her. Immediately he whisked her up, turned on the faucet, and held the burn under the cold water. Tai's body was dangling from under his arm. She just smiled up at him, feeling as if she were floating.

Papa Job placed her feet on the floor again and unplugged the iron. He told her not to do any more ironing today. Tai watched Papa Job dunk the mop into the metal bucket. With his hands he squeezed the ropes of the mop. He wrung it so strong, the ropes dropped dry. He had strong yet gentle hands like a magician. He touched everything carefully and he made everything he touched come clean. He was concentrated on the floor and all the other floors in the house that needed to be as clean as he was.

Tai slid a ladderback chair over to the kitchen counter. She climbed up and turned on the television set. It was a small black-and-white television talking on the linoleum counter next to the sink. Television cameras revolved on Tarzan who swung like an ape from his frazzled string in the jungles of Africa. At the same time, Papa Job swung his mop. The ropes slapped down and spread out like a million fingers. Blue water and foam streamed out. Tai stood on the chair as if she were in a tiny boat being lapped by the water and suds of Papa Job's mop.

Suddenly the lapping stopped. Papa Job was staring at the television. He held a faint, fixed smile. When his laugh came, it came suddenly from the belly.

"Umph," he laughed. "Look at the way they do Africans."

Tai leaned back and laughed after him; not knowing the joke, but just laughing to be laughing with him.

Papa Job shook his head and grunted, still thinking about that thing that made him to laugh.

"They like to show us like that."

By midday the house was clean and smelled of ammonia and damp wood. In the yard, all three lines were filled with cloth and wooden clothespins. These hot days the children liked to soak in the wide claw-footed bathtub where the water was cool. After bathing, the boys got a haircut. Toomi was always first. Papa Job wore a white sleeveless T-shirt, black pants, and black suspenders that hung down both sides of his pants legs. Taiyewo settled on the floor underneath the kitchen table, cradling her ibeji doll. And Balinga stood near Papa Job, with one foot curled on top of the other, holding on to the handle of the broom. Balinga's job was to sweep up the hair when it dropped on the floor. Toomi sat straight and still while Papa Job draped a towel around his neck. Balinga and Tai watched.

Papa Job's scissors began clicking while the other hand began combing. He was clicking and combing. He made fun with Toomi same time.

"Toomi, why are you pretending you have no girlfriends?" Papa Job asked him, a small smile on his lips.

"Toomi's girlfriend lives in the compound," Balinga reported.

"She's not my girlfriend," Toomi frowned.

"Then what is she? Your boyfriend?" Papa Job asked, his eyes glimmering. "So you go to the compound and talk to her and laugh with her, eh?"

"No," Toomi said.

Papa Job paused, holding the scissors and comb in midair. "Then you fight with her?" he asked.

"No."

"Then you loooove her," he said, snipping away at Toomi's hair.

Tai leaned back her head and laughed. "He looooves her."

"How many girlfriends do you have?" Papa Job asked Toomi.

"Zero."

"Oh-ho! Zero," Papa Job laughed. "So the girls, they don't like you?"

Toomi shrugged.

Papa Job brushed the hair off the towel. The black hairs floated onto the floor. "Stop pretending and tell us, Toomi."

"Ho-ho, daddy! I'm remembering something!" Balinga said. "You know the girl in the compound? She said she liked his spot."

Toomi had a flat black mole on his cheek.

Tai clapped her hands and giggled. She crawled out from under the kitchen table and tried to touch Toomi's mole but Toomi grabbed at her hands and held them fast.

"What about you, Balinga?" Toomi said. "You are always chasing girls around the compound. The girls even run from you screaming."

Now everyone laughed.

The boys' clean-shaven heads were practically bald. Papa Job, the boys, and Taiyewo sat at the kitchen table. A lantern burned at the center of a faded white tablecloth. Outside the screen door, fireflies flinched back and forth, looking in. Papa Job opened a mathematics book. His pink palms touched the pages as gently as his soft, warm, dark eyes behind his wire-rimmed glasses. He was going to teach them some mathematics. He was the kind of teacher who went slowly over every problem and seemed to be learning as they were learning. First he'd read the mathematics problem out loud, following the numbers with his finger. Then he'd write out the problem very neatly on a sheet of paper. Then he'd take that problem and work it out, turning it this way and that, looking at it from different angles. He could sit with them and discuss one mathematics problem all evening until it made sense even to five-year-old Tai.

Toomi already had his paper and pencil ready. But Balinga was emptying his bookbag on the table, trying to find his paper and pencil. Out rolled a tennis ball, then came two nubby pencils, rumpled paper, comic books, and candy wrappers. Papa Job looked up and frowned.

He said, "Balinga, bring me the contents from your bookbag."

Balinga scooted back his chair. He came and stood beside his father, his arms clasped behind his back.

"I can see you, Balinga. What I want to see is the contents from your schoolbag. Bring them."

Balinga went back and got them. Papa Job laid them out in front of him on the tablecloth.

"Balinga, don't let me see comic books in this schoolbag. I only want to see school books in this schoolbag, okay? And no tennis balls. Okay?"

Balinga nodded. "Yessir."

"Now, tell me. Where did you get candy?"

Balinga stared at the candy wrappers in Papa Job's hand.

"Balinga?"

Papa Job waited.

"What is this that I am holding in my hand?"

"Candy wrappers."

"Where did you get candy? Hm? This is maybe ten or eleven wrappers here. Sizzy doesn't buy this. I don't buy this. So who bought it?"

Balinga replied something that was too small in sound to hear.

Papa Job cleaned his ear with a finger and cocked his head to one side. "What?" He asked Toomi and Taiyewo, "Can you hear what he is saying?"

Toomi and Tai shook their heads. "No."

So Papa Job said, "Go out on the porch, Balinga. Stand out there. I want to hear your voice from way out there."

Balinga stood outside the screen door. He peered inside like the fireflies.

"Now. Where did you get this candy?"

"A friend," Balinga called through the screen.

"Okay. I am hearing you now. Come inside again. I want you to be speaking up loud. Speak loud here. Okay? Don't whisper."

The screen door whacked behind him.

"Now. You say a friend gave you candy. How many times?"

"Once," he murmured.

"What?"

"Once," he said a little louder.

"A friend gave you eleven pieces of candy at once?"

"Yessir."

"When?"

Balinga hesitated. "A long time ago."

Papa Job looked at him closely and for long. "You are lying," he pronounced. "And if you are lying, then you are also stealing. Telling lies is the first stage in a thief's life. First he will be telling lies. Next he will be stealing things. You are a thief. When did you steal this?"

Balinga began to cry. "I didn't steal it."

Papa Job laughed. "Don't lie for me. I know you are lying. And I know you are stealing. So this is what you want to be. A thief."

"No, sir."

"But you are a thief."

Papa Job held out the candy wrappers and frowned at Toomi.

"Toomi, did you see your junior brother steal this candy?"

"No, sir. But I've seen him take candy from the store before."

"And you, Tai, have you seen your brother stealing candy?"

"No, sir. But brother gave me candy before."

Papa Job nodded as he looked Balinga up and down. He told Balinga to hold his arms up in the air. He was not to let his arms bend but to keep them straight up in the air. Balinga held up his arms, sweating.

"Stand up!" Papa Job said. "Stand straight! Don't let me see you doing that, lowering your arms."

Then Papa Job turned to Toomi and Taiyewo. "In a court of law the judge would find you two guilty as well. You knew he was stealing and yet you didn't report him. That makes you thieves as well. Go. Stand up. Raise up your arms."

In no time all the children were sweating and crying. Their clothes were soaked right through and their arms were paining them. Papa Job spoke to them all the while.

"There are two ways a person can learn in life," he said. "He can learn by someone else's painful experience, or he can experience pain himself. But it is better to learn from someone else's experience. There are people who come to the world to be a bad example for other people. That is their sole purpose as soon as they come into the world. I hope," he said, "None of you came to the world for that."

Then he let them lower their arms and he poured each of them a cup of cool raisin juice.

"Now let us begin the math lesson."

Sizway returned from the market with a large basket of potatoes on her head. She opened the squeaky screen door. Everyone was silently reading by the light of the lantern, even Papa Job. Sizway groaned as she put the basket down on the floor and wiped the sweat off her face.

The children turned around in their chairs. They came to greet her.

"Good evening, mumma. Are you thirsty?"

"Yes, very. The basket is heavy and the path from the market very difficult."

Tai went to the refrigerator to get Sizway something for her thirst. She came back holding a cup of cool raisin juice with both hands. Sizway squatted. She turned her back to the children and drank.

"Sizway," Papa Job said, gently closing his book. "Did you know that Balinga has been stealing things?"

Sizway stood up and came to Job. She placed the empty cup on the table.

"Not again."

She looked in wonderment at Balinga.

"Why, Balinga?"

And Papa Job said, "So he has been stealing before? This is very bad. Very, very bad of you."

He was speaking of Sizway now.

He told everyone to sit at the table. Sizway sat at the head of the table, opposite Papa Job. Though Sizway's hair was still black and her skin blackberry smooth, she suddenly appeared old and feeble. Balinga looked at her and started crying. Papa Job turned to Balinga. "Why are you crying? You think I should praise you for this? Why do you always think you should be praised when you need to be condemned? Why can't you work hard and earn praise?"

And Sizway said, "What is the matter with you, Balinga, that inside you there is so much stealing? Why are you so full of something like that?"

"Why does any thief steal things?" Papa replied her. "Because he is selfish. And you—you yourself—are helping him to steal. In a court of law you would be found guilty as well. The stealing he was doing inside the house, he is now doing outside the house. This is very serious. Very, very serious."

"What has he been stealing?"

"Candy."

Sizway looked to Balinga again. She was shaken. "If you wanted candy, why didn't you just ask for it, Balinga?"

"Excuse me, Sizway," Papa Job said, raising his finger. "Don't tell him that. If candy is what is causing him to steal, then he shouldn't have any candy. I don't want you to be feeding his bad habit. Don't let me see candy here."

Sizway nodded. She looked even more tired.

Tai asked, "Mumma do you have a story for me?"

Sizway gazed at Tai, heavy-lidded. "What will you give me for the story?"

Tai got up and went to the kitchen shelf for her mother's packet of tobacco. She came with it. Sizway picked it and filled her pipe with it. When the pipe was lit, Tai scooted onto her laps. She lifted her chin to watch the puffs of smoke like clouds floating over her head.

"I will tell you the story of Iyo," Sizway began. "There was a boy named Iyo who was the first and only child of his parents. But at an early age he started stealing things. He stole from everyone who lived near him. The families in the compound complained to his parents. But his parents would just beg them and repay them for what their son had stolen. The boy's parents would say, 'Listen, my son is still a child. He doesn't realize what he is doing. Don't be so harsh on him. He is our only one.'

"Now the boy grew up but he kept stealing things. He would come home with the stolen things and pile them. He'd pile them. And his parents always gave some excuse for him. But one day the father died and the mother was left alone to raise Iyo. She had to work even harder, laboring all day to repay people for the things her son had stolen. One day she, too, died and her son was arrested for stealing.

"Iyo went before the judge. The judge found him guilty. The punishment for stealing is to cut off a finger. It was the law. So the judge fined the boy a finger. They cut it off. Eventually Iyo stole again and he was fined another finger. He stole again and another finger was gone. Soon the judge had offed all the fingers on the left hand. Then he had offed all the fingers on the right one as well. Now Iyo's life was useless, he couldn't do anything. Eventually he just died."

Sizway sighed. "Now, what is the lesson in this?" she asked them.

Tai tilted her head back, looking up at mum. She said, "I think the lesson is that people shouldn't steal."

"Yes, that," Sizway nodded.

She waited to hear from Balinga and Toomi.

"Balinga, what do you say?" Sizway asked.

Balinga had his head lowered. He didn't answer.

"Hm," Sizway said. "Maybe Balinga doesn't learn anything from this story."

She turned her eyes to Toomi. "Toomi? What of you?"

"Well," Toomi said, clearing his throat, "I think the story is teaching us that people should be held responsible for their actions."

"Hm, you are speaking up well," Sizway nodded.

Papa Job also cleared his throat. He said, "We are not just speaking of people here. We are speaking of the family's responsibility. A family has a responsibility. That responsibility is not to hide a child's bad behavior. Iyo's parents helped to ruin his life. His parents refused to see his bad habit and they made excuses for it. His parents didn't kill him, but they helped him to kill himself."

Sizway nodded. "Mm, your daddy is really telling you well. First Tai said a person shouldn't steal. That is right. Stealing is immoral. It is against every law. It can never be good.

"Then Toomi said a child should be responsible for his actions. That is true. That is the dream of every parent, that their child grow to be responsible. A child must first of all be responsible to himself. Being responsible means behaving well even when no one is looking. When you are at home, can I or Baba be there? Can we know what you are doing there? A responsible child behaves well even if his parents are not looking.

"And Kibaba said a parent has a responsibility, too. My mother used to say, if you don't hide a person's disease you are getting closer to a cure. You can't cure what you are hiding, can you? No. Iyo's parents wanted to hide his disease. In hiding it, they killed any chance for his future. They didn't kill him but they helped him to kill himself."

Papa Job leaned over with his elbows on the tablecloth. He said, "Toomi, Taiyewo, if you hate your brother then don't report him when you see him stealing. But if you love him, report him to me as soon as he does it and I will handle him. Okay? Do you love Balinga?"

"Yes, daddy," Toomi and Taiyewo said all at once, glancing over at Balinga.

"Then if you love him, you will support him when he does good things and refuse to support him when he does bad things."

Sizway lifted Taiyewo off her laps. She stood up. "I must go and wash. I am tired."

"Do you know another story?" Tai asked.

"Perhaps I will think of one."

Sizway went to the bathroom and softly closed the door.

Some time later Sizway took the children with her to the food store in town. She only bought a few things from Chachi's because most food the Ki grew themselves. The front window of Chachi's was filled with porcelain houseware, lace tablecloths imported from Italy, and all sizes of statues of the Virgin Mary. The inside of the store was hardwood floor with long, tunnel-like aisles. The shelves reached the ceiling and most items could only be reached by climbing a ladder. In the back of the store was a refrigerator of milk, eggs, and soft drinks. Also in the back was a refrigerator of frozen fish and meat. That's what Sizway wanted today, meat.

At the front of the store the old woman, Chachi, ran the register. Chachi was a thin white woman with sharp green eyes and flat red hair. Her store was one of the few that had air-conditioning. It was quite cool and one could hear the air conditioner's motor clanging from the ceiling. A customer was at the counter talking to Chachi. Sizway walked up behind the customer with her purchase of meat. She waited in the coolness while the sweat on her face dried.

Finally Sizway and the children stepped out again on the scorching hot street. Balinga started talking right away. He was telling his mother how well he was doing in his lessons. But she was smelling a sweet something in the air coming from his breath.

She asked him, "Balinga, where did you get candy?"

He said, "What candy?" (It was even in his mouth at the time.)

So she asked him again, "Where did you get candy? Tell me."

He said, "I had it, mum."

She asked him a third time. And do you know, he had taken it from Chachi's? He was stealing even as she was with him.

In the kitchen Sizway sat across from Papa Job at the table.

"Kibaba, you talk to him again and again. Nothing. What else?" Her eyes were rimmed with dark circles.

Balinga was in his bedroom when he heard his name being called. He responded, "Yessir!" and ran into the kitchen where his father and mother were sitting at the table.

"How are things going with you, Balinga?" Papa Job asked.

"Fine, sir."

"What happened today?"

"Nothing."

"So which means your mother lies."

"No, she doesn't lie." The whites of Balinga's eyes slid swiftly over to Sizway and back. Had she told his father?

"So what did you do wrong?" Papa Job asked him.

Balinga dropped his head. He mumbled something.

"If I have to ask you to speak up, I will beat you," Papa Job warned him.

"I—I stole from the store, sir."

Papa Job looked at Balinga and laughed. "You are without sense. You don't know that this stealing and disgracing you are doing, you only do for yourself? You don't know that if you leave this family and do wrong thing, you do it for yourself. When you rob someone, you are only robbing yourself. You are robbing yourself of your future. They say every day is for the thief but one day will be for the owner. One day the owner will catch you. You are wicked. Your mother and I, we already have what we want and if we don't have it we know how to work to get it. But you, now, you have nothing but what we give you and you don't know how to work to get it yourself. You only know stealing. The prison is the only future for a thief. When they catch you and take you to prison I will tell your mother not to visit you there. If she visits you, I will disown her. Why do you bother going to school if you want to go to prison? Why? Hm? . . . Answer!"

"I don't want to go to prison, sir."

Papa Job frowned. "Don't tell me that. You are a thief. What will you do after you serve your time in prison? Will you look for a job when you get out of jail? What will you do when your employer finds out you have been to jail? What will you tell your employer? Will you tell him your daddy and mommy restricted you so till you started stealing? Do you think your employer will care for that? They don't care for that. They only care for your own record. Not your daddy's record. Not your mommy's record. But your own. He won't want to hire a thief."

Papa Job paused, looking Balinga up and down. He was thinking of the next thing he would say. "Balinga. Tell me. Why are you even going to school? Why are you wasting time trying to get good grades? You don't need good grades in jail. Your friends in jail, some of them had good grades, some of them had bad grades. Some of them even had university training. But they didn't need any of it in jail."

Balinga looked at his father.

Papa Job sighed. "I can see you now. I know you will not stop stealing. This is what I will do for you. Since you want to be stealing and you want to make stealing your career in life, I will just have to warn people about you. I will have to tell everyone to watch their things when you are near. I will have to report you to the school and to the principal and teachers and students—everybody—to the relatives, all the Ki people, everyone, and let them know whom you are. We will inform everybody that a thief is in their midst."

Papa Job turned to Sizway. "All we can do is limit the spreading of his stealing. When he returns to school in the fall, write notes to all of his teachers and tell them he is a thief. And all of his schoolmates, we must tell them, too. He is a thief. They must watch their things. And we will have a family meeting in the compound to inform everyone that he is a thief."

"You know there are many types of schools, Balinga. But there is one school that everyone must go to no matter if they are literates or illiterates. Do you know which school that is? . . . Then I will tell you. It is the school of life. Every day you wake up you go to the school of life to learn. Life will teach you hard, Balinga, what you are having trouble learning at home."

Papa Job didn't intend to tell anyone about Balinga's stealing, but he said it so that Balinga would fear the next time he wanted to steal.

The kitchen found Sizway and Papa Job at the table again, leaning on folded arms.

"Kibaba, you talk to him again and again. But nothing. He has stolen again."

"That is because Balinga is a goat, not a lamb. He doesn't need talking, he needs beating. If you scold a lamb and shoo him away from something, he won't come back and bother it. Goats are hardheaded. They are selfish and greedy. Even when you swat them with a stick they come back to the same thing. You can even cripple a goat from swatting him, still he comes back. Balinga is a goat, not a lamb. I will deal with him. But first I will eat."

Sizway prepared his dinner and then went to the children's bedroom. There was a tall, four-paned window that ran from floor to ceiling. The bottom half of the window was wide open to let in any air that might be moving that night. Three unfinished dressers stood against the wall, spaced apart. In between the dressers were three rolled sleeping mats, leaning against the wall.

Toomi knelt and rolled out his sleeping mat. He looked at it. Peered under it. He looked over at Balinga, who was putting on his striped pajamas, and said, "Have you taken anything that belongs to me?"

"I don't know what you are talking about," Balinga answered, "I haven't taken anything of yours."

"Well, something that belongs to me is miss. I kept it here, rolled in my sleeping mat."

Balinga buttoned his pajama top. "Why does everyone blame me when something is miss? Ask Tai when you miss something. Don't ask me."

Balinga turned around and noticed Sizway standing at the door of their bedroom. Balinga tightened the drawstring of his pants and his frown deepened. "Mumma," he said, "Toomi is asking me if I have taken something of his."

She shrugged. "Well. Answer him."

"But I didn't take it."

"Why are you complaining? When something is miss, we suspect you. Even if you didn't do it, everyone will suspect you."

"But Tai could have taken brother's thing."

"And so? People will be stealing things when you are around. If your body stinks, people in your company take the advantage to fart."

Balinga unrolled his mat next to Toomi's. Then Taiyewo unrolled her mat. Then . . .

"Balinga! Get up!"

Papa Job had entered the bedroom, wiping his fingers on a napkin. He had done eating.

"You are going to get a beating. Bring your friend."

Balinga got up from his mat and started begging. "Daddy, I won't steal anymore."

"Bring it!"

Balinga got "his friend"—the switch that was behind his dresser. Papa Job took the switch and told him to off his pajama pants.

"You think because I haven't beaten you for stealing, you could just go on stealing? I see, now, that lectures are like fairy stories to you. They don't help you. Anyone who tells you stories aren't helping you. And anyone who lectures you isn't helping you. You are a goat, not a lamb. You only understand hard things, not soft things."

"I'm sorry, daddy."

"You are sorry? I don't marry sorry. You are without sense."

"I promise I won't steal anymore."

"Don't promise me. If you won't do it anymore I won't beat you anymore. But if you do it I will beat you. I will have to beat you today because you did it today. Remove your cloth!"

Balinga slowly began removing his pajama pants. "Daddy, I—I promise, I—"

"Balinga. I don't want to hear that. You do it I beat you. You don't do it I won't beat you. Simple."

"Kibaba—" Sizway started.

"Not now, Sizway."

Before leaving the bedroom, Sizway glanced back at Balinga, the beautiful one, who looked most like the one who had died at an early age.

After Balinga's beating, Papa Job told him to keep the switch behind the dresser. "This switch is your friend," he said. "It is the only friend you have because it is the only friend you will listen to. Your friend will teach you what you are having trouble learning. Keep your friend behind your dresser."

Their bedroom was dark. Sizway stood by the ceiling-high window, pulling her arms through her nightgown. "Kibaba, do you think beating will solve Balinga's problem?"

Papa Job stared at her for a while. "What are you asking me?"

"Maybe too much beating will just make the child to be stubborn. It will make the child too used to beatings. Eventually when the child does something wrong, he'll say, 'I know what my father and mother will do for me. I know what they will always do. They will just beat me. I am used to that. I am used to hard things. What else can they do for me besides beating me?' Soon the child will no longer fear beatings."

Papa Job faced her in the dark. He was in shadow but she was washed in moonlight. He thought, she wasn't asking him question, she was telling him.

"Okay," he said. "Sizzy. Father your children the way you want, okay?"

"Am I to be the mother who fathers them? You are not hearing me, Kiba."

"I don't want to hear you."

He went to the bureau and began undressing in the dark. He was angry and she was angry. In her thought she blamed him for taking Kehinde and Taiyewo to the hospital in town. Because of Kibaba Kehinde had died and Taiyewo's spirit was badly wounded. Sizway unrolled a seldom-used sleeping mat instead of sharing the wide one with Papa Job. This is the one she would be using from now on. It wasn't Balinga's beating foremost in her mind, but the child she would never hear cry again from any beating. She turned on her side on her mat, giving her back to Papa Job. For that, he himself began to take less and less part in the children's upbringing.

When Papa Job opened the screen door the next morning
the heat hit his face like a furnace. The leather seat of his
pickup truck burned his skin and the windshield wipers stood
motionless on a dusty arc. He started up the motor and headed
for the downtown. He drove past the alleys, the bank, the
church, Jake's Party Store, the Quik Service Cleaners, Rosey's
Barber Shop, and the dry cleaners run by Mr. Phelps. The downtown was full of honking traffic and slow-moving people burnt
black by the sun. Papa Job parked in front of his used furniture
store.

Sitting on a barrel next to the screen door was Jim, a black
man cradling a guitar. He wore a dark suit and a limp tie. His
sweating fingers left rings of dampness on the wood.

"Mornin, Job."

"Mornin, Jim."

"Got one for you, Job." His fingers slid down the guitar
strings, striking a blues chord.

> Ya know, I seen ole Miss Gaines
> Sittin at the road mailbox
> I seen ole Miss Gaines
> Sittin at the road mailbox
> Got a battery TV set
> Waitin on her welfare check.
>
> If it don't come she set there
> Till the sun done come down
> If it don't come she set there
> Till the sun done come down
> With her battery TV set
> Waitin on her welfare check.

Jim bapped the wood of the guitar to end it. He caught Job's eye and soundlessly laughed. Papa Job smiled and dropped some coins in Jim's tin can. He smelled the man's sweat on the air. Jim brought a brown bottle to his lips. The suction of the bottle fizzed and then pooped as he took it away. His eyes were always red from drinking. Jim pulled at his shirt collar, trying to make himself comfortable in his sweat, then he sounded another blues chord. He said, "Say, Job, how do de Islands sing, eh?"

Papa Job was unlocking the screen door of his shop. "In soprano. The men don't sing no more."

The furniture store was filled with dusty pieces stacked on top of each other because the space was small. The one-room shop was dimly lit by antique lamps that sat on a few tables and bureaus. There were ladderback chairs, drop-leaf tables, dressers with mirrors, bed frames, cupboards of all types of wood. Far into the back of the store were pieces of furniture being repaired, and in the corner, in the back, was Papa Job's desk and swivel chair. Papa Job worked long hours at his business. As night fell he was still working on a piece. He knelt on newspaper. He dipped a paintbrush in a can of paint. He wiped the brush on the top edge of the container to remove as much of the paint as possible. He stroked the brush on newspaper. Then he applied the paint to the leg of a chair.

An hour later he was done painting and was cleaning his paintbrushes. He stood by the worktable, near his desk and swivel chair, dipping the brush into a can of turpentine. The bell of the store clamored when the door was opened, and a man entered in a tailored suit, hat, and a cigar stuck in his jaw.

He couldn't see Papa Job for all the furniture. Still he called out, "Hello, Papa Job."

He moved past furniture, side-stepping pieces, and stepping over pieces to get to the back of the store.

Papa Job looked up when the man's head peered around a tall dresser. "Moneyman, how are you?" Papa Job was drying the bristles of the paintbrush with a rag.

Moneyman gave a broad smile and patted Papa Job's shoulder. "Good-good. I see you're working late again."

"Just cleaning up."

"Where's your assistant?"

"Gone home for the night."

Papa Job's worktable was crowded with old cans and mason jars of paints, enamels, varnishes, turpentine, shellacs, lacquers, stains, and linseed oils. On the wall behind the worktable, carpentry tools were suspended on nails hammered to the wall.

Moneyman admired the chair Papa Job had painted. It was a brilliant cobalt blue.

"I see you finally finished the chair. It's a nice color."

"Yah," Papa Job nodded, glancing at it.

"How'd you finally get the legs off?"

"Hot vinegar. I softened the old glue with it."

"Yeah? Humph. You know, I got an old chair at home but the screws won't stay tight."

Papa Job nodded. "Remove the screw and plug the hole with matchsticks."

"Matchsticks!"

"Yah."

"Humph. Well, hell, I'll try it." Moneyman thought for a minute. "How'd you learn all this furniture stuff, anyhow?"

Papa Job nodded at the shelf full of books behind his desk. The desk itself was also piled with neatly stacked books. There was a green desk lamp as well. Moneyman went to the shelf and began leafing through the pages of a book. After browsing for a while he asked, "If you were to get in a used piece, what do you do with it first?"

Papa Job shrugged. "First thing, repair it. Where you find it broken, repair it. Then remove the old finish. Work the thing well with the sandpaper or the chemical remover. Smooth it over. Then refinish it. You'll see a beautiful work. But imagination is the most important part. You have to be able to imagine what the finished piece will look like when it is still rough."

Now he wrapped a few thicknesses of newspaper around the bristles of the paintbrush. He tied it with a string and hung it on a nail on the wall. He removed his leather apron and placed it on a hook behind his desk. He wore a white shirt, bow tie, and suspenders. He seated himself at his swivel chair and clicked on the desk lamp. He slid the looped arms of his spectacles behind his ears. Moneyman sat on the edge of the desk. Papa Job wrote some figures in his account book.

Moneyman sighed. "You're a hardworking man, Papa Job."

Papa Job didn't say anything.

Moneyman said, "Thought I'd get together with the guys for a game of blackjack tonight. How'd you like to come along?"

Papa Job had heard about these gambling games before. "I don't know anything about gambling, Moneyman."

"Well, you're talking to the right person, cause I know a lot about gambling."

But Papa Job gave a small smile. "Maybe some other time."

The talebearer grunts and tightens her blanket around her shoulders. "Even a good man will do what he'd never do if it's too hard to go home in the night, if the home is a place of fighting. One night Papa Job followed Moneyman to a gambling game."

Papa Job locked up the store. His truck was parked at the curb. Papa Job and Moneyman climbed into the cab of the pickup. They drove to the edge of Sojourner, until the road changed to dirt. Moneyman told him to leave the truck; they should walk the rest of the way.

The two men trudged long on the dirt road in the dark. The cold moon seemed to pulsate and splash their shadows out before them. Papa Job wore his black suit jacket and bow tie. Moneyman also wore a black suit. Their pockets bulged knuckles. They were headed for the crossroad and a cardtable around which sat a circle of men. Men who enjoyed shooting the breeze, good talk over whiskey. No thought of extended family, no fences, no gods, because they believed themselves men without fences, men who had stooped on this dirt road all their lives to make the clacking bones of whiter men feel at home. While the white men walked tall, the men at the crossroads conspired by night, drinking palm wine and beer and honey beer, folding their quivering hands and waiting out time . . . or cursing it.

Papa Job and Moneyman proceeded through the darkness. Finally their footfalls slowed and stopped at a sign pointing in four directions—the crossroads. Beneath the sign sat a circle of men around a cardtable. Whiskey bottles winked under the moonlight like miniature glass cities in the dark. The men at the table wore black suits and striped shirts, a dull egg-white. An empty chair waited for Papa Job. He sat down. A whiskey bottle skittered across the table, halting in front of him. It seemed to shiver in the moonlight. Papa Job pulled his wallet from his pocket and removed a roll of bills.

Papa Job began to stay out late gambling. But Sizway said nothing. Papa Job won lots of money and lost lots of money, but still Sizway said nothing. Papa Job brought home a whiskey bottle from his late-night gambling group, though he didn't drink any of it. Sizway saw it and said nothing. Finally he stepped out of the night and into the glow of the porch light in the backyard. He came with another whiskey bottle peeking out of the pocket of his suit jacket. He paused to straighten his black tie, then strolled over with his hands deep in his pants pockets. He bent to kiss Sizway's lips lightly. It was on his breath. Sizway smelled it and looked up from her sitting position at the bottom of the stairway. Her white cotton nightgown glowed in the dark against her chocolate-brown skin.

Sizway frowned. "I've been worried," she said.

Papa Job answered, "Worried for what?" He thought she meant worried for his gambling and drinking.

"The boys left the house and haven't returned."

Papa Job shut his eyes briefly, grunted, and half-smiled. He looked at her. "Where did they go?"

"I don't know. They said to the library, returning books. They left at five. It is now ten o'clock. Could the library be open for so long?"

Papa Job stared at her and then looked away. "So you didn't know the library closed at five?"

"Closed at five?"

At that moment the boys entered the backyard.

Sizway jumped up shouting, "Toomi! Balinga!" She quickly forgot Papa Job. And he turned his back and proceeded up the stairway, with his hands in his pants pockets.

The boys slowly came toward Sizway.

"Where did you go?" Sizway demanded.

"To the library," Toomi said.

"You are lying. You didn't go there," Sizway said.

Toomi frowned. "We did go to the library."

"When it closes at five?"

"How could we know it closes at five?" Toomi answered.

"You told me you knew the hours."

Toomi's frown deepened. "I didn't tell you that."

"So, I am the liar?"

Toomi didn't answer.

"Little boy, you are getting on rude," she said. "Just because you have a mouth and you can open it, doesn't mean you shouldn't think."

Toomi stared through her, unseeing.

"And Balinga, what of you?" she said, turning to the eight-year-old.

He looked sullen. "I didn't do anything."

Sizway looked from one to the other. "Why?" she asked. "Why you don't see how hard I am trying? You don't care that the trouble you children are causing is killing me? Are you so selfish that you can only think of yourselves? You can't think of your parents? I caught you stealing, Balinga, but did I beat you? No. I told you to promise me that you wouldn't do it again. The following day you stole again. You were stealing before I could dry my tears. You don't care. And you, Toomi, I told you to be bringing home your homework from summer school. Every week

I get a note from your teachers. They all sing the same thing: Toomi doesn't do his homework. You are selfish. If you don't forget how to remove your jacket, then you shouldn't forget your homework—"

The sound of a woman complaining went on and on.

Inside, the house was dark. Papa Job sat motionless at the kitchen table. Taiyewo came and climbed onto his laps. *Long time ago a red candle burned and Sizway's breasts swayed full instead of fallen. She drew in the dust of the floor and told Papa Job that every generation of every people become what they've been taught by those who make them a man or a woman. She spoke of family and the old ways.* Water glimmered in Papa Job's eyes. Tai sat sideways on his laps, attentively staring at the glimmering water, as if he had wept and not blinked to let them fall. She held an empty can with ribbed sides in both hands. She placed it against her father's cheek. She patiently waited. The water fell. She put the can to her lips.

The family lived and lived. Prayers for rain turned to prayers for air. In the night, Sizway stood on the back porch while the rain dripped from the rafters. She was showered in moonlight. She wore a white ankle-length nightgown and her black hat. Papa Job entered the fenced yard. The rain had stopped and the mugginess began to rise. Papa Job held onto the railing as he climbed the stairway. He was damp with rain, running sweat, and breathing heavily. His shoulder slightly brushed Sizway's on his way inside the house, but Sizway softly called out to him. "Kibaba?"

He kept his hand on the door of the screen. His voice was soft as well. "What is it that you want, Sizzy? I am tired from talking."

"I want to know . . . Are you tired? Are you tired from drinking?"

Papa Job turned and stared at her calculatingly, then looked away. "Yah," he nodded, "I am tired from that."

It was on his breath.

"Will you stop, then, to rest?"

He answered, "This drinking doesn't want me to stop."

"Can you talk to the drink? Can you tell it your wife is suffering? your children are suffering? that you ignore the children?"

Papa Job frowned. "Yah, I tell the drink that. And I tell the drink that when I don't ignore the children, my wife also complains. What is it that you want, Sizzy?"

She opened her lips.

But he stepped close, tense in the summer warm dark. "Your 'I' is for yourself. Right now, all you can think of is yourself and the child that you lost, not our children that live."

"I think of how our children see their father drinking."

Papa Job said nothing. Sizway frowned. "There is help for that, Kiba. If you are unable to stop, there is someone in the camp. I can get you medicine for that."

"What you give me, Sizzy? Ogun? Obatallah? Allah? A toad to hang round me neck, eh?" He spread open his arms and shouted at the moon. "Hey! My wife collects bottles and bones, juju and candlesticks." He lifted the scent bag of myrrh and human hair from her breasts. "Hm. This is to ward off the bad spirits. This will cure the arthritis, eh?" He looked at her and laughed and his laughter was like the crackle of thorns under a hot pot.

"There is medicine for drinking."

"I don't want your medicine."

"Then what do you want then? to fold your hands together and eat your own flesh?"

His smile was slowly fading as he looked at her in the moonlight. He murmured, "Yes, that's right. I want to fold my hands together and eat my own flesh while you continue to live for the dead and not for the living. You know, you, too, need medicine. You don't know the difference between the living and the dead. You don't know Kehinde has died."

She looked past him. "Kehinde travels."

"Humph. He has died. He has died."

When Papa Job called Death for the third time the bad spirits roused themselves like a cave of bats roused by firelight. They flew out of Papa Job's killing words.

Sizway saw them. She stepped back first and then stepped around Papa Job. He caught a glimpse of the fear on her face.

"Where are you going?"

Sizway half-walked, half-ran from the yard.

At Kehinde's grave Sizway built a fire and sat cross-legged in front of the flames. Her head was lowered, covered by her black felt hat. She slowly rocked back and forth. She chanted to Bakuu who presides over the giving—pregnancy—and the taking away. She called out to Bakuu.

As she rocked, her body took on a jerkiness of movement, her eyes a fixity of gaze. Her white gown stuck to her body skin as if she had been doused in water. Black of skin and white of gown, she trembled and rocked herself.

She called out to Bakuu to block and ward off evil. The bad spirits have heard. They will go and tell the matter.

"Block them," she chanted. "Ward off the lie. The boy is still small. He will not know the truth from the lie if they tell him he is dead."

Her face became wooden, rigid expression; high cheekbones became stiff mounds. Her nostrils quivered. Bakuu had finally descended to her head. Sizway picked up the empty clay bowl and held it with trembling hands at the level of her womb. Her golden eyes swelled to accommodate the inner eyes, the eyes of Bakuu.

Bakuu spoke in a hoarse voice. Bakuu placated Kehinde's spirit.

"There is life here. There is life always. Take it, child, take it, child, take it, child, take it, child."

Sizway's eyes, little by little, took on their normal size, but she continued chanting. "Take it, child, take it, child . . ." She heard a truck drive up to the cemetery. She heard the truck door open and then shut. The driver of the truck walked through the cemetery, approaching her fire. He stopped a few feet behind her. Then he crouched on his haunches. His eyes held the same worried frown she had had earlier that evening. "Kehinde's okay now."

Sizway stopped rocking, stopped chanting. "How do you know?"

"I know. My spirit is stronger than your own."

His frown deepened. "Why did the bad spirits pursue him? What did this Kibaba do to bring this on my son?"

Sizway stared at Kehinde's grave. "Why do you call him your son?"

"He is my own."

Michael hadn't changed over five years. He was still tall and built strong for farm work. He still wore a cowboy hat over a head of black curls as thick as grapes.

Sizway knelt to put out the fire. She wanted to return to her husband and children. But as she poked a stick at the flames the stick fell from her hand. Her hand hung limp at her wrist and her whole body weakened. She slowly sat back.

His eyes were fixed on her yet gentle. "Don't be scared," he said. "You won't be able to move for a while but nothing will happen to you. I won't let it."

He stood up. There was still a small flame. He came around and squatted in front of her. He watched her for a while. She was kneeling, sitting back on her buttocks. He addressed her. "What do you see, Sizway?"

The darkness spread out like a thick fog, exposing the cemetery trees like black shadows. And in the dark sky the clouds parted like grey smoke, exposing the white moon.

Michael continued to watch her. He addressed her again. "What do you see? Tell me."

His mind was spreading open to her, like the spreading apart of darkness, like the floating apart of clouds. And his mind pulled her in. She saw things. She saw him lift her as if she were as light as a child. She saw him turn her body so that her back was against the strong wall of his chest. They were sitting like that in this cemetery. She saw him bow his head, his lips near her ear, and whisper to her, while his fingers held her and her sweat-soaked gown.

She closed her eyes to shut it out.

"It's okay," he murmured. "It's okay to look."

She opened her eyes. Her breathing increased. Her small brown lips parted, taking in rhythmic, sharp gasps of air. She felt his fingers gently knead the rounded parts of her flesh and she felt his breath close to her ear. His lips brushed her lobe, making her want to turn her head, making her want to taste the strangeness of his mouth. But she shut her eyes again. She swallowed. That's when his mind slowly released her.

He studied her with serious expression. "Will you remain here with me or return to him?"

She didn't answer.

"You know I could take you with me, tonight. But I won't take you. I'll give you this."

He held out two stones, the same ones he had offered her when she was carrying the twins.

"Promise me this. If the marriage to the man that you live with is lost, you'll leave these stones here. And you'll remain with me, you and our children."

She waited.

"Promise me," he said.

She scooped the stones off his palm. She looked down at the stones.

He said, "There are men in the world . . . men born from the dreams of a small girl."

She nodded and murmured, "But I am no more a small girl."

"And I am no more a dream. You should know now. You and me, we are the same."

She closed her fingers on the stones. She stood up. Slowly he stood up.

He walked through the cemetery with Sizway following behind him. His truck was parked on the road. He opened the door of the passenger side. But Sizway didn't enter.

She said, "You say we are the same. What then can you teach me? and what can I learn from you if we are the same? Kibaba and I are not the same. He can still teach me; and I can continue to learn."

"There are things I could teach you. My spirit is stronger than your own. With all your wisdom and knowing, I know there is still a small girl inside, a girl who's scared sometimes, who isn't always strong."

Beneath her black hat, her face was all angles and high cheekbones. Her braids hung down her back and her gown stuck to the sticky sweat of her body.

"There are many things I could teach you," he said.

The evening sky god yawns, slowly stretching black arms out upon the sky, his yawning mouth a hole for the moon. Spiderwebs of moving hair threads curl in the night wind around the talebearer's face.

"The world change," she murmurs. "It will change on you. And a rope twist round like a snake. . . ."

A blackbird flashed, a bit of vivid color in the moonlight, and landed on the porch rail. Feather-tipped brows frowned, wings fluttered, eyes like polished black beads darted in the night.

Across the fence from Papa Job's house, a porch door opened and yellow light tumbled onto the floorboards. A man in shirt and pants and a woman in nightgown emerged from the light, bringing with them the sounds of a heated argument when voices rise over each other and no one listens to what another is saying.

Black marbles blinked, blurred, then blinked. The crow backed up on the rail, lifting clawed toes high. Ebony feathers reflected the light of the moon like gleaming wet paint. The bird tilted his head, picking out a few words from the jumbled screams across the fence.

Bastard. Fool. Bitch. Nag. Don't never come back. The man yelled, "You was a fool for ironing my shirts." She yelled, "Well, you won't be the fool for wearing them." And ripped up the shirt in her hand. The man clamored off the porch and down the street. The woman turned back inside the house, but not before hollering at her children to get back to bed before she slapped them silly.

Moonlight lifts the talebearer's head. "You see, teeth grow in the mouth sharp and pointed," she says. "Claws appear where fingernails used to be. A woman lay in bed with a man. Before the night is over she wail out on the back porch, beating her breasts. Her husband storms off the porch, baDambang, baDambang. The woman falls on her knees, begging, begging. What? Hmm. This man and this woman die slowly all the while they lay together. They decay on the bedsheet like the residue you leave on the lip of a jar. And so, what used to be a man or a woman, who walked upon the earth with two legs, crawl on four . . . tiktik, tiktik, tiktik. . . ."

The blackbird ducked his head under his wing. His small body quivered as he pecked and pinched the tiny bugs hidden in the feathers. Then he lifted his head, eyes blinking up at the porch ceiling, watching the slow swing of a naked lightbulb hung low on a wire from the rafters. The bird opened his orange beak. "Kwok!" He backed down the porch rail, "Kwok! Kwok!" lifting high his skinny raw legs and fluffing feathered wings. Whining, the screen door turned on its hinges. The blackbird blinked, leaped, flew.

Toomi, Balinga, and Taiyewo stepped outside, followed by their mother. They began to descend the stairway when the screen door creaked open and Papa Job's slurred voice came out at Sizway, pushing aside the darkness. "Where are you going with my children?" he asked.

Sizway held the hands of the two youngest ones, the eldest stood behind her.

"I will return soon."

They took a few more steps down the porch. Then they turned to the wire mesh at the same time. The door whined on its springs and slammed shut.

A dimly burning wick and a bottle of Jamaican rum was an island on the wooden kitchen table. Hunched over on his elbows, Papa Job sat in the late-night room. Brown rattan shades blew up and then back, air-sucked to the screen window.

Papa Job was wasting away like wool that is moth-eaten. His hair and mustache were speckled with lint. His naked belly strained against his belt. Food smears hardened on his pants legs. His bare feet were dirty, ashy, his toenails chipped like plaster walls.

He sat on the edge of his chair, his eyes watery and running, and pulled out a small object wrapped in newspaper. He uncovered an old spot-rusted harmonica. The silver metal flashed in the candlelight. Carefully he rubbed it between his palms. He slid the square holes between his lips, shadowed over by thick mustache. The first notes were scratched out, tentative. He paused, blinking liquid-dark eyes. The back of his hand ran over his wet lips. His chair scraped back. He left the harmonica on the table.

Outside, twilight had sifted down upon the peaked roofs along the street. Papa Job stood out on the porch, naked from the belly up; one hand slid down in his pants pocket, pulling aside his open zipper, the other grasped his bottle of rum. The stale odor of sweat and liquor blew out from his skin, stirred by the evening wind.

He shuffled off the porch and into the center of the yard. He stood in a thousand warm shadows. He began to circle the chicken wire that surrounded Sizway's vegetable garden. Slowly he went—round and round, liquor moistening his bones until his legs began to wobble, until his muscles softened like oily dough. It was not long before his mind beheld strange things and his tongue uttered things turned the wrong way, until the night took him in laughing softly to himself.

His yellow eyes curled inside wrinkled lids; white teeth smiled; spit flying through his teeth when he gasped. He walked over to the fence that separated his yard from his neighbor's yard. Blades of grass pricked up from his neighbor's lawn and waved their machetes in the air, whispering. Pine trees stood over him, pointing their fingers. Papa Job trembled. He felt a gold needle pricking his bladder. Opening his belt buckle, he peed across the fence on the deep warm grass of his neighbor's yard.

"Kibaba?"

Papa Job hurriedly zipped himself and turned, squinting in the dark. It was Sizway and the children.

"Take the children in the house!" he shouted. He didn't want them to see him drunk.

After a while Papa Job stumbled up the stairway of the porch. He fell back in a hard chair. He blinked and then gasped out between gusts of laughter that were shaking his whole body. He shook his head and leaned back in his chair, looking up at the night sky.

He swallowed a gulp of rum and stared out before him. His wet lips glistened. He stared down at the floorboards and his eyes beheld strange things and saw things twisted the wrong way. He saw filmy images of his three sons, Toomi, Balinga, and Kehinde, the dead twin, rising up in smoke fumes from the cracks in the porch floor. Their images squatted on the floorboards, an ethereal tribunal.

Toomi and Balinga wore jeans and were barefoot. They each wore a single long braid at the back of their necks and black felt hats like the older Ki males. Kehinde resembled the ibeji carving. His belly extended to a point, his legs squat and slightly bent. He was naked. His filmy, weightless body floated upward and settled on Papa Job's laps.

Papa Job trembled.

"Something don't seem right," Kehinde whispered. "Baba have a big bottle of dark juice. He done the whole bottle of it."

Toomi's teeth were silver pointed knives when he spoke. "Don't worry. He's been drinking his rum, that's all," he said.

And Balinga's eyes were white moons in the dark. "Yah, he is too drunk now to hurt anyone."

Then the dead twin looked at his brothers and frowned. "Which one of you will be able to put our father out of his misery and into his grave? Hm?"

Kehinde lifted from Papa Job's laps like a blown feather. He wavered down to and fro, to and fro, before landing in the center of the group on stumpy wooden legs. He sat down. He raised one half of his buttocks as if he were passing wind. Fumes of burnt rubber filled the air. From his buttocks dropped excrement that steamed on the porch floor before hardening into the form of Papa's muddy brown shoe.

Toomi and Balinga stretched out their feet; they both had the clawed feet of blackbirds. First Toomi slid his clawed foot into his father's shoe. Kehinde pressed his thumb down on the toe of the shoe. Toomi's curled toenails were about two inches away from the tip.

"Hm. It needs half an inch to catch," Kehinde muttered.

Then Balinga measured his own clawed foot. It started spilling out all four sides of the shoe.

Kehinde shook his head. "Too wide."

Kehinde sighed and thought for a moment. He said, "I will have to consult the oracle."

Papa Job swallowed hard.

Now filmy images of wooden barrel drums were rising up in smoke fumes from the cracks in the porch floor. The drums walked in between Toomi and Balinga's knees. The boys took more sly glances at their father. Papa Job felt the oily sweat spreading out under his clasped armpits.

Toomi began beating on the sides of the barrel drum with the sides of his knees. "It is the truth I sing," he said.

> I need a good tailor, you know.
> That black sausage up there, he go
> To make me so mad
> Me pants burst
> Ja, ja, ja . . .

"Well, I need cocoa butter to cool my anger," Balinga frowned, with his eyes fixed on Papa Job.

> Baba say if you don't have no money you can't have
>   nothing
> Baba say that, say that
> Baba tell us to work our guts out
> Baba say that, say that
> Yet he get up so early each workaday morning
> And chase after rum like a dog after shit
> Baba is loco, he go-go so loco
> Baba is that, is that.

Suddenly the sound of great thuds, like rolling pins, filled the porch. The dead twin was tossing divining bones along the floorboards to consult the oracle. And they were the bones of a full-sized man. The skull rolled this way, the neckbone rolled that way. Kehinde plucked off a toebone from a foot and dropped it into his mouth.

"Here is his fate," Kehinde said, pointing.

Before he read the oracle he crunched down on the toebone that was still in his mouth. Then the boys gazed at their father's fate. Slowly they turned and stared up at him and their eyes were black holes in the sockets.

Papa Job stood up, shaken. He pulled open the screen door and the filmy images of his sons followed him inside, sprinkling him with holy water spit. All the lights were out in the house. Papa Job bumped into the stove. He turned up the fire on a burner that held a black kettle. He watched the white flames lick the black man's bottom. He felt the spirit dead running

around him in the dark and never stop running and he listened
to a distant voice ring in his ears.

> We know the man who loves his wife,
> He is Kiba-baba.
> We know the man who loves his wife,
> We cry out, Thank you, Baba!
> Who makes his son to die?
> Who makes the skin to show through me pants?
> Who is the man who makes the house fall?
> Oh, thank you, Kiba-baba.

At dawn the rooftops were like black steeples in the sky.
Papa Job was sleeping with his head on the kitchen table. He
roused. His expression screwed and tightened against pulsing
veins. He squeezed shut his eyes then opened them wide seeing
white spots. He straightened his back. He was sick from the rum,
sick of the drinking that he couldn't put down. He felt for the
bottle in his pants pocket. He got to his feet. Sizway was standing on the threshold of the kitchen door, watching him. Papa
Job saw her and slowly straightened stooped shoulders. He
sniffed and wiped his arm across his watery eyes.

Sizway said, "Kibaba, why? Why?"

"Why what?"

"You drink and drink. You never stop to rest. The children
are suffering. I am suffering. This has gone far enough."

"Don't talk to me about it," he muttered. He plopped down
again in the chair at the kitchen table.

Sizway came closer. She spoke quietly. "When did you become like the fathers in the town? They are dead yet breathing.

They are breathing for nothing. Their children are living under a dead father. These fathers take no part in their children's upbringing."

Papa Job laughed. "Isn't that what you wanted? for me to have no part in the children's upbringing? You don't know what you want. And when you get what you want, you want something else. Why are you complaining?"

She shook her head.

He shouted, "You wanted it! You wanted a useless man, a useless father!"

She slowly sank to the floor, placing her forehead on his knees. She wept softly.

"Cry, Sizzy. That's right. Cry for yourself."

Sizway prayed, "Eshu-Elegba, may we walk well. Eshu-Elegba, keep the road to my family and community open. Keep—"

Papa Job took the rum from his pants pocket. He unscrewed the cap.

"The spirit in the bottle, Kiba, it is a bad spirit," she said. "Some men can drink it. But your spirit—"

Papa Job ignored her.

Sizway reached out and gently held on to the neck of the bottle. "No," she begged him. She was on her knees. Papa Job jerked the bottle out of her grasp. But the bottle snapped back, striking her like a sledgehammer on the forehead. She cried out and clapped her hands over her face. He dropped the bottle. He came down on his knees and removed her hands. Thickly the blood ran from her forehead, covering her face like a veil. He sobered. "Sizzy. I'm sorry."

Tears surfaced in her eyes. "My mother is alive. My people are still alive. I don't know why I stay here with you. I will go back to my own people."

Before the morning had broken, she had taken the children. She had left Kibaba Job.

"They say night time is the meditation God gives one from the hard lessons of the day. God gives us a backdrop of darkness, moon, and stars and lonely sounds that creep out of darkness. Night covers a man as he sits inside what he calls a house. But his house at night seems like flimsy cardboard and all his cries seem vain. Night time makes a man feel his smallness. To be in the world is to know night time and darkness, to barely see one's hand in front of one's face, to barely see where one is going."

---

chapter seven

Late in the night, Papa Job lay in fetal position on the bedroom floor, smelling of drink. After a while he felt people enter the small bedroom. He heard voices whispering. The visitors squatted around him on the floor. He felt that they were many. Papa Job didn't move from his place on the mat. Were they human or spirits?

"What is wrong, Kiba?" Abel asked.

Papa Job lurched up from the mat, dazed. "Who is that? Abel? Ho, God. I . . . I thought you were spirits again. . . ."

The visitors exchanged glances.

Papa Job looked around him in the dark, squinting through blurred eyes. There were many there—Abel, Sinsi, Ashe, many Ki relatives, squatting in the dark.

"Kiba," Abel said, "did you know there are bad spirits in what you are drinking? You can't talk to these spirits."

Papa Job fell back on his mat, holding his head.

"My head is hurting me."

"Your wife came to us. She is living in the camp. She told us you have put up this house for sell. Why? Why are you selling your children's inheritance?"

"To pay debt."

"Which debt?"

"Gambling debt, brother."

"Why are you gambling? Why are you drinking and destroying your life?"

"Drinking? I drink."

"And you dent the family's image. You know, we are all family here. We share the same family. The family name is important. It belongs to each of your children. The name of your children shouldn't be disgraced. Behave like a man who reasons."

"What are you talking about?"

Then Sinsi's voice came close. He felt Sinsi's hand press down on his chest.

"There are three types of men, Kibaba Job," Sinsi said. "One man is all appetite. Anything his appetite wants he takes it. That's the first type—all appetite. The second type of man is in between. If he is in the company of a man who is all appetite, he too will not know moderation. And if he is in the company of a man who reasons and weighs things, then he will reason and weigh things. But this second type of man is not stable. He is too easily influenced by whomever he is with." Sinsi came closer. His long braid hung over his shoulder and his breath was warm on Papa's face. "And then there is the third type of man. This man will reason before he does anything. He will ask himself, 'If I do this thing, how will it affect my own future and the future of my family?' Tell me, brother, which type are you?"

"I reason."

Sinsi tapped Papa's chest with his finger. "Then be proving it. Are you a father here?"

"Yes."

"Then you are the head of the home here?"

"Yes."

"Then if you are the head why are you destroying your body? So, you didn't know that your family is your body? Isn't a head attached to a body? A body will feel what the head feels. When you destroy your family, you destroy yourself. You are drinking. Why? Is this the history you want to make?"

"I drink, Sinsi. What else?"

"Drink for shame."

"What are you trying to say?"

"Not what I am *trying* to say, but what I *said*. Brother, if you continue, you will leave only a history of shame for the whole of the family."

Papa Job was angry now. "Did I ask you—any of you—to come here?"

Abel just looked at him and spoke with low voice. "This problem has gone beyond your own yard. It is the whole of the family's problem now. We don't believe in closing our eyes when we see our own destroying himself."

"Then talk to Sizzy. It is she who destroyed the family. Didn't she leave for the camp?"

"So, you don't want her?" Sinsi asked.

Papa Job didn't answer.

"Umph. One day you will want her," Sinsi said. "What will you do then?"

Sinsi flicked his braid behind his back and stood up. "Let us go," he said.

Dawn rose over the crest of forest-green trees and dew sprinkled the faces of leaves. The air was chilly and frigid and open. Manji emerged from her house of jagged stone and shuffled to the edge of the low-hanging porch. She stepped down and onto the ground one foot at a time. Her hair was snow white. She wore a loose-fitting dress and shoes missing shoelaces. Her leggings had fallen in layers around her ankles. She stooped at the waist with a burlap bag of chicken feed in her hands.

"Chick-chick-a-dee," she screeched. "Come here and eat and come if you want to eat."

She pointed her thick finger as she spoke, spraying the ground with meal.

Papa Job emerged from the thick green growth of trees surrounding Manji's house. He came into the clearing and her chickens scurried away from his shuffling feet.

Manji climbed onto the porch. The floorboards echoed with each footfall. Then she turned to face Papa Job. He placed one shoefoot on the low-hanging porch, the other one was on the ground.

They talked with low voice. They continued like that and Papa Job went to deny things. They didn't agree. Papa Job wrung his felt hat and his words flew at Manji but Manji didn't take it to heart. After a time, Manji took her hand to scratch her knee which meant they had talked the talk done.

Papa Job turned on his heels and left.

Many more nights passed and more dawns before Papa Job came again to Manji's stone house in the woods. Early morning shadows lined her porch.

Papa Job's one shoefoot hit the floorboards, the other foot on the ground. Manji leaned against the doorjamb. Papa Job stood outside looking in. Manji stood inside looking out. Her eyes were grey, clear, and shiny like marbles.

"When can I see Sizway?"

"Sizzy say she don't want."

"What you mean, she say she don't want?"

"I, man, I tell you what she say," Manji said.

"Send Sizzy out here, mumma. Please. I just want to talk to her."

"That's fine for you," she replied. "There's nothing wrong with that."

Papa Job breathed in the still air. The silence came in around him.

"Do you love me, mumma?"

"Mm. I very love'a you."

Beyond Manji, the room was dark. Papa Job watched the darkness.

"If you love me then you will tell Sizzy to come out from in there."

Manji waited. She shifted her weight from her tired foot to her rested one.

Papa Job hit his hat against his thigh. "Mumma, you make a fool of me."

"Umph. I make you nothing. To bow to an old woman won't prevent you from standing straight."

"So, you won't allow me to talk to her?" Papa Job asked.

"So you can kill her?"

"I didn't mean for the bottle to strike her. If I had known—"

"But If-I-Had-Only is a late-born child."

Papa Job tried to discuss it again.

But Manji said, "You see this saliva in my mouth? I don't want to waste it on you. I will talk to your family, not to you. Bring the elders in your family."

And then the darkness in the room separated. Sizway's white dress came forward. A white gauze patch was taped to her forehead. The darkness receded. He saw the high cheekbones, the sunken jaws, the long angled nose, the thin dripping braids.

His eyes watered.

"Ho, Sizzy."

"You and me be mismated shoes," she said.

"I love you. I came all the way to Sojourner for you."

"And I very love you."

"Then come home with me."

"I can't. You are still drinking. You may strike me again."

"I didn't mean to strike you."

Sizway eyed him closely and then dropped her eyes.

Papa Job was thin now, almost fragile, in his limp black coat. He looked worn out by life. His eyes peered helplessly out at her through his wire-rimmed glasses.

"Listen, Sizzy, I know I have to stop drinking. I don't want to drink. Last week I almost stopped."

Manji interrupted. "My son, can we eat 'almost'? If you almost kill a rabbit, can we eat 'almost'? Almost doesn't kill anything."

"Yes, I know," he told her. "Almost isn't enough. I know that."

And Sizway said, "If I go with you, you will turn back. I want us to solve this family problem once and for all. It isn't just your drinking. The problem didn't start with your drinking. But I want it to end. Go to the old woman Kehinde. The one who married you to me. Tell her you want to solve this problem between us. And bring the elders of your family. The old ones who married us. They are the only ones who can help us now with this problem."

Papa Job sold their house to pay off his debts and left for Detroit to find his relatives, while Sizway and the children lived on in the compound. Once Papa Job left for Detroit, Sizway could leave her mother's house. She entered the central part of the Ki camp, carrying a large basket on her shoulder. Soon she merged in with the crowd of other Ki women heading this dawn to the market.

In the open-air marketplace, Sizway spread out her beautifully embroidered rug and set out rows of herbs in brown glass jars to sell. Her first customer that morning was Eva. Eva came in a cotton shift, loose-fitting hosiery, and run-down heels.

"Mornin, Sizzy. What you got in those jars for me today?"

Sizway gave a small smile. "What you need, ma?"

"Something for constipation."

"Are you constipated?" Sizway asked.

"A little," Eva said.

Sizway nodded and began sorting through the jars. Eva settled her thin body on a waiting stool.

Sizway was mixing different dried herbs into an empty jar. "Have you tried tomato and sauerkraut?" Sizway asked without looking up. "You can even get it at the store in town."

Eva cocked her ear to one side. "What's that?"

"Two parts tomato juice and one part sauerkraut," Sizway repeated. "It is good for constipation."

"Oh, no. I don't drink that."

"Why?" Sizway asked, gazing at her curiously.

"Well, when I see tomato juice I just see blood. I can't hold it down."

Sizway nodded. The explanation seemed reasonable to her.

"I can give you some herbs," Sizway said. "Borage leaves and flowers, some dandelion, sticklewort, and witch grass. You take it unsweetened in mouthful doses." And then Sizway gave her the other side of the remedy. "We don't just give herbs, we have to go to the root, mumma. Constipation comes when we don't want to let go of old ideas. We are stuck in the past, so the stool becomes stuck as well. Umph, we strain. It won't come out. Why? We have to be able to let go of old thinking. Once we do that, the stool it will flow, eh?"

Eva nodded. She took the jar and gave Sizway three dollars for it. But Eva's mind was already wandering far from thoughts of remedies. Eva said her sister dropped her off and then had driven over to Beulah's farm. She said her sister would stop by this way to pick her up. She would just sit here and wait for her sister to come get her.

Sizway nodded and turned to her next customer. While Sizway was busy listening to someone else's ailments, Eva looked around the market, peering through cat-eye glasses. She spotted somebody. Her eyeglasses slid down on her nose. "Sizway, do you see that man over there?"

Eva pointed.

"Is that Jim-Walter?" she asked.

Sizway looked up from beneath the brim of her hat. She shrugged. "I don't know, ma." She turned back to her customer.

Finally her customer left and Sizway sprinkled tobacco in the bowl of her pipe. She slowly puffed. Eva had taken on her talkative posture, sitting with her knees clasped together, her back straight, and her pocketbook on her laps.

"Certain thangs happen, Sizway, and you just wonder why. . . ."

"Mm?"

"Well," Eva said. She thought for a moment. She said, "You know, I been sitting on that end seat for years. I can't tell you how many years."

"Which end seat, ma?"

"Oh, the one at church. It was my seat for years. Well, one day a new woman come to church. She wants to take the end seat, see. Every Sunday, you know, she stroll up the aisle, stop at my pew, wanting to move me over. I turn sideways, like this, so she could step in. But, no, she wanted me to move over. I went and asked somebody who knew her from another church. I said, I'll find out from him if she sit at the end up there. She used to attend Church of God in Christ, so I asked him. Do she take the end up there? 'No,' this man said, 'She never did take the end up there.'" Eva shook her head and pulled her purse closer to her. "So, thangs happen, you know, and you just wonder why."

Sizway puffed slow streams of smoke, her eyes lowered. She looked up when another customer came. She listened to the problem the customer was having and sorted through her jars. When the customer left, Eva folded her arms and kept her eyes on her tightly clasped knees.

"You know where Jim-Walter's probably going tonight, Sizway? To that new church down near the auto-body place. Only got sixteen members in all. He go to that church, see, and the preacher just put his hands down everybody's pocket. That's all that preacher want is folks' money. Jim-Walter say, he say, 'Well, I guess I'll go on down to the church tonight.' I say, 'Mmm.' You know, I just set back and let him do the talking. He say, 'But I got to take a little *green* with me.' Then he get him some money. I thank he give money to that preacher so the preacher can lean on him, you know. He don't have no friends, see. He want the preacher to lean on him. So then he ask me, 'You need a little money, Eva?' I never do act anxious. I say, 'Well, if I had it, I guess I could spend it.'

"Now my church, the one I go to, been around for years. I was talking to Lena on the phone the other day. You know, Lena and me both on the stewardess board at church. You probably don't know so much about it, but the Holy Ghost Baptist Church and the Baptist Speaks been separate for years, years. Tornado came and blew em both down. After the tornado, they build a new church for both church members. They called it the Holy Ghost Baptist Speaks. Elva, May, Rosa and Hannah railroad the pastor cause he didn't want the ladies to have a Christmas bazaar. He gone now. He didn't believe in all those church chicken sales, all those chicken pies and such. He say, 'Put your money in the offering. That'a way we keep the church going.' He talk sense. We get along fine. He tell me thangs and it stop there."

"You think Sizway want to hear all of that?"

Both women looked up at the same time. Jim-Walter, Eva's husband, shuffled up to them.

"Afternoon, Sizway," he mumbled, tipping his hat to her.

He wore sagging pants, a thermal undershirt, and a battered hat. It looked like he had just been roused from sleep and he was frowning deeply.

He said, "Eva, I come all the way down here to ask you one question. What you mean by taking furniture out the house?"

Eva didn't skip a beat. "Jim-Walter and me, you know, we separated. I'm staying with my sister and her husband. If I took some furniture I guess I'm entitled to it."

Sizway's eyes moved from one to the other. Her lips held away all sound.

Jim-Walter went on, "You and your sister come by this morning, sneaking around, taking out furniture."

Eva continued looking at Sizway with a frozen smile on her face. "I guess I'm entitled. It's half mine. I guess so."

"I can't deal with this kind of thang no more, Eva—the backbiting, the pettiness, the hatred, the hate—" His voice cracked. "I can't deal with it no more."

"Well," Eva responded. "Guess that's another country heard from."

There were tears in her husband's eyes. His voice shook and his body shook. Finally he shuffled away.

Eva's smile remained wooden, her eyes fixed straight ahead. "I guess he's the same thang he's always been—old and cheap. Talkin bout furniture. My sister say, 'Oh, I'll get a divorce attorney for you.' But I've always gone to this lawyer, Conners. I told my sister I'd been to Conners before. I didn't tell her how many times. When Conners saw me in his office, he said, 'Oh, Eva, *you* again?' He said, 'What is it you want?' I said, 'Separation.' Then Conners, see, he made me fill out some papers. I told my children, it ain't nothing to worry about. It's the same thang it's always been—money. Old and cheap, that's all he is. Old and cheap."

Sizway suddenly turned and looked down the line of Ki women.

"Children!" she shouted.

The children didn't stir.

"My children don't hear well," she said. "I'll have to get it myself. Excuse me."

Sizway hurriedly left Eva and made her way beneath the canopy, weaving in and out between Ki men and women selling things. Many Ki children were sitting around a communal bowl. She tapped the shoulder of her youngest son, Balinga, who was eating with the others.

"Balinga. Come," she said.

Balinga stood up in his brown shorts and shirt, licking his fingers.

"Where is your brother?" she asked.

"Not far from here. There," he pointed.

Sizway searched with her eyes the crowds of people milling about, haggling over prices, clutching brown paper bags. Then she caught sight of Toomi and another boy strolling past a farmer's stand of oranges. Toomi gave the boy some fruit. The boy bit into it and Toomi giggled like a hyena, saying, "I pissed on it, and you ate it."

Sizway frowned. "Go and get your brother."

"But, mumma, when am I going to finish eating?"

"You will eat something. Let me worry about it."

Sizway walked to the very end of the Ki line of sellers. She sat where it was quiet and waited. Soon the two boys were hurrying toward her. They were both tall and slender and very handsome. Toomi was thirteen and Balinga was ten.

"Good afternoon, mumma," they said.

"Sit down. You show bad manner, Toomi. Very, very bad. Just sit."

The boys sat facing her. She watched them for a while and then addressed them.

"Have you learned your lessons well at school, Balinga? and you, Toomi? Hm? Which one of you can tell me what a noun is?"

Balinga puffed out his chest with importance. "A noun is the name of a person, a place, an animal, or a thing."

"Okay. And a verb?"

Toomi raised his hand as if he were in school.

Sizway gazed at Toomi.

"A verb shows action," Toomi said.

"Ahh, it shows action," Sizway repeated, eyeing both of the boys closely. "Children, love is a verb, not a noun. You hearing me? Love is a *verb*, not a noun. I want you children to know that I love Baba. Baba is going to come home. We are working on it."

The boys' faces were sober. Balinga's eyes began to water. "I don't want you and Baba to fight anymore."

Sizway nodded, lowering her eyes. "No children will like to see their parents fighting. When the elephants fight, the grass suffers. Parents are elephants, children like grass."

Both boys nodded.

"But if you ask two people to live together, you ask them to fight sometimes. You know the teeth and the tongue? they live together but sometimes they fight. The teeth will bite the tongue."

Then something caught Sizway's attention. A sick feeling like a wave went through her stomach. She saw Eva wobbling past on bowed legs with another white-haired woman. She remembered the tears in Jim-Walter's eyes. She turned back to her boys.

"Children," she said, "as I mature I see that most things we fight over are not worth fighting over. It is not important. We fight through the night and forget that we may never see tomorrow. We don't know tomorrow. The One Spirit owns tomorrow. We may meet our death tonight."

"I don't want you and Baba to die," Balinga cried.

"Yes, but who is dying now? Just listen. Do you know when you go to sleep you forget about everything else. Your fingers let go of whatever you hold in your hand. You forget about the belongings in your room that someone can break in and rob. You forget about the people in the next room and the people outside. All the things you worry about when you are awake, you forget about when you sleep. Where do we go when we sleep? Will we ever come back from sleep? We don't know. That's why we have to have the ability to stop fighting. Death may come before we wake. Now I called you to me not to discuss Baba's and my problem. That is for us. I wanted to talk to you about your own problem. You know you have a problem, don't you? . . . So, you didn't know?"

The boys waited and watched her.

She leaned over and cupped Balinga's chin in her palm and said, "Look at me. And listen. I will talk slow so you can listen well, okay? You have a problem, Balinga. Stealing will only lead you to prison. Are you hearing me? Don't answer, just listen. Stealing will only destroy your future. Your future is more important than what you think it is. When Baba comes home again and we find you stealing again, I will tell Baba, 'Just kill him. We don't need liars here. Just kill him. I can have more children.'"

Then Sizway turned to Toomi and held his warm hands in her own. "Toomi. Look at me. Your future is more important than what you think it is. With the last report sheet you brought home there was trouble. There is always bad report. I don't care for the B grades in your subjects, when the grades in manner are down. What good is it to be smart and have bad manner? Your citizenship is always down. Under the part where they judge self-control, you got a 'C' there. You always fool around. Under the part where they say, Listens well, 'D.' You don't listen. Works well alone, 'D.' You don't work well alone. You always want to talk. Shows effort, 'C.' You don't show effort. You are selfish."

She carefully slid her braids behind her ears. She eyed each one of the boys thoughtfully.

"Hmm, I can see many things I did wrong for you, children. You know a woman's womb? It is a road. All kinds of people pass down her road. Some people may be good and some people may not be good. But it makes no difference to the road which kind of person uses it. A road is like a woman's womb. Do you understand?

"My womb has carried many children who will grow up to be good children and children who will grow up to be bad and waste their life. But the only child I can claim is the one who does well. I don't claim any other kind of child. Listen to me," she said, "your life with me will never be like it was before. For me, now, there are only two kinds of children. There is the kind of child who does well, and when it is time for him to leave home I will cry for him. And there is the kind of child who causes so much trouble that I will even beg him to leave. I will be happy. Which one are you? Eh? I will cry for the first child because I will miss him for all the good things he has done at home. But the other kind of child will have done so many bad things that I will even *buy* him a suitcase and *help* him to pack. Which one are each of you? Which one do you want to be?"

Each child murmured in turn, "The first one."

"Then be the first one."

She said, "I think back to the time of your birth, how we started our journey together. There were times when I sat you both upon my laps. There were times when I carried you on my back or in a sling at my front. All of you, even Taiyewo, you are too long-legged now. I can't put you on my laps for five seconds now before the blood will leave my leg. There were times when I gave you baths. Now you lock the door of the bathroom. You don't want me to see your penis. They say, When the leaves begin to change colors winter is not far away. The season has changed for us. You are moving past being boys. We started our journey together but now we are on separate journeys. We don't journey together anymore, we only have a tie, a bond. You know what can make our bond stronger?"

The boys shook their heads.

"—for you to be responsible and to turn out well. That is how I can claim you."

When Sizway came to live in the compound, her boys remained with her but her daughter went to live in the house of the old woman Kehinde. Kehinde herself asked for the child. Kehinde was over one hundred years old. Her nose seemed more hawked and bony than ever but her dark skin had no crinkles in it and her black beady eyes were still bright.

Kehinde's house was quite cozy. The floor was firmly packed ground. In the center of the ground was a firepit encircled by chalky white stones and she kept a constant small fire burning there. Around the walls stood crude shelves and long, narrow benches. Near the firepit were small mats with wooden bowls and spoons and an iron pot with the evening meal inside. Kehinde carved her utensils out of wood and she made woven mats and baskets from reeds. The mats were laid out near the firepit for resting and sleeping. Kehinde always slept with her feet toward the flames. As she slept, the air whistled piercingly through her nose like strong wind through a chink in the roof.

Kehinde was usually silent and so Tai also came to live mostly in silence. They would sit for long hours in front of the fire, Tai reading and Kehinde sitting, thinking her own still thoughts. Tai at seven years went to school in town with the other Ki children, but as soon as she returned home she swept the yard, she cooked the evening meal, she cleaned, and then did her homework. Kehinde came to like Tai very much because Tai was a child who knew how to be quiet.

Each morning at sunrise, Kehinde left the compound with her largest basket and searched the woods for wild berries and mushrooms, beech, hickory, and chestnuts as well as acorns and sunflower seeds. At her age she took small steps, her tiny frame tilting from side to side and her elbows jutting out on either side. Kehinde knew every tree, every rock, every bird, and every plant and flower. She knew their language and could talk to them. She knew the healing art of every herb and would often mumble unintelligible words over them—the language of the herb—before she gently dug the herb up by its root from the ground. She lifted a root that was as long as an alligator's tail, only gnarled and twisted.

"When you see a twisted root like this within a charm, you know that the charm is very, very strong—you cannot touch it. But this one," she said, lifting a vine, "will capture bad forces and guard the households that own such charms."

Kehinde put the roots in her basket and continued walking. Tai was able to find on her own many of the roots and herbs her mother asked for. When Kehinde tired they settled in a clearing. A fire was built and Kehinde tossed leaves on the fire until it be-came smoky. She told Tai to go and sit on the other side of the fire, facing her. Tai did as she was told. She watched her mother toss in more leaves while warm, white clouds of smoke spiraled up toward the trees. It left a strong smell of burning pine in the air. Finally Kehinde crouched over, her elbows resting on her knees, her thin braids hanging over her eyes, and her eyes glistening black through the plaits. The smoke became so white and thick that Tai could barely make out Kehinde's form through it. Then a sudden wind came and blew the smoke to one side. That's when Tai noticed that Kehinde was no more there. There were only flattened leaves left by Kehinde's buttocks. Yet when the smoke returned upright, undulating here and there, she made out again Kehinde's black beads of eyes, her steady sharp gaze, watching Tai.

"Come here," Kehinde told her. "Your eyes are getting watery."

Tai stood up. The smoke spread out and spiraled. Tai walked around the fire. But again there was no one there, only flattened leaves. Tai stared curiously all about her.

"Come here, child."

Tai turned around. Kehinde was sitting on the opposite side now, the place Tai had just left. Kehinde slowly got to her feet. They sat again under the tree where they had left their basket. Kehinde told her to close her eyes and place the cool leaves there to remove the stinging. While Tai did this, Kehinde told her, "Long ago the white people had power. They could make things disappear and reappear, they could talk to animals and gain their assistance, they could talk to green things and get healing from them. They had many kinds of power. But now they have lost it or forgotten it. They put their magic in science. But we still use it the way they did in ancient times. We haven't forgotten how."

Tai removed the leaves. The stinging had gone.

"People with power use it only when it is necessary to use it. It may be necessary to move out of the path of danger."

"Mumma, which is greater? power or wisdom?"

"Mm. Wisdom, daughter, is greater. A person with power who isn't wise is like a person who walks hard but can't think. But few people are wise. Wisdom is a gift the One Spirit gives one when they come into the world. But most people don't come to the world with that gift."

Tai wasn't born wise. Wisdom was put into her ears. The Ki believe that if a person is not wise they should go and sit in the company of wise people. They should keep shut and listen. They say it with a proverb: A child who knows how to clean her hands will be allowed to eat with the elders. And so Kehinde began to allow The-One-Who-Knows-How-to-Be-Quiet to come closer and closer into her circle of elders and into her knowledge of power. Tai was soon called The-Old-People's-Child.

When there was no school, Kehinde allowed Tai to go out and play with the other children in the camp or in the woods. Tai would run along with them. She knew how to run and play games but she rarely opened her mouth to talk. To be quiet had become a part of her nature. Eventually her schoolteacher came visiting because Tai wouldn't talk in class. Kehinde sent Tai out of doors and settled down by the fire. She gestured for the schoolteacher to sit next to her. Then the schoolteacher started. She said, "Tai never puts her hand in the air to answer questions, and when she is questioned directly she just stares at her desk."

So Kehinde asked the schoolteacher, "Is she completing her lessons?"

"Yes, very well."

"Is she passing her exams?"

"Yes."

"Hmm. Do you think she can hear you? Is her ears working?"

"Yes. I think so. Yes."

"And is her voice working? Have you heard her speak at all?"

"Well, yes. She speaks a little."

Kehinde scratched her head. "You know, I am old," she said. "And I am an illiterate. What is it that you want to see happen?"

"Well, in terms of overall development, I think she needs to verbalize more, socialize more."

"Okay. I will be telling her to do it," Kehinde said. Then Kehinde held her cheek in her palm and wore her familiar tired expression, as if she had been sitting for long with crying children.

Kehinde used to say, "Silence is the best answer for foolishness. If you argue with foolishness, you become a fool, too." She didn't want to argue with the schoolteacher. And Kehinde would never encourage Tai to be talkative. To Kehinde, a child who was patient with her tongue was walking toward wisdom.

Kehinde was a woman with power but what she valued most was patience. She always told Taiyewo that if a person wants power they must first learn patience. The tongue must be patient, she said. Nowadays the pen and paper that the white people invented has become another kind of tongue. The pen and paper will tell all a person's thoughts without limit, it will just be talking and talking. And the pen is even worse because words written on paper are permanently recorded but words spoken can be later forgotten. So the pen and the paper must also be patient. It is better, she said, to be a fool who has patience than a person with learning who has no patience at all. If a fool is patient no one will know he is fool because he will keep his tongue inside and he will keep the cap on his pen. But a learned person's tongue will be wagging and wagging, exposing all of his foolishness. That is why we say, Even a fool with patience can appear to be wise.

One evening as they were sitting in silence by the firepit there came a knock at the door. Kehinde went to the door. Standing there in the falling dark, hat in hand, was Papa Job. Kehinde placed the flat of her hands on her backside, while puffing up thin, white wisps of smoke.

Papa Job was washed and shaven but smelling bad of rum. "Mumma, I need you to help me," he said.

Kehinde stepped past him and sat on the step. The sun had fallen behind the trees and the dark was beginning to stand up. She motioned for Papa Job to come sit with her.

"Come here, my husband."

Papa Job hesitated.

Kehinde laughed craftily. "So you think you are not my husband? I am your wife. I married you to our daughter, didn't I?"

Papa Job settled down on the step next to Kehinde.

"My husband," she said, holding the pipe slightly away from her mouth, "the family name is important. It belongs to each member of the family. The family name must not be damaged. Everyone in the family will make a name for himself and add to the name of the family. Some will be the first doctor in the family, another will be the first university teacher. What will you be known for? What history will you make for yourself and your children? the first drunkard in the family? I don't want you to dent the family's name. If you want my help, I will give it. But you will have to stop drinking before I can help you. Do you want to stop drinking?"

"Yes, ma."

"Then I will help you to stop. I will give you something for that," she said. "But the power I have is not enough. Power can't work without a person's will. Your will to stop drinking has to be working with the power I give you."

"Yes, ma."

Then Kehinde got up. "Now. Come inside. I will make you something to eat," she said.

Papa Job slowly followed Kehinde inside. The room was dim and smoky. Tai was reading near the pit where the smoky fire was going. When she saw her father, she put aside the book. She greeted him by bending her knees, the way Ki girls greet their elders. She took his hand and led him to the firepit, where he sat on the ground. Then she hurried to the shelf, got a saucepan, and scooped some food for him on the pan. She handed the saucepan to him with both hands, again bending both knees. Papa Job took the food. She knelt a distance away from him but he didn't touch the food. As strong and wiry as his muscles were, his physical body, he seemed shriveled and very small.

Papa Job looked over at Tai. At seven years she was tall and thin. Her bright cheerful smile of childhood was replaced with an old woman's blank calm. She wore a plain, limp dress and a scarf tied in back at her neck. She was becoming more and more like Kehinde.

Kehinde was sitting in a dark corner of the room. In her laps were some plants and roots, which she was sorting and peeling and preparing for Papa Job. She muttered to herself as she picked through the roots and plants. "This one for this one, that one for that one . . ."

After some time she called out to Papa Job without looking up. She said, "My son. You are not eating my food."

"Please. Let me just sit here," he said.

"Why are you not eating?"

"I am just tired, ma."

"You say you are tired?" she called.

He nodded. "Yes, ma." He said, "Tired of life, maybe."

Kehinde laughed craftily. She bit off the tip of a root and spat it out.

"No. You are not tired," she said. "You haven't lived long enough to be tired. Your life is just beginning. It just started today. The Ki have a saying, When two people are fighting and they are not tired of fighting no one can come and settle the thing. But when they are tired, even a child can come and settle it. Eh? What do you say to that?"

The Ki elders came in mass to settle the family problem. The old people sat in a wide circle on the ground of Kehinde's house with the fire burning in the pit. Papa Job's uncle Jake, the only elder from his side, was there. Uncle Jake's voice rattled when he talked, it even rattled when he slept. But he was aware of the problem and came all the way from Detroit to help Papa Job to solve it. Kehinde was there and Manji, along with many of the grey-haired and aged from the compound. Sizway and Papa Job felt humbled in the presence of so much age.

Before talking of things, the old people prepared themselves by making offerings. One elder filled his pipe and handed it to the other elder, who lit it and offered it to the sky and earth, and so on. The room was dim and hazy from pipe smoke. After smoking, the old people were ready to talk.

They said: "Let us start by hearing the problem well from you, Kibaba Job. Explain things to us. Let us hear your side."

So Papa Job started. He ran his hand down the back of his head. He interlaced his fingers. He said, "This summer our son died." He paused and swallowed hard. "All you who are here, I don't deny that I became a drunkard. I armed myself with anger and drink and gambling. I asked myself why I should continue to be a father to this woman's children when she doesn't want me to father them. Our child was stealing. I was handling him. I used all-all the little knowledge I had to handle his problem. But my wife undermined me. Every discipline and training I gave to the children she undermined me. In doing that she taught them to hate me. She lost one child to death. But I lost all of my children." He lowered his eyes and his long lashes shadowed his cheeks. He removed his round glasses that had clouded over and wiped them.

Then the elders turned to Sizway. They said, "You, my daughter, it is your turn. Explain things to us. Tell us so that we can understand. Let us hear your side."

Sizway interlaced her fingers. She said, "My husband speaks truthfully. This problem has lived since early summer. I had a child who stayed for a while, then died. He didn't remain long with the living. After his death, I forgot the other children. When they did wrong thing, I looked the other way. In doing that I undermined my husband. He started gambling and drinking. Even if I wanted him to father our children, he could no longer father them. And he's lost our home to debt. But it started as my husband said, with the death of Kehinde. Before, when my eyes were open, I couldn't see. Now that the family has fallen apart, I see many things clearly."

The elders nodded. They said, "We people of spirit, we will all die. As we are called to live, we are also called to die. You, Papa Job, were wise in building a business in town, but a man must also be wise for his own home and consider his family. Eshu-Elegba warns us to rest at the cool of the crossroad and there consider life before action."

After much talk, the elders concluded, "What has happened has happened. Now let us look at the point where you can again start beginning."

The next day the Ki got together and started building a house for Kibaba Job and Sizway in the compound. Workmen used timber to put up the four walls and all through the camp was heard hammer and nails. Before the roof was finished, Sizway and Kibaba entered. They looked this way and that. Then they looked up at the night stars glittering through the unfinished roof. Sizway placed the kerosene lantern in the grass. She laid out her large rug of ancient work with a beautiful border woven into it.

"Let us sit down." She showed him this good place for sitting.

They sat side by side beneath a million stars. She dug with a stick a little hole in the ground. She opened a pouch at her waist and removed two stones—a purple amethyst and a black onyx. She buried them. Then from her pouch she removed a large leaf, the size of a hand. It was soft and smooth. She opened a small jar of sweet sauce and dipped in the leaf. She folded it and put it into her husband's mouth. She folded another leaf, dipped it, and put it into his mouth. Papa Job set the pouch aside and pulled her down with him while enfolding her in his arms. She found his body thin and almost fragile, like that of a woman. It was as if she were holding herself.

After three days the house was built and the family settled into their new clapboard raised on stilts. Evening went and found Sizway and Papa Job sitting on the front steps of their new house. Cooking fires were dying out and house windows were lit yellow by oil lamps. People in the compound were going to and fro, visiting with one another. This night Papa Job played beautiful songs on his harmonica. He asked Sizway, "Why are you crying when I play this?" And she answered, "I cry from remembering." And the people of the camp said, "Let us go and listen to the songs Kibaba plays on that instrument." And they went to listen to the music he played on his front steps.

They said, "We want to hear your music. Play. Make us hear."

Papa Job composed different songs, until the people began to know the songs little by little. Then Papa Job said to the onlookers, "Let us entertain one another. Let one of you take the harmonica."

"How can we play this?"

And he taught them to play. As for himself, he brought out his favorite, his bongo drum, which he now called the Black Gypsy.

Dusk had turned into dark. Toomi came and stood beside his father who sat on the steps talking to a visitor. The visitor was named He-Who-Was-Born-Laughing. He was about Papa Job's age. He was never known by anyone in the camp to be down, he was always laughing. He looked over at Toomi in the dark. "How are you?"

And Toomi simply said, "Hi," failing to show the proper respect. He just said, "Hi," as if he were greeting one of his own age group. He didn't greet the man well.

"Go inside, Toomi," Sizway said.

"Mumma, I'm not tired. I want to sit with my father."

Toomi remained standing beside his father.

Then He-Who-Was-Born-Laughing asked, "Where have you been, Toomi?"

"I have just come from the woods. I found sunflower seeds."

"Give me some."

Toomi reached in his pocket and dropped them in the man's hand.

He-Who-Was-Born-Laughing winked. His cheeks contained his laughter. "Probably maybe you've been visiting your girlfriend in the woods, too."

"No. I have nothing to do with them."

"You are lying."

"You are silly. I don't have girlfriends."

Sizway immediately looked to see who was calling an old man "silly." Seeing that it was Toomi, she turned to his father in the dark. "Please, Kiba. Slap this child. Is anyone silly here?" Sizway was drinking anger.

Toomi glanced at his father, with fear beating at his heart. "I'm sorry, Baba," he said. Then he turned to He-Who-Was-Born-Laughing. "Sorry, sir."

But Sizway said, "You are sorry? I don't marry sorry. If someone strips off all of your clothing in a public place and everyone ridicules your nakedness, but in private that person who stripped you comes back and says, 'I'm sorry,' and even offers you new cloth, do you think that will remove your disgrace?"

"No, ma."

"You are stupid. Why can't you look around you before you open your mouth?"

Papa Job told Toomi to go inside. Then he turned back to He-Who-Was-Born-Laughing. "Forget the boy," Papa said. "Let us talk of other things."

When Papa Job finally came inside he told Sizway she had a price to pay. He said, "The boys for a while will be relating to other people the way they have become used to relating to you.

Changing yourself will change the way they relate to you and how they relate to other people."

"Umph, you should have slapped him," she said.

"I don't have to slap him every time. The boys are even now at an age when they will be talking back to you sometimes. Toomi sees you are a woman. He will be testing you and talking back. If you want to live long, you will ignore most things. If you don't, the bones will be coming out of your neck. Don't ignore the major things. But try and ignore the minor things. Your sons have passed the age where they will do your bidding without talking under their breath. Let us just work together."

The night was lit by bonfires and by the bright red, orange, and yellow of the Ki's cloth. The people gathered in the great open space. Papa Job, Sizway, Toomi, Balinga, and Tai all sat together in the circle. They were celebrating Tai's twelfth birthday and praising the guardian of twin spirits, Ibeji. The celebrants had started. Food was passed round and gifts. Everyone was purposefully going about well-practiced rituals. Women used ritual fans as they danced. And the positive breeze of the women's fans was like a ripple of water. The fans were rounded, decorated with a richness of beads, cowry shells, jingle bells, and peacock feathers.

Tai sat quietly watching the festivities. Her hair was braided in spirals around her head. Heavy copper earrings hung from her earlobes and copper bracelets circled her arms to the elbows. She wore a bright red dress cut from Sizway's old wedding dress.

All the drums were being beaten all around. Papa Job had dressed himself in rich, gilded fabric and had become beautiful. He wore a glittering gold tunic and pants that ballooned around his legs and a gold cap. His skin shone clean, his teeth white as milk, and his eyes clean and open. His knees hugged a cunga drum while the celebrants pressed close.

The muscles in his arms flexed and his hands moved like fluttering wings. His fingers widened on the drum. The tips of his fingers were red, beating out rhythms rapid-fire. And the other drummers responded in rapid-fire cross-talk. Everyone moved with the drumming, their palms clapped and became worn out from clapping. Other people danced, but Papa Job's eyes were on Sizway, trancing her as he tranced the crowd.

Suddenly Tai sprang up as if she heard her name being called, a cry calling out over all the loud drumming. She left the circle. She went to the house of her old mother, Kehinde.

She entered the house and found a veiled woman there, a half-dream, sitting on the dirt ground near the slow-burning fire. Tai came close to her.

"Is that you, mother?"

The veil moved slightly from the faint breathing beneath it. The breathing had the rhythm of sleep. Tai knelt before her.

The veiled woman handed her a green-leafed plant. "Eat," the woman said.

And Tai replied, "Please, I must ask my mother."

Tai ran out into the night and back to the ceremonial circle.

"Mumma, I want to eat with the stranger."

Sizway said, "Eat with her if you want."

Tai returned to the veiled woman.

Tai ate the bitter plant while the veiled woman watched her. Tai had a hard time keeping the bitter plant down. When the plant was fully eaten, the old woman gave her a gourd to drink from.

"Drink it," she said.

"Please, let me go and ask my mother," Tai answered.

Tai again returned to the ceremonial circle. She said, "Mumma, I want to drink with the stranger."

"Then drink with her if you must," Sizway said.

Tai came back and drank the bitter liquid.

Then the veiled woman plucked a frog from a jar. She tied the frog's legs with string. She sprinkled salt on the back of the frog. After a while, she rubbed palm oil on the back of the frog. A little while later she put on the frog the power of oshu. At first the frog was happy. Then the frog cried like a human.

"Turn your back to me," she told Tai.

Gently she made twelve cuts on Tai's scalp with a razor, dipping the blade in the juice of the frog. She wrapped Tai's head in white cloth. Then she told her to turn around and face her again. Tai knelt before her.

The veiled woman lifted a white cloth on the dirt floor and slid out a whole chicken's egg.

"Eat."

Tai was to eat the egg—shell and yolk.

"Now you will remember everything you have seen with your eyes and heard with your ears," the veiled woman said.

After Tai ate, the veiled woman lifted the white cloth again and slid out a knife and a glass bottle. She handed Tai the knife. "Strength," she said. Then she handed Tai the bottle. "Courage," she said. "Eat."

"The knife and the bottle?"

The woman didn't answer, as if Tai were asking something foolish.

"Mumma, what is strength and what is courage?"

"Courage is being able to withstand pain. It is never ceasing from doing good when things don't go your way."

"And strength?"

"Strength is when you are able to say no or yes to a thing and not turn back nor regret it later. It is when you take a decision and stand on it."

Tai lifted the metal knife to her teeth and bit into it. It yielded to her teeth like butter. She ate the knife. Ate it all. Then she lifted the bottle. Starting with the neck she crunched down on it like it was very fine crackers breaking easily against her teeth. Now all that the veiled woman had given her would be forever in her blood.

When she had ate it all, she looked at the veiled woman. The woman knew her thoughts. She said, "Don't ask me what you must do. You are still a child. Bring honor to your family. That is all a child need do."

The veiled woman had no more to give her. Her job was done. Tai's was just beginning.

Tai left the house wearing a white headwrap stained with blood. She did not go back to seat herself in the ceremonial circle. Instead she entered deep into the woods outside the camp. When she came to a clearing she stopped. Above her head was a black sky full of stars. Tai's chin uptilted toward the black night, up toward the stars and the easy wind.

———————————————

"They say shooting stars are spirits darting cross the sky," the talebearer murmurs. "Tai must do what she had been taught. She took the stones in her hand. . . ."

———————————————

The girl knelt on the grey, pebbled ground. She made a circle out of white stones. Then she extracted a nubby piece of chalk from the pocket of her white dress, dust-whitening her fingertips. Placing her left arm behind her back, she drew with the right a large cross on the dirt in the middle of the circle of stones. She chanted in a low voice as she drew, "Alabe Oshun, uh-huh-mmm, Awade lode, ya-ah-hmm, uh-huh-hmm . . ."

The talebearer squints wrinkled lids, she puffs up rings of pipe smoke in the twilight.

"The one line she draws be the boundary. The other leads across the boundary to the cemetery, linking the above with the below, God and man, God and the dead, the living earth and the dead white clay. She stood on the cross between life and death. . . ."

Tai's legs straightened and paused in their rising. Her knees were embedded with tiny pebbles and sticks, which she picked off with her fingers. She stepped into the middle of the circle, in the middle of the cross, pressing her face once more against the black garment of sky.

―――――――――――

"You see," the talebearer says, "a person's life has no end, it is a circle. The crossroad is the point of meeting between life and death, hot and cool, male and female, the individual and the many faces of family. Wholeness comes to a person who understands the ways and powers of both worlds."

―――――――――――

At the ceremonial fire, the Ki sang blessings to the orisha of twins, Ibeji, guardian of twin spirits. They praised Taiyewo —Come-to-Taste-Life—and Kehinde—The-One-Who-Came-Behind, and their spirited voices carried through the woods.

> Come-to-Taste-Life, you will live in the very middle of
>   our life
> Where love between man and woman was made
> Where love for children was made
> Where stories of family were first heard
> You will live in the very middle of our life
> Where we are whole.

―――――――――――

The talebearer empties the ash of her pipe on the ground. When she leans forward, the ibeji necklace swings away from her neck.

"It was on the night of Ibeji that my inner eyes were opened," she says, tapping the bowl on the ground, "and my memory became long as the veiled woman foretold. I took everything in with my eyes and my ears and I didn't talk. Not for many years. On that night I learned that the one who raised me had died. Kehinde had died even before the Ibeji celebration had started. Mumma Kehinde had never been sick. They say people with power don't die of sickness. They know the time of their death and they enter it with their eyes open. Many years later, after my birth mother died, I began to tell stories the way my mothers told me.

"My wish is that you will remember this story and tell it after me. Remember the family. Remember the old ways. This is a parable, not a tale. A parable. But we pretend and call it a tale."